GILBERT MORRIS
AND BOBBY FUNDERBURK

THE FAR
FIELDS
SERIES #1

BEYOND
THE RIVER

GILBERT MORRIS
AND BOBBY FUNDERBURK

THE FAR
FIELDS
SERIES #1

BEYOND THE RIVER

STARBURST PUBLISHERS

P.O. Box 4123, Lancaster, Pennsylvania 17604

To schedule Author appearances write:
Author Appearances, Starburst Promotions, P.O. Box 4123
Lancaster, Pennsylvania 17604 or call (717) 293-0939

Credits:
Cover art by Kerne Erickson

We, The Publisher and Author, declare that to the best of our knowledge all material (quoted or not) contained herein is accurate, and we shall not be held liable for the same.

BEYOND THE RIVER

First Printing, March 1994

ISBN: 0-914984-51-9
Library of Congress Catalog Number 92-84016

Printed in the United States of America

Dedication

To *Denny* and *Dory Davis*
for
forty years of faithful friendship.

Contents

PART ONE: THE CITY   9
  One   **The Trouble With George Washington—!**   11
  Two   **The Reliever**   25
  Three   **The Far Fields**   39
  Four   **Memories**   55
  Five   **A Way Out**   67

PART TWO: THE FIELDS   85
  Six   **Color And Light**   87
  Seven   **Storm**   99
  Eight   **Haven**   113
  Nine   **A Trip To The Market**   131
  Ten   **Light Of The World**   147
  Eleven   **A Kiss After Dying**   159
  Twelve   **A New Life**   173
  Thirteen **An Unwelcome Message**   189
  Fourteen **To See Jesus**   199

PART THREE: THE FLOCK   213
  Fifteen   **The White Tower**   215
  Sixteen   **A Bridge From Hell**   229
  Seventeen **Warrior**   247
  Eighteen **The Coven**   261
  Nineteen **The Prophet**   271

Part One:

THE CITY

Chapter One

The Trouble With George Washington—!

"I must be as crazy as they say I am—paying 500 Credits a month for this apartment!"

Starr had not spoken the words aloud, but as she awoke the thought came to her as it did almost every morning. A streak of irritation ran along her nerves, for she hated self-doubt, and as she sat up, she muttered, "It's my own business what I do with my Credits!"

Throwing off the light coverlet with more force than necessary, she sprang off the narrow bed, then stood there staring defiantly around her living quarters, which consisted of a single room, ten feet wide and twelve feet long. It was listed under Accommodations as LA-1, Luxurious Apartment, First Class. She had waited fifteen months for the privilege of paying 500 Credits each month, more than two-thirds of her total income. The walls were a neutral beige, as in all the other apartments, but the two oil paintings and the blue curtains on the single window added splashes of color. As she let her eyes rest on the one to her right, she steadfastly refused to think of what it had cost. It was very old, of course, coming out of a period which was her speciality—pre-NuAge history, but this painting went far back even for that period.

Now as she looked at it the strange sense of peace and serenity came to her as when she had first seen it. She remembered the moment when she had found it, on a visit to an antique shop in the Fringe. An old woman with blackened teeth had allowed her to go through the attic of her decaying shop, and she had discovered it sandwiched between stacks of yellowing newspapers and magazines. She had been searching for papers and periodicals, but when she had lifted an old magazine with the quaint title of LIFE and seen the oil painting, she seemed to enter another world.

It was a simple painting—a landscape with an OldAge farm in the foreground. A white house with a porch running the full width was in the center, and to the right a red barn with a pair of dappled horses. A huge oak tree stood on the left. A swing dangled from one of the massive limbs and two small children were being pushed by a woman wearing a long dress. To one side a man was smiling at the three as he stood holding the reins of a beautiful black horse. A blue sky, white clouds, and the rolling hills of green trees formed the setting. Something in the painting had moved Starr even then.

Looking at the painting she remembered how she had fought to keep it. She had bought it from the crone for only 50 Credits, but the Curator of the Past—a tall, thin man with narrowly spaced eyes—had given her a hard time. "It's not a *healthy* picture," he had argued. When she had asked why, he had snorted, "You're a Remedial Historian. If anyone should know the danger of the kind of rampant romanticism this painting glorifies, it ought to be you!" The Curator of the Past then gave her a stiff lecture on how Old World had perished because people wasted their time swinging children instead of serving the State—but in the end he had let her have the picture. He had let her have it for *only* 500 Credits, and Starr knew that most of that would go into his own account. But as she let her eyes rest on the painting and felt the sense of peace it always brought, she was glad she'd won that battle.

Starr glanced quickly at the other painting, one which her best friend had done. It was a strongly executed portrait of a young girl. Looking full face out of the frame, there was an air of innocence about the child that never failed to catch Starr's attention. One of the few people who had ever been in her apartment, a Clinical Dream Master named Lon Beta, had insisted, "You ought to get rid of that painting, Starr. It's a wish-fulfillment thing." He had grinned broadly at her, adding, "You're always wishing you could go back and be a little girl again. I think you've read too much about that old fable of Adam and Eve in the Garden of Eden." He sobered, gave his head a shake, then admonished her, "That was a nice story, Starr, but it's just a myth. Maybe all of us at one time or another would like to find a place where everything's perfect. But we never will. That's why we have people like me. If you want to dream about Eden—or a place like that old farm house in the other painting, I can help you."

Starr shook her head, "I don't need any of your little dreams, Lon. I like to look at things straight-on." He stared at her with a peculiar look in his grey eyes. "Everybody needs dreams, Starr. Life would be terrible if we didn't have dreams. I've seen a few people try to hold out, but they all came around. You will, too."

Turning from the paintings, Starr went to one of the two doors in the apartment which opened into the tiny bathroom. Stripping off her nightgown, she stepped into the shower, and for her allotted time let the warm water run down her body. When the water shut off, she longed, as always, that she could have a shower that did not shut off automatically; but as she dried and dressed she smiled, remembering how before she had her own place she'd shared a communal shower.

Starr walked to her kitchen which was a section of cabinets three feet wide on one end of the room. The designers had included a two-burner stove, a microwave oven, a tiny sink and dishwasher, a refrigerator no more than 18 inches square, and a cabinet for her food. Her friends thought she was insane to go to all the trouble of cooking, when pre-packaged meals were cheap, while *real* food was expensive and difficult to find. But as she dropped a piece of real bacon into the small frying pan she knew it was worth it. Starr enjoyed seeing the bacon curl as it fried, and smelling the rich robust aroma. She cracked the egg and carefully fried it in the grease, just enough so that the yellow would be nice and runny, then warmed a roll with sesame seeds on top. Finally she sat down at the tiny table with the meal before her, as she looked out the single window and past the structures of the skyline of the City. Always at that moment something came over her as she sat in her own place with the good food she'd prepared. Her study of Ancient Religions of America had revealed that people in OldTime had said "grace," a prayer of thanksgiving to their God. Starr had no superstitions about God, but there was something in that moment that caused her to think that she could understand those people who lived so long ago in such a simple time.

After making breakfast last as long as possible, Starr cleaned up the kitchen, then changed into her uniform. Standing before the full-length narrow mirror, she studied herself with a jaundiced eye. She saw a tall young woman wearing a light brown skirt and tunic with a dark brown leather belt. Over her breasts was a pair of crossed leather straps; a pair of calf-length nylon boots adorned her feet. She gave her slim figure a critical eye, deciding that she could use another two pounds. Then she leaned forward slightly, peering at her face. It was a squarish face with a strong jaw and high cheekbones. The complexion was smooth and the olive tone was not the result of a tanning booth but came from some distant aborigine as did the mass of auburn hair. A pair of steady grey eyes looked back at her. They were wide-spaced, deep-set, and shaded by heavy black lashes. It was not a beautiful face, but, she thought with satisfaction, it was durable, and would cover the strange passions that rose in her from time to time.

Suddenly, a fragment of poetry came into her mind like a small bird darting into a room though a window carelessly left open:

There will be time, there will be time
To prepare a face to meet the faces that you meet—

Her lips drew suddenly tight, almost hard, then she wheeled and left the room quickly. And, as always when she left, there was a small stab of fear. She had long known what it was, for she was a woman who had learned to know herself better than most. The apartment, she had long since realized, was her harbor. When she left it she left safety and peace behind. When the day was over she would scurry back with the same urgency that small furry animals seek their underground dens when snowflakes begin to fall and storm winds gather. Starr realized it was a weakness, but she could not change it. As she moved out of the apartment into the hustling world of the City she forced herself to stand straighter, putting on the face that others would see—one filled with a confidence that she did not feel.

A covey of people waited for the elevator, so Starr turned into the stairwell and walked down the nine stories to street level. She disliked crowds—which set her off from most people. Most of her friends had discovered that she liked to be alone—a habit that some of them found dangerous and anti-social. Most people, she had long ago discovered, were afraid to be alone with themselves, and found it necessary to be with others around the clock. This was not illogical, since most denizens of NuWorld were born in crowds, lived in crowds all their lives, finding isolation only in death— and even then their dust was mingled with the ashes of others in the Great Urn.

The hollow sound of her boot heels striking on the concrete stairs had a sepulchral quality that rang in her ears. When she reached the door a red light flashed and she spoke clearly, "Hello, Starr Omega." A hidden microphone picked up her voice, transformed it into an electric signal, then fed it into a computer bank. Her voice print was identified, approved, and returned to a speaker over the door which said, "Good morning, Starr. Have a wonderful experience today!"

The door slid open noiselessly, and as Starr passed through it she wondered if others felt as she did while going through the exit procedure. She accepted the fact that security was necessary to keep Undesirables and Barbarians out of the ordered life of the City. But somehow speaking into a machine made her feel like an idiot. And the fruity voice that answered her with a platitudinous phrase angered her. At times she had to restrain the impulse to say something obscene to the door, but that would mean getting her name on a list somewhere in the Department of Concern.

Stepping out of the building, she walked to one of the small vehicles marked CARRIER and got inside. The interior was all light tan plastic, including the vinyl seat which was no more than 40 inches wide, room for two people. There were no levers whatsoever for controlling the carrier, only ten small buttons and one large red button marked START. Starr pushed 37.04 and a 71.25, the latitude and longitude where the Department of History was located, and then the START button. The carrier moved off at once, its electric engine emitting a mild high-pitched whine. From time to time the guidance system made corrections, such as slowing to avoid another carrier or turning down another street. Most of the passengers Starr noticed in other carriers were either reading or staring blindly ahead.

Starr never read while riding, choosing to examine the scenery that floated by or the activity that went on daily in the City.

More than once she looked up to where the huge geodesic Dome made of clear plastic covered that section of the City. She was always impressed by the scientific genius that had produced the Domes, for they were miracles of architecture. As she looked up to the peak nearly a quarter of a mile overhead, her practically flawless memory brought into her mind part of an essay she had read concerning the building of the Domes. It ran through her mind in orderly fashion, sentence by sentence, so that she could have read it and recited it as easily as she could have read from the original text. It was that gift which made her such a good historian, the ability to read and recall bits and pieces of information stored in the grey cells of her mind. As she noted the way the sunbeams were refracted by the interlocking triangular plates so that all of Section G was bathed in the smoky brown haze of a muddy light, she ran through the article in her mind:

According to the old legends, the world was destroyed by water in the distant past. While no one believes that myth in these days, we are conscious that the earth did suffer a catastrophe no less severe than Noah's flood. And it came not without prophets, for in OldAge many pointed out that unless man ceased to pollute the atmosphere he would destroy himself. But the system of OldWorld was built on commerce, and commerce ran on fossil fuels. Although the techniques of solar power, wind power, and other forms of power were known, there was no country willing to lead the world into a program of restoration reform.

So one day the world died.

Not as in the days of Noah, of course. Not in a seven day week. But there came a day when the atmosphere could take no more. The tiny bits of burned oil and other polluted atoms that had gathered in the skies and were held in place by gravity reached a saturation point.

So Planet Earth suffered the Greenhouse Effect.

This meant that the age-old biological and botanical processes simply malfunctioned. The earth was trapped inside a container of poisonous gas with no way to break out.

So men and women and children strangled to death, slowly and horribly, their lungs seared by the air which had become toxic. Once it had been miners who had died of black lung, but now the denizens of the planet were dropping dead by the millions.

The end of the world had come.

But man is a god. And a small group of scientists proved that man can save himself—and it was the Domes that proved to be the salvation of mankind.

In a mad race against death, which halted technological process in other areas, a few desperate scientists hit upon the concept of a hermetically-sealed Dome (which had been done on a small scale many times) and created gargantuan Domes. Inside these Domes the air could be purified. Plants could create carbon dioxide. Purifiers could create safe waters. The first Dome proved the theory was good, but it was only a small one, covering about twenty acres. But when it demonstrated that life could go on under glass, larger ones were built. The geodesic Dome is the simplest of all structures, and one of the strongest. Now the scientific community threw itself into a massive program which made the building of the pyramids look like childish toys! Soon entire towns could be contained in a single Dome, and even the largest cities on earth could be contained in ten or twelve Domes linked together by hermetically-sealed passages.

Starr's carrier pulled up to a towering windowless building made of high grade plastic. A metallic voice said, "Eleven Credits, please." Starr extended her left hand, palm-down into a slot and waited until she heard a tiny clicking sound, and when the metallic voice said, "Thank you. Be all you can today. You owe it to yourself," she removed her hand. The laser had read the tiny chip implanted in her left palm, then fed the information instantly to the Bank. On her next statement would be an item labeled "Carrier" with the date and time of the reading and the eleven Credit charge showing. Getting out of the carrier and entering the building she wondered idly what it must have been like in OldWorld, having to carry money. Or even trouble with the old credit card system. One of the first adjustments made in NuWorld was to issue every individual a number which was implanted in a tiny chip in the palm of his left hand. No need for cash then, every service or item could be instantly charged.

Starr entered the building, then spoke to the guard who nodded casually. Taking the elevator to the sixth floor she went at once to the Office of Remedial History. But R.H. was more than a single office; half of the entire floor was broken up into small cells for individual workers.

Her own Division, American History, was a cluster of these smaller offices, and she went at once to her Director, Emmett Tau, who was sitting behind a gray desk staring at the screen of a computer. In front of him was a console. From time to time his hands would flicker over it almost lovingly. Starr knew he was auditing the work of his staff. And she also knew that he was not finding any mistakes in their work, for he looked glum. Only when he caught one of them in a mistake did his eyes gleam with joy.

"May I talk to you before I go to work, Emmett?"

The Director looked up from the screen, his dark brown eyes fixed on her. "Go ahead." His eyes kept flickering back to the screen, but there was no way to stop him from doing that. *If a Roman orgy took place in my office* Emmett Tau was fond of saying, *I wouldn't even look up!* He was a man of one dimension, and his god was the work he did.

"My Mentor at the University says that I'm ready for the dissertation, Emmett. Will you allow me to take some time off to do the paper?"

Emmett tore his eyes from the screen and studied her. "What will your subject be?" he demanded. He had a harsh voice, surprisingly loud in a man so small. What he was really demanding, Starr understood, was to know if her research would benefit Emmett Tau and the American Section of the Remedial Division of the Department of History.

"I'll choose a subject that will be of use to us here in our Section," Starr nodded, putting a strong note of enthusiasm in her voice which she did not feel. Her plan was to do a paper on a subject that was based on English history during the Middle Ages of OldWorld, but it would be fatal to tell Emmett Tau such a thing. "I thought we might get together and you could help me choose a proper subject," she added demurely.

Emmett stared at her, his mind almost whirring as he thought how he could get every possible benefit from this situation. He noted the slim beauty of Starr Omega, thinking that maybe he would have to offer her a six month Loving Friend Contract. He added to her physical charms the bit of information that she was the best junior remedial historian he'd ever had. And it all added up.

"Why, I think we can work something out, Starr," he said. "Why don't we get together later this week and see what we can come up with?"

"Fine!" Starr smiled, then at once said hurriedly, "Hey, I'm going to be late!"

She turned and walked out of his office, going directly to her own, which was simply a space eight feet square with four walls and a ceiling. There was a hook on the back of the door for her coat. But the room had no other ornaments or decorations of any sort.

Two pieces of furniture were located in the middle of the room—a small wooden desk and a straight back chair. On the desk were four monitors and one keyboard.

There were no books, maps, or charts in the room. The small computer on her desk interfaced with the megaputor which occupied the first three floors of the building. There were no documents, magazines, or books in the entire Department, for all information was stored on tiny silicon chips. By simply touching the keys of the console Starr could bring up on the screen a copy of the Declaration of Independence, a letter from Lord Byron to his mistress, or the number of inches of rainfall in the ancient state of Nevada during the year 1969. Three of the monitors were for reading information from Megaputor; the fourth was for her own writing.

Since there were no windows or any other form of distraction, Starr went to work at once. That was what was intended, of course, and she didn't resent it. She was one of those rare individuals who could close out every outside stimulus so that her entire attention could be concentrated on a single task. Starr had read once that great hitters in baseball could do that. Many of her friends needed drug therapy to give them that sort of power. But that required the use of stronger and stronger drugs—which meant that ultimately they lost almost all power to concentrate.

Starr brought the computer to life with a touch of her hand, an act that made her feel like the huge figure of God on the ceiling of the Sistine Chapel. She enjoyed the power of having at her fingertips the history, achievements, and power of not only NuWorld, but of OldWorld as well.

For the next four hours she sat at the desk, pulling from the microscopic chips far below her feet, documents, letters, journals, maps, books, drawings and a host of other fragments of information. She saw them as part of a huge jigsaw puzzle, but much more difficult since most of the pieces she examined did not fit into her project and had to be discarded. That was what destroyed promising historians. They were not willing to wade through a thousand items to find one that would fit into the whole they were trying to construct.

The particular task that Starr was engaged in was to "remedy" a certain historical item—the religion of George Washington, the first President of America in OldWorld.

It was a problem more difficult than most, for the inhabitants of NuWorld were fascinated by OldWorld history. Naturally, for their roots were there, most of them. The Greenhouse Effect had one effect of its own, and that was to melt the polar caps. This meant that the waters of all oceans rose. And this meant no more Florida. No more Gulf Coast. No more Southern California. If an OldWorld inhabitant could be raised and shown a map of NuWorld he would have had difficulty recognizing it. But changed as it was, it was still the homeland, and people wanted the story of OldWorld. Indeed, they never seemed to get enough of it!

But knowledge is power, and the new rulers of NuWorld had no intention of letting anyone get powerful enough to bring destruction on their new society. OldWorld had lacked control, and that had brought its doom.

And that was why *remedial* historians such as Starr Omega were needed.

It was easy enough to find out that certain events transpired in OldWorld, that certain men or women performed certain deeds. "That's no problem for a good historian," Emmett often told his staff, then his eyes would glow with a zealous light. "But history must be put in such a form that it will do no harm to those who read it."

Case in point— Mr. George Washington. He was the General of the Continental Army of the United States. Yes, no problem.

First President of the new republic. Fine. Served two terms and died in the year 1799 (OldTime) Quite right.

But Washington had one tragic flaw. He was a man who believed in God. A man who prayed. It was difficult to put him into an ecclesiastical structure, for he did not lean to such things. Nevertheless, there was a mountain of evidence, sound historical evidence, to prove beyond a shadow of a doubt that George Washington did believe in God. And, unfortunately, did not keep this belief to himself. He displayed it often in full view of eye witnesses.

And now that NuWorld had come there was no need of God.

So the question that Starr had been struggling with was simple: How do we give the history of George Washington to the people without letting them know of this unfortunate blot on the great man's character?

That was the nature of a remedial historian. To take historical material, and when it conflicted with the philosophy or beliefs of NuWorld—to find a way to amend the material.

It would have been simple for Starr to simply ignore the facts of Washington's religious bent. But that was the method of a heavy-handed amateur. That method was used, but the problem with that approach was that it simply didn't work! Someone was always digging up information and revealing facts long after NuWorld remedial historians thought they were safely destroyed.

Starr was one of the new breed of remedial historian. She felt that the facts were sacred. But when they did not fit into the system, it was her job to find a new method of *presenting* them so that they would dovetail with "truth."

"It"s a matter of selection and interpretation," she often said. "Facts are hard, but when they are placed in the crucible of selection and interpretation, they become flexible and then can be correctly grasped.

And it was her fiery and stubborn determination to face the whole "truth" that made her a valuable member of the Department.

"If Starr writes it up," Emmett Tau said firmly to his superior, "There won't be any skeletons in the closet for anyone to find. She'll find them herself and pick them apart bone by bone!"

But George Washington was not cooperating. Starr had doggedly pursued the man with every ounce of her intellect. She had examined literally thousands of pieces of information, some from his friends and many from his enemies. She had thrown upon his behavior and his life a harsh searchlight—

And had found nothing!

Finally, she reached out and switched her machines off, and then in a rare display of raw anger she struck the table with her fist.

"Blast you, George Washington!" she cried out, trembling with fatigue and anger. "You really *were* the greatest man of your day! And the whole thing would probably have fallen through if you hadn't held it together!"

Then she put both her fists on the table, leaned over and with her eyes closed, said in a hard, flat voice:

"And you *did* believe in God! And nothing I can say or do can change *that!* The trouble with you, George Washington, is that you didn't have the good sense to be an atheist! All you could do was save your country!"

Then she flung herself out of the room and left the building without speaking to another soul.

"What's wrong with Starr?" Emmett's assistant asked.

Emmett gave him a certain smile. "George Washington is giving her a bad time. But she'll get that rascal pinned down! You'll see!"

Chapter Two

THE RELIEVER

Adolf Hitler was on the right track, Starr thought as she left the gleaming black obelisk, *but he had that single flaw that prevented him from fulfilling his potential. He was insane. Washington believed in God. Hitler was insane. Well, thank Freud I don't have to remediate Hitler! Some poor fraulein was probably fuming over that right now. How do you amend the attempted extermination of an entire race of people in the name of Christianity when the alleged Christ was a member of that race? Good luck Gretel or Heidi; you'll need it.*

Starr felt the hot anger flowing through her and knew it was counterproductive, so she did what she had been doing more frequently to control any outburst of emotion—thought of the painting in her apartment. On the front steps of her mind was the light. Had there really been light like that in OldAge or was it only the imagination of the artist? Those lovely shafts, like transparent gold from the sky, striking the leaves and exploding in green-gold starbursts! She looked toward the Dome far above and the muddy glow that seeped through it, bathing the City in a perpetual brownish haze. Surely there had been no world like that painting!

As Starr came back to herself she was walking on the narrow strip of concrete between the sidebelt and the carrier track. She looked around self-consciously and stepped onto the sidebelt.

Directly in front of her was the Astral Mall with its massive rainbow-shaped entrance decorated with the twelve signs of the zodiac. She decided to grab a quick lunch before she made her afternoon house call.

As usual the mall was a sea of human bodies. The palm readers and fortune tellers were doing a thriving business. A barker in front of the Crystal Palace, dressed in a shimmering silver robe with the hood thrown back from his shaved head, was hawking business for his assortment of quartz crystals. "Kneel to your own self. Honor and worship your own being. God dwells within you as YOU!" He bowed and motioned her inside, but she shook her head and continued on. She had bought a crystal once but never could seem to use it correctly. One day she stepped on it in the dark and cut her foot. Then, with a vengeance she flung it down the disposal chute in her bathroom.

Starr stopped in front of the Dog Shoppe, which always amused her. In the display window the dogs were bouncing and chasing each other and barking their metallic little barks. Everyone thought it was a fad destined for the same fate as the Hovershoe and the Static Darmsbow, but the craze had lasted as long as Starr could remember. She stepped inside and put her hand over the rail into the play area and immediately the sensor of the closest dog picked it up. He was a Beagle, and his long ears flopped wildly as he bounded over to her and licked her finger with his wet and remarkably fleshlike tongue.

They were cute, she thought: Dalmatians, Shepherds, Chihuahuas, Great Danes, all four inches high and perfect in every detail. Real dogs, along with cats and most other household pets, had vanished of course—sometime during the Season of Black Skies when people were starving by the millions. She was tempted to buy one, but decided she must put away childish fancies if she were ever to achieve the proper Level of Ascended Consciousness.

The shopkeeper, wearing a tan smock and an unbearably pleasant smile, approached her from behind the counter. "May I interest you in one of our cuddly little darlings? The Beagles are on special today." He reached down and scratched the miniscule dog on the back and its right hind leg became a frenzy of motion. "The batteries have a lifetime guarantee and there's absolutely no maintenance."

Starr looked at the Beagle, its hind leg slowing down as the scratching stopped. "No thank you. I'm out a lot. I'm afraid he'd only get lonely."

The shopkeeper frowned and shrugged his shoulders. "Strange times we're living in," he said, returning to his counter.

As she left the shop, she glanced at the logo above the door, a rainbow ribbon of light containing the words, "God is dog spelled backwards. Dog be with you."

Like most in the City, the restaurant was a typical fast-food affair designed to provide you with the proper nutrition in the shortest possible time. The food was virtually tasteless, as most food was everywhere, but no one seemed to mind. Soon she would treat herself to a meal in one of the run-down cafes in the Fringe, which was the only place left that she knew of where food could be consumed for pleasure as well as energy.

What Starr liked about this one was the loft area that was accessible by a spiral staircase. There was seldom anyone there because of the wasted effort of climbing the stairs. As she climbed, Starr looked out over the fifty or so clear plastic tables and booths, all filled to capacity. The men and women were dressed in the same type of uniform that she wore; only the colors varied, reflecting occupation, and rank was indicated by symbols sewn on the right shoulder.

Starr sat at one of the three tables that looked out over the shoppers, bustling along the slate-covered floor of the mall. A series of fountains ran down the center as far as she could see and people were sitting on the circular benches that surrounded them. They were lighted by recessed florescent tubing, powered by a system of electric pumps tied into the massive dynamos in the bowels of the City and covered by plastic bubbles to keep the water secure. She tried to imagine children playing among the crystal and chrome and black plastic columns of the mall. She couldn't.

A slot was positioned under the right edge of the table and Starr slipped her hand in, palm down. A lighted menu appeared in the table top. She touched "Salad and two smaller adjacent squares for extra vitamin C and extra iron." Almost immediately she heard a whirring noise in the black column next to the table, a panel clicked open and she reached in the opening and took out a tan plastic container and spoon. She took the cover off and looked at the six green globs of paste-like substance arranged in a circle on the plate. *They've hired a chef from the City's Culinary Department, she thought, and replaced the cover. Well, at least there's the loft and the walls don't talk to you.*

"Greetings Starr Omega. Power and life to you." A small young man with a terrible complexion and sad brown eyes walked up, grinning at her. He worked in one of the offices in her building, and pestered her whenever he happened to see her in the restaurant.

"No need to be so formal. We're all merely citizens under the Dome." She had no sooner said it than one of the Manuals in his slate-gray overalls flicked by her line of vision and disappeared into the nearly invisible hinged panel in the far wall.

"Hey, Starr, what about it? You ready to get with me? My Theosophy professor says a hands-on experience with a Reliever is a must for anyone wanting a well-rounded education. I'm even thinking of majoring in Relief." He stood almost at attention in his tan office fatigues with a hopeful expression on his face.

She wished she could remember his name. "Pimples" was all that ever came to mind. "I'm afraid getting clearance from the proper authorities would be next to impossible in a situation like this. The Department of Extreme Concern has to approve them all now."

The young man paled under his acne. "Well, gee, it's not all that important I guess. There's always other areas of interest. Goodbye Starr Omega." He spun around, took the stairs two at a time and walked briskly across the restaurant and into the office.

Starr sat at her table, watching the masses moving below in their uniforms of muted shades of green and gray and brown. She sat and thought of the painting and of the light and the marvelous warmth and color of it, and she felt the soft breeze that stirred the leaves and set the light rippling and shimmering in the trees. *What in Freud's name am I doing?* she almost said aloud. *I have those pitiful citizens waiting for Relief and here I sit, lost in a dream of a forgotten world! You'd better start taking your responsibilities more seriously, Starr Omega! People are depending on you to fulfill dreams and lift burdens.*

As the harsh glare of the hidden florescent tubes drew her to the present, Starr lifted the plastic container and pushed a red button on the table's edge. A panel zipped open in the column, she tossed the container in, then stood up to leave. As she took the first step, a voice tinkled from underneath the table, "Thank you very much, Starr Omega. Please visit us again soon." A look of disdain came over her face. "Well, scratch another restaurant off the list," she thought as she headed for the stairs.

✦   ✦   ✦

The carrier came to a whining stop in front of the Department of Adjustment. It was closer to the Rim than the Department of History and the Astral Mall. Consequently, the buildings were somewhat shabbier and there were scraps of paper about. Starr even saw a plastic spoon lying in one of the narrow alleyways. Rumor had it that some of the undesirables who had eluded Peacemaker Units were seen on these very streets in the early morning hours.

Above the main entrance, in block letters on the building's gray plastic exterior were the words, "To Protect and Serve." Starr entered the main lobby and saw a crowd around the bank of elevators. She disliked the vacuum tubes, but since her daydreams had put her behind schedule she turned right down a narrow hall and stopped near the end. She placed her palm on the white circle on the wall and the panel whooshed open. Stepping into the narrow cylinder, she sat in the contoured seat, leaned back into the headrest and folded the curved and padded bars around her. "Sixty-seven, please," she said and closed her eyes. There was eight seconds of high-pitched whining and a heavy weight pressing down on her.

As Starr left the tube she heard a familiar and unwelcomed voice, "Hey, Starr. Come here a minute, will you." Sammy Chi was crossing the room toward her. She knew precisely what he was going to say.

"How about a three month Loving Friend contract? You'll only have half the fun, but it's better than nothing." His white teeth stood out against the dark face as he smiled broadly.

"You might as well ask for three years, Sammy," she called out over her shoulder as she continued toward her office. "You've got as much chance at that as you do three months, or three seconds."

Sammy's face reddened slightly, but he was not put off. Catching up with her, he took her by the arm and turned her around. "C'mon, Babe, Don't be so hard on yourself! Give it a chance." The smile had returned as he leaned on one of the many gray plastic desks in the common area, running his hand through his curly black hair.

He was interesting, but vain to a fault Starr thought, and she didn't have time today for verbal fencing. "Is that a gray hair I see, Sammy?" she asked, glancing toward the dark mass of curls.

The smile vanished. "Where? Show me where, Starr," he said in a sudden panic, bending his head down. "Pull it out!"

Starr turned and walked away, and as she entered her office she saw Sammy hurrying into the dressing room. "That'll occupy him for ten minutes," she thought. "Then he can pester someone else."

Her office was much like the one at the Department of History, except there was a gray plastic table instead of a desk and she had only one monitor. The space was eight feet by ten feet. There was an extra chair in one corner and a black cabinet in the other.

Starr sat down and touched the keyboard. The screen came to life. *1107723-Southeast Sector-Unit 43-Tube 49-Rim. Religious Dissident. Attitude untenable. That means only one thing,* she thought. *1107723 has gathered some scraps of Christianity from Freud knows where and refuses to have them expunged from his psyche.* She had never relieved one, but she didn't relish the task for these "Neo-Crossbearers" were the only clients never given the mind soothing chemicals that made them pliant as putty. They must face the most staggering of the "Unknowns" totally unassisted.

How bits and pieces of this ancient religion kept turning up and why some would cling so tenaciously to them was an absolute mystery to Starr. All other religions were tolerated and even encouraged, yet every effort was still being made to eradicate this pernicious behavioral plague that had proven so destructive to cilvilization in OldAge. All the artifacts relating to it had been destroyed (but the scraps kept surfacing)or, according to some, were stored in secure vaults in the White Tower above the Department of Concern. That, however, was only conjecture and she gave it little credibility.

Starr remembered the words of Freud, who loathed all religions, but, even in NuAge, had maintained his preeminence as the god of Behavioral History. *The whole thing is so patently infantile, so foreign to realilty, that to anyone with a friendly attitude to humanity it is painful to think that the great majority of mortals will never be able to rise above this view of life.*

Starr knew almost nothing of Christianity. She had dumped it into her "dustbin for religions" along with all the others she had been exposed to. To her, they were all the same. She had the mind of Goethe, who said, "He who possesses science and art also has religion; but he who possesses neither of those two, let him have religion!"

"Well, to work," she murmured, summoning her resolve. She pressed a button in the right edge of the table and waited forty-five seconds. There was one knock on the door and a stentorian voice from the other side announced, "Peacemaker delivery for Starr Omega."

Why must they be so loud? Are they all required to attend Bellowing School. "Come in," she said.

The Exactor was about six feet tall and dressed in a uniform similiar to Starr's, except that it was white with white nylon cross straps and white boots. Like all Peacemakers, he wore a white helmet with a mirrored visor that was always pulled down over his face. "Delivery accomplished," he said in a flat metallic voice.

Placing his hand palm down on the white circle on the top of the table the door opened. Then, he slammed the door as he left the room.

The man he had brought with him was dressed in the ubiquitous slate-gray overalls of the Manuals. He was about five-ten and bald, except for a gray fringe around his temples and down the back of his head and neck. He had pale blue eyes, thin lips and a nose that had been broken sometime in the past. His age was difficult to guess, maybe fifty-five. He weighed about one hundred and sixty pounds (the Metric System had never been accepted, even in Nu-World). His hands were strapped to a plastic transport belt around his waist.

Starr thought of him as harmless a person as she had ever seen. She was required to offer the dissidents who were not relocated a final opportunity to recant their beliefs, but she was taken aback by this one and was trying to formulate an opening statement. She had expected terror, not serenity. This, like all inappropriate behavior, was disturbing to her.

"My name is Philemon," he said.

"Philemon! No one is named Philemon," Starr replied without thinking.

"I am," the man said in a quiet steady voice.

Starr looked at him and tried to regain her composure. *Why is his presence so unsettling, she thought. I'd rather they came in screaming and thrashing about!*

"Aren't you supposed to talk to me?" the man asked.

After a thoughtful pause, Starr gave him the required appeal: "You can still be of service to the City," then looked at him closely. " What did you say your name was?"

"Philemon."

"Yes, Philemon. As I was saying, your situation is not hopeless. You need only denounce this insidious philosophy that has seduced you and the City will forgive your rebellion, embrace you and nurture you."

The man looked at her with those pale weary eyes that held no fear, that were filled with a kindly light and something else. "I'm a simple man," he said. "I don't understand your words."

Starr still couldn't place it as she looked at him. "I shouldn't tell you this, but all you have to do is make a statement. It doesn't have to change what you believe. Just don't talk about your beliefs."

The man smiled and Starr felt something. *Assurance, that's it she thought. That's what he has. He's so absolutely sure of something.*

"If I don't share what I have, I lose it," he said. "Let me share with you the . . . ."

"Stop!" Starr said. "I won't hear this. I offer you life and you throw it back in my face. Enough." *Someone must have given him a drug somewhere along the circuitous route they all take, to make him easier to handle. He's not rational.*

"I'll pray for you," Philemon said softly, but Starr was no longer listening to him.

I must learn to control myself, she thought. *This is worse than that George Washington business!* She touched the proper sequence of numbers on the cabinet, opened the heavy door and removed a white box the size of a man's heart. She placed the contents on the table: two pressurized syringes four inches long and the diameter of a pencil, an alcohol swab in a foil package (Why make it sterile?), and a two-inch by three-inch booklet entitled "The City—Departure Message."

Philemon's head was bowed and he was praying. All Starr saw was a man in extremis babbling to himself.

"I'm required to read this to you," Starr declared. The man raised his head and she saw that the assurance was unchanged. Starr read the brief message, ripped the foil package open and swabbed his left arm above the elbow. She held the first syringe to the sterilized area and pushed the button at the end. There was a pop like a distant air rifle and, as Starr turned away, she noticed Philemon's pupil's were normal.

Starr sat in her chair with her eyes closed. *I won't think about this,* she said to herself. *I'm a member of an honorable profession and the City has trained me well for it. I provide a valuable and indispensible service to our citizens.* And after a few seconds, *He won't be any problem now.*

The drug had taken Philemon out of the room, the City— and the world. He sat limp and docile. Starr took a pair of heavy scissors from a drawer in the table and cut the plastic thongs on his wrists. Then she had him stand, removed the plastic transport belt and laid it on the table next to the white box. Taking the second syringe and setting the timer for ten minutes, she tucked it inside her tunic and said, "Follow me."

Starr led the way down a dark narrow corridor and entered the third door on the right. Normally the entire procedure was accomplished here, but none of the standard rules applied for dissidents. The room was dim with a soft green light emanating from the top of the opposite wall. To the left was a reclining chair covered in a dark green fabric.

"Sit down, please," Starr said, and Philemon lay back in the plush chair.

Starr touched a sensor on the arm of the chair and the entire wall in front of it sprang to life. Even after witnessing it dozens of times, Starr felt that she was actually rushing at incredible speed through deep space. Giant asteroids zipped by and the entire solar system could be seen at a great distance with the sun's overpowering brightness and the steady shine of the planets.

Looking away from the screen, Starr took the syringe from her tunic and walked to the opposite side of the chair. She looked down at Philemon. His eyes were closed and his lips were moving. *Poor thing,* she thought, *He's babbling to himself.* She placed the syringe against his left arm and pressed the button. There was a soft pop as the air pressure sent the clear liquid into Philemon's veins. There was nothing left to do.

It's gone extremely well, Starr thought as she left the room. *No complications whatsoever.* She closed the door behind her.

Two floors down, Lido, a Manual assigned to housekeeping duties was startled by the sound of the slamming door. "No one closes doors that hard," he muttered and continued on his way in one of the service shafts that honeycombed the building.

Starr entered the break room and walked directly to the coffee service built into the wall. Taking a tan cup from the shelf, she held it under the spigot and touched the "Black-extra dark" sensor. The steaming liquid filled the cup one quarter inch from the rim. The room was empty and she sat down in a hard plastic chair next to the coffee service and closed her eyes with her head resting against the wall.

"Maybe I came on a little strong, Starrkins. You think we could start all over?" Starr groaned inside at the sound of Sammy's voice. *Good Freud! Will this man never learn!* She didn't respond in any way, merely sat there with her eyes closed holding her cup of coffee.

"Starr, are you asleep? Did you hear me?"

"Unfortunately I did, Sammy, ' she replied, keeping her eyes closed. "And to answer your questions chronologically: No-no-yes."

"I don't understand," Sammy said with a puzzled look on his face.

"I believe that, Sammy. I truly do."

Sammy sat in the chair next to Starr. "Is there something wrong with me?" he asked in a hurt voice.

Starr thought about Sammy and men in general. Maybe there was something wrong with her. She had no inclination to establish a relationship with anyone. "No, Sammy. There's nothing wrong with you. Not even any gray hair." She heard him laugh.

"That was a good one. Kept me looking in that mirror for ten minutes. How about going to the Sensory with me tonight? I hear they've just about got taste perfected in this new one. The other four have always been good, but I'd just about as soon have the OldAge movies the way this taste thing was going for awhile there."

Starr heard the drone of his voice, but none of his words. She was thinking of assurance; pure, fearless, perfect assurance. And she saw a light in pale blue eyes that was somewhere still shining.

Chapter Three

THE FAR FIELDS

Bernard Alpha's office was larger than most. As director of the Department of Adjustment, with its four separate bureaus: Geriatric, Infant, Disease and Dissident, he was allowed two hundred square feet of space. He also had the only window in the building and it was huge by NuWorld standards, four feet tall and spanning the entire outside wall of the office, a distance of sixteen feet. Inside it looked like the rest of the tan wall. When he touched a sensor on his desk, it became transparent, but the dull black surface outside, which was kept polished to a sheen before the shortage of Manuals, remained unchanged.

The window was a status indicator with little practical purpose. The view it provided was of the blank wall of the adjacent building only yards away. As space was at a premium under the Dome, growth was vertical rather than horizontal and the proximity of the buildings made sweeping vistas impossible. Bernard could, by standing at the extreme left of his window, look up and to the right, and see the slow curving fall of the Dome toward the Rim. On a particularly bright day, there seemed to be a slight tint of gold to the dirty brown light that filtered through.

Bernard touched his keyboard and Starr Omega appeared on his monitor. "Starr, would you come to my office please. I have an unscheduled duty for you."

Starr was leaving her office with the white box and the transport belt. She looked back at her monitor. "Yes sir. I'll just drop these off at Supply."

I hate to assign this unpleasant task to her, Bernard thought. But she is competent and hasn't had field experience yet.

Bernard opened the right bottom drawer of his desk and took an eight by ten black and white print from a hidden slot. *It wouldn't do for a man in my position to evidence any sentiment for OldAge.* He always used the print to calm him before any disagreeable chore, and during his lunch hour he locked his door and lost himself in it while he ate.

The photograph showed a park with acres and acres of trees surrounded by office buildings. There was a stream flowing through the open meadows and woods and people walking on footpaths and over bridges that crossed the stream. Boys and girls played on swings and slides and merry-go-rounds and families were picnicking on blankets spread in the shade of the trees. All this in the very heart of the city!

There was a single knock on the door of the office. "Come in," Bernard said, hastily replacing the picture.

Starr entered and took one of the two hard green straight-backed chairs in front of the desk. "You wanted to see me sir?" She liked Bernard Alpha. There wasn't a hair on his head. His eyes were fringed with blonde lashes and brows and he was the most pleasant man she had ever known, in a position of authority.

Bernard lifted his five-feet-two frame from the chair and sat on the desk next to Starr. "Someone has to make a house call and I'm afraid you're the only one available," he said in his soft clear voice.

Starr frowned and replied, "I've never been in the field before. You're sending me alone?"

There was a chuckle from Bernard. "Don't look so anxious, Starr Omega. I do believe you've heard too many wild stories in the break room."

"There's a rumor going around the office that someone has to make a 'house call' to the Rim today."

"It's not a rumor. It's also not dangerous or I wouldn't be sending you, or any one for that matter, alone."

"Going alone to the Rim doesn't concern me. I visit the restaurants in the area once in a while," Starr said, crossing her legs and leaning back in the chair.

Bernard placed both hands on the edge of the desk and leaned forward. "What's the problem then?"

Starr looked into his kind eyes. He truly was a different kind of bureaucrat. "Just a feeling I have."

"I watched you with the Neo-Crossbearer today. He got to you, didn't he?"

"It went perfectly." she said, unable to meet his eyes. She noticed the broken nail on her left ring finger.

"That's not what I asked you."

She was silent. *Must have happened during the Relief Procedure she thought.*

Bernard had returned to his chair. "You haven't answered my question, Starr."

"I'm sorry," she said, looking up.

"Never mind," Bernard said. He touched a sensor on his desk and swiveled his chair half around.

Starr was watching the wall become transparent. "I didn't hear the question."

Bernard didn't repeat the question. He had seen this happen before. "I was monitoring your Relief Process today, Starr. I trust you give no credence to the OldAge concept of death. That should have surfaced in the training period."

"I have no such illusion," Starr said formally.

"How do you view it then?"

"The same way any rational person would." Starr looked at the back of Bernard's head, then beyond him to the dark wall of the next building. "There is no such thing as death."

"Please continue," Bernard said as he swung his chair around to face her.

The face that Starr looked into was becoming harder. "There is only an endless recycling of the soul into body after reincarnated body," she said, returning her gaze to the broken nail.

"Exactly! And since there is no death, it only follows that there are no victims," Bernard said, not believing a single word he spoke. Beliefs didn't matter, or perhaps he no longer had any beyond his own immediate circumstances.

"It should have been different," Starr said. "I didn't expect him to act that way."

"Even in this age of enlightenment, human behavior is sometimes unpredictable, Starr," Bernard said.

"Yes." she said, unable to look up. "I understand that. It's only that he was so like . . . like a child. That's it. It was like working in the Children's Bureau, except he was a man."

"You need to reacquaint yourself with the basic precept of the Department, Starr," Bernard said, worried that she would not meet his eyes. "Do you recall it?"

Starr knew she must regain control of herself. "Yes sir," she said sitting up straight and meeting his eyes.

"I'd like to hear it, please."

Starr recited "All our clients are no longer *karmically* in balance with the greater society. Therefore, we are rendering them the greatest possible service by enabling them to enter the next life."

"Excellent," Bernard said. "It is imperative that we free ourselves of the atavistic emotional baggage of OldAge if we are to cleanse the Earth and bring about the fullness of the New World Order."

Starr was in control again and looked coolly into Bernard's eyes. "I'm honored to be an integral part of the *Purification Process,*" Starr said, feeling her confidence returning with the words.

Bernard smiled and took a "field kit" from his desk drawer. It was a slim white box with the logo of the Department of Adjustment on one side and a clip on the other. "The address is inside," he said. "I'm sure you'll enjoy the trip."

"Thank you, sir," Starr said. She clipped the box to her belt and left the office.

After Starr was gone, Bernard considered the effect that such a brief experience with the man named Philemon had had on her. He had encountered only a handful of these "Crossbearers" and knew virtually nothing of their philosophy, as it was forbidden in NewAge. He believed them, as well as their predecessors in OldAge, to be a part of the ignorant and unwashed masses. That is until a few months ago.

He had been called to the White Tower on an urgent matter and, after its conclusion, visited an old friend who worked in the vaults. Quite by accident, he had been left alone with some of the artifacts of OldAge. Among them were portions of the writings of a man named Paul who had lived in the first century, by OldAge reckoning of time. He was evidently one of the exponents of this philosophy, and though he had had only a few moments to scan the writings, Bernard knew that this had been a brilliant and learned man.

Too many nights since then Bernard had lain awake with an unrelenting desire to read the complete works of this eloquent man who had written so long ago, of concepts unknown to him, of sin and grace and salvation, and of someone called Jesus.

Bernard Alpha stood at his window and looked down at the narrow carrier track and the base of the building opposite his. What he saw in his mind's eye was a color version of the black and white print in his desk. The people were moving about the park and he could hear the shouts of the children and smell the food on the tablecloths that were spread on the cool green grass in the shade of the trees. It was getting easier and easier for him to envision this scene. He felt that soon he would be able to join the people, eat with them, stretch out on the cool grass and fall into a long dreamless sleep.

The harsh buzzing of the monitor on his desk snatched Bernard from the vision. He was disturbed by the reality of his daydream. He crossed to his desk, but before answering the call he retrieved Starr Omega's personnel file from Central Records to his monitor, typed a brief entry into it and locked it in with the security code.

✦　　　　✦　　　　✦

"How's my favorite Reliever today?" Ken Gamma asked Starr as she entered the station.

"Fine, Ken," Starr replied. The sleds running on time today or should I catch a nap?"

"You got about ten minutes. Wanna go on up?"

She hated this part, another vacuum tube. But there was no sense in prolonging it. "Might as well," she said, enjoying the way he always catered to her with no demands attached.

Ken was on permanent duty at this station and he was her favorite. He had short brown hair and a round face and was always in a good mood. His uniform, which was a replica of the Peacemaker's, without the helmet and visor, was too tight for his pudgy body. For some reason this was not offensive to Starr, even though the NuAge ideal was the classic ectomorph body type. He reminded her of something she had run across during her research at the Office of Remedial History. It was in an OldAge children's book and was called a "Teddy Bear."

Starr sat on a bench and watched Ken go through the check list of the vacuum tube that would catapult her one hundred and fifty feet vertically to the loading platform that was a part of the Dome Sled track.

Stations for the Dome Sleds were located on the top floors of buildings that formed a geometric pattern throughout the city and at towers located around the Rim. Access, for the most part, was limited to official business. The sleds themselves were bullet-shaped stainless steel tubes containing five two-person benches, one behind the other. They had open windows that curved up into the roof and they ran on tracks that were attached to the underside of the Dome.

"All ready," Ken said as he bowed to her and made a gesture toward the tube with his left hand.

Starr took a deep breath and walked toward Ken. "I wish that tube wasn't clear. I'd rather not see where I am. Can't you paint it black or something?"

Ken chuckled. "Don't worry 'Starry Eyes,' I haven't lost a customer all day."

"I've got to get a job with more horizontal travel," Starr said to Ken as she stepped into the cramped chamber. Then there was a brief rush and the blur of the city all around her.

Standing on the steel eyrie of the loading platform, Starr looked down a thousand feet to the canyons between the buildings. Hundreds of carriers were sliding along their tracks like gray clots moving slowly and silently through the arteries of the City. To her left, the Dome rose slowly and inexorably toward the White Tower. It was a two hundred foot high white pyramid atop the thousand foot black tower that housed the Department of Concern. The entire structure had come to be called the White Tower and it stood in the exact center of the City.

At this height the light was much brighter as it came through the thick clear acrylic panels of the Dome, and it seemed to gather darkness as it descended. It glimmered and gleamed and moved in slow waves all around her and Starr felt she was in a city beneath the sea.

As she stood there gripping the cold steel of the hand railing, she thought of all the great cities of the world that had disappeared in the Season of Waters. *She saw an enormous shark, its eyes dead and cold as the depths of space, glide slowly through the murky waters of the Rotunda in the Capitol, a hundred feet beneath the surface of the Atlantic. Crabs were scuttling across the sandy bottom in the streets of Leningrad. She thought of New York and London and Tokyo, of Cairo and Barcelona and Melbourne, all taken by the sea.*

The Dome Sled creaked heavily into position at the loading platform. Starr remembered the words of a poet, or perhaps he was a visionary, from OldAge, *A savage servility slides by on grease.*

The long descent to the Rim began. Starr was enjoying the ride as she marvelled at the Dome Sled System. It was built during the leanest period of the energy shortage, before the grain fields came into full production, and harked back to OldAge techology. An interconnecting series of cables and pulleys was designed to transfer the energy released by a descending sled to one that was ascending. This "gravitational" energy source had to be supplemented by electric power, but it was seventy-five percent self-sustaining.

Because of the nature of her "home visit," Starr was given an "Express Sled." As she passed the loading platforms along the track, she could hear bits and pieces of conversations:

"Peyote buttons? How in Freud's name did you manage that?"

"I have this friend who works at the Greenhouse and . . . ."

". . . at this precious little antique shop. It's an authentic Ouija from OldAge with . . . ."

"Holistic health shops are passe, my dear, and I'll tell . . . ."

". . . and having originated in the Lyra nebula, I'm able . . . ."

She soon tuned them out and heard only the low hum the sled made against the track and the occasional creaking as she shifted positions for a better view.

As far as she could see the stark windowless buildings stretched in unbroken columns, following the invariable downward flow of the Dome. The government buildings were black, commerce and industry (which were government-controlled) were gray and the residential were tan. There was very little variation from this color scheme.

Ten feet above her Starr could see nests built on the surface of the Dome and birds of all sizes and colors were flying into and out of them carrying insects and worms for their young. Over the years debris, brought in by the winds and the birds, had collected in various areas and formed a kind of loose soil. To her amazement, Starr saw grasses and plants (and trees as tall as twenty feet high) were growing on the Dome. She was enthralled by the sight, for all the flora of the City was restricted to the government greenhouse and only authorized personnel were allowed admittance.

Starr tried to identify some of the birds and trees, but her knowledge was limited since there was virtually nothing on this subject in the general information pool. There was a plethora of files concerning the artifacts and mentifacts of OldAge, but information (especially visual) regarding its flora, fauna and terrain was practically non-existent.

A squirrel skittered across the smooth surface of the Dome and climbed a small tree that Starr believed was a variety of oak. He sat upright on the base of a limb and began eating a small nut of some kind. Starr could not identify it. She saw how the light hit him and gave off a reddish glow like something she had seen a long time ago but had no name for.

The sled was passing over the zone that marked the transition from Central City to the Rim. The tallest buildings here were three stories and there were no carrier tracks in the streets. But the streets were filled with people! This never failed to excite Starr and she loved to walk among them whenever she made a trip to one of the restaurants and she always came alone.

The black market flourished. You could buy jewelry and liquor and outlandishly colorful clothes of every design imaginable. There was a bustling barter system, and few of the people ever took part in the credit system of the City.

And entertainment! It was even more outlandish than the clothes. There were jugglers and acrobats and magicians on every street corner, or so it seemed. There were dancers and musicians on the streets and in the clubs, and plays were performed in the theatres. There were no Sensories. *Perhaps because of a lack of power,* Starr thought.

For years, the Peacemakers had tried to bring order and conformity to the Fringe, as this area was called, but it finally became a game of diminishing returns and they turned their efforts elsewhere. Anyone on the run from government authority was likely to be found here. Most of the stations along this section of the track were closed.

What Starr liked best were the artists. There were few studios. They mostly set their easels up on the streets and painted portraits and scenes of life in the area. Families gathered around their tables sharing meals, people dancing and drinking and celebrating at various events (it seemed they were always looking for a reason to celebrate).

One event in particular intrigued her. Someone had told her it was called a wedding. She had researched this and found it to be a custom of OldAge, but she was unable to grasp any real purpose for its continued existence.

It was a stimulating and mysterious area. And one mystery in particular attracted Starr—the paintings of one artist. He had a small shop near a restaurant she visited, but he would never speak of his work. "They're for sale, not for discussion," he had told her. There were scenes of vast plains and rolling hills and lakes and rivers. Some depicted a barren and desolate mountainous area. And some were of gold and green fields, broken by stands of huge trees that seemed to go on forever.

Starr had reached the final station. The heels of her nylon boots rang against the metal surface of the stairs as she descended into the very heart of the Rim. What struck her first was the laughter. Not the ringing, raucous laughter of the Fringe, but a warm, melodic sound that flowed over her like the showers she enjoyed so much.

People crowded the streets here, as in the Fringe, but they were dressed in the slate-gray overalls of the Manuals. She stopped two women as they walked by her.

"Pardon me. Could you tell me how to locate this address?" she asked, showing them the address she had taken from the box.

The women looked at the logo of the Department of Adjustment and their smiles vanished. "I'm sorry, I don't read," the older one said. "But you might check there."

"I'll read it . . ." Starr said, but the women had turned quickly and melted into the crowd.

Starr looked at the building the woman had pointed to. It was a long, gray, one story affair constructed of sheet metal. There was a double line of these structures, all identical, curving along the base of the Dome as far as she could see. She opened a heavy iron door that swung easily and quietly on its hinges and looked into an enormous room filled with gleaming metal tables and chairs. The walls were lined with benches, and men and women sat and stood and walked about the room. Their expressions and actions seemed out of place in the cold stark environment of the great hall.

In a far corner of the room was a cubicle of transparent plexiglass panels. Inside it, Starr could see a row of gray metal filing cabinets, a desk with papers scattered on it and a lamp that glowed yellow in the white glare of the room. Above the door was a white panel with the word *Office* in black letters. A man with thin brown hair combed tightly to his skull sat at the desk, his head bowed over the papers.

As Starr crossed toward the office the people nodded and spoke to her. She returned their greetings, but felt uncomfortable doing so. She stepped into the open door frame of the office and the man looked up from his work. When he saw the emblem on the white box, he rose quickly from his chair.

"May I help you?" he asked.

Starr decided not to use the address. "I'm trying to locate a woman named Martha Epsilon."

"Yes, we were expecting you."

"You were?" Starr asked.

"Well, Martha was anyway."

"I see," Starr said, although she didn't.

"If you'll follow me, please," the man said as he walked around her and out of the office.

Starr followed him out a door directly opposite the one she had come in. It gave onto a narrow alley of bare concrete eight feet wide. The adjacent building had an open doorway and she could hear the sound of splashing water and the low rumble of a hundred separate conversations at one time.

The man turned left down another narrow alley between the communal bath houses. She followed him, her boots thudding on the smooth concrete. At the end of the alley, the man stopped and pointed to the right. Starr was unprepared for what lay at the end of the alleyway. She saw hundreds and hundreds of metal cylinders stacked at the very base of the Dome. They curved out of sight in both directions and were arranged in double rows of ten high and ten wide, back to back with the open ends out. They were four feet wide and eight feet long and appeared to have been welded together, forming single units of two hundred.

Men and women were going to and from the bath houses and climbing and descending the ladders that provided access to the cylinders. Most of them were barefoot. Some were in overalls and some had towels wrapped around them. All were dripping water and leaving wet footprints on the bare concrete floor. Starr looked to where the man was still pointing and saw the white panel with black lettering at the base of stack, *Southeast Sector–Unit 43*.

"Martha lives in tube seventy-three," the man said. "Will there be anything else?"

"No, thank you," Starr said as she stood in the controlled bedlam of the Rim, stunned, looking at the endless stacks of tubes. She noticed that the base of the Dome, to a height of fifty feet, was of opaque black acryllic and that, above it, the thickness of the panels and the angle made seeing through it impossible.

Starr followed the four foot wide passageway between the tubes. Some of them had cloths hanging over the ends; some were open. She noticed a pale woman in her mid-twenties sitting at the edge of tube number forty-nine. The woman had blonde hair and her light blue eyes were fixed on a picture she held in both hands.

Further along, to her right, Starr found tube number seventy-three, the home of Martha Epsilon. The lower rungs of the solid steel, forty foot high ladder were worn halfway through.

"Martha Epsilon?" Starr called, and waited.

Eight feet up a woman with short white hair that looked as if it had been cut with heavy shears looked over the edge of the tube. She had dark, olive skin and an open, unassuming expression on her face, which was surprisingly free of wrinkles. When she smiled, Starr noticed that most of her teeth were missing.

"Are you Martha Epsilon?" Starr asked.

"That's me, honey," the woman said. "Come on up."

Starr felt the smooth cool steel on her hands as she went up and thought of the untold climbs before hers that had worn the rungs of the ladder so deeply.

"Come on in. I'm making us some tea," the woman said.

There was a threadbare blue carpet on the floor with padding underneath to fill in the hollow of the curve. Three cushions lay along the right wall and two blankets, an extra pair of overalls and some odds and ends of clothes and other articles were stacked neatly at the rear. A cloth bag with a strap sewn on the side, packed as if for a trip, stood against the opposite wall. Near the clothes, on the bare metal floor was a small one burner stove. A copper kettle sat on the stove.

"Do you know why I'm here?" Starr asked.

The woman took two chipped plastic cups from behind her and placed them next to the stove. "Yes I do. You're going to take me to the Fields. That's why you're here."

Starr watched steam rise from the spout of the kettle as the woman poured the dark liquid into the cups. "I'm sorry there's no sugar. Times are hard right now," the woman said as she handed the cup to Starr. "Be careful. It's hot."

"I'm not here to take you to the Fields," Starr said. "I don't even know what you're talking about."

"The Fields," the woman said. "The beautiful green Fields where I was born. They're so far away I can't make it by myself. You've come to help me."

"I'm a Reliever," Starr said. "Do you know what that is?"

The woman looked puzzled. "Yes."

"I'm here to do my job."

"But I've done nothing wrong."

"I know that. I'll help you enter your next body. You're through with this one."

"This is the only one I'll ever have. When I leave this one I'll be pure spirit."

Starr saw there was no use talking to her. "If you'll lie down now, I'll help you."

The woman sat her cup down next to the stove. "They came and took me away from my mama and my daddy when I was ten years old. I worked for them sixty-three years cleaning their buildings. Now I'm too old to work. Please let me see my home before I die, my beautiful Fields, my beautiful green Fields."

Starr had seen deranged people before. "Please lie down," she said.

"I will, child," Martha said. "I'm not afraid to die. I just thought I was going home first. I'm just an old woman, a silly old woman. I don't know why I thought that."

As Starr prepared the syringe, she looked at Martha. She was staring up at something that was not visible and she had a smile on her face that seemed to brighten the air around her. "I'm so tired and I'm going home. I'm finally going home."

Starr decided to use only one syringe. She used it and sat back and waited.

Martha lay back against the opposite wall with her head resting on the cold steel. Her coveralls were threadbare and the white socks on her feet made them look like a child's. A blue shawl, faded from countless washings, was draped around her thin shoulders. "How beautiful the heavens are," she said and lifted her arms upward. "Lord Jesus, receive my spirit."

Starr had never heard the name before and the sound of it caused her to shiver. She was swept away by the immutable flow of eternity. Someone from long ago was calling her name and, in the echoing sound of a child's laughter, she was falling, falling into hands that were strong and gentle and sure.

Martha lowered her arms and turned her head toward Starr. "I forgive you, child," she said. "Lord, lay not this sin to her charge."

And when Martha had said this, her head moved slowly to the side and she fell asleep. Starr sat in the home of Martha Epsilon for a long time. And when she went down the ladder, she saw two men in white suits waiting at the end of the dark alley.

Chapter Four

Memories

Starr was trembling and couldn't stop. She stood in front of her bathroom mirror in the harsh glare of the neon tube. Her face was drenched with sweat and her hair curled in dark wet tendrils about her face, ears and neck. She touched the white dot on the counter, then splashed water on her face with both hands until it stopped running. Her face in the mirror looked strange, as though it belonged to someone she hadn't seen for a long time and couldn't quite remember.

The dream had come to her for the third time in as many nights, and the mood that descended on her afterwards was the same as last night and the night before that. No matter how hard she tried, she couldn't think her way out of it.

She stood in a small grove of trees and looked out across the Fields that stretched in an unbroken sweep of relentless green from horizon to horizon. At the top of the tree Starr stood under, a fox squirrel was eating an acorn and the tiny cuttings were falling on her like soft dry rain. The skies were dark and threatening; thunder rolled across the land like the sound of distant cannon. Far out in the field, an old woman with rough-cut gray hair, and wearing tattered overalls, was walking slowly away from her.

"Wait for me!" Starr cried out as she walked toward the old woman.

As the wind came, Starr began to run after the woman.
"Wait! Please don't leave me!"

She ran through the green, endless Fields as the wind grew stronger, flattening the Fields and tearing the tops of the trees. In the rushing of the wind was the name that the woman had spoken. The name was the same as the wind. When the woman spoke the name, the heavens opened and she left her body lying in the Fields and rose like a star into the bright open sky.

The wind subsided, along with the clouds. The woman also was gone, except for the flesh that she had been. Under a hard pale sky, Starr stood in the endless green Fields, realizing that now she was all alone in the earth.

Lights from the great height of the Dome that burned during all the hours of darkness gleamed softly on the blank walls of the buildings. They were purposed for combatting the crime problem, but Starr enjoyed the air of fantasy they lent the City. They softened the stark reality of day and created an atmosphere where she could escape into her mind.

The view from her window was sparse, her own block and parts of two others. It couldn't contain the worlds she imagined. But tonight, and for the last two nights, the dream had taken those worlds from her.

As she looked out she thought of an old newsreel she had seen in the course of her research—the Battle of Verdun in France in September of 1916. The constant shelling had blasted away all the trees; what remained was a moonscape of charred, twisted stumps, and trenches and bunkers packed with cold, weary, hungry men. That scene came to her tonight. She saw the desolate battlefield, with a dry wind blowing across barbed wire and shell craters; she saw torn bodies—and felt how very much like her soul this place was.

✦   ✦   ✦

Starr stood next to Sammy Chi in a long line of people waiting to get into The Pentagram Club.

"It's the hottest thing in town, Babe," Sammy said as he
moved to the rumble of the music coming from the building.
"You're gonna love this place. I guarantee it."

Starr was familiar with Sammy's guarantees, but she was not
going to stay home and wait for the dream. *I must really be desperate,* she thought as she watched Sammy gyrating next to her.

Inside the club the music was deafening. The rhythm was a
frenetic hammering that threatened to crush Starr's eardrums, and
if there was any melody at all, it lay crippled and helpless under
the driving, pounding drums and percussion. Behind it all, Starr
could hear what sounded like the wavering wail that came from
minarets in ancient cities on the opposite side of the world.

"Whadda you think, Babe?" Sammy screamed into her ear.
He had told her to dress in white, the "in" color for this week she
supposed, and he had on a baggy white coat and pants covered in
sequins.

He didn't want to hear her answer, Starr thought. She pointed
to her ears, shrugged her shoulders and continued across the
crowded club. She had on a white silk jumpsuit with a red belt and
high heeled red boots. She had bought them for the occasion, determined to liven up her life. The salesgirl had assured her the outfit
was the perfect choice.

She noticed several men staring at her as she passed. She also
saw the frown on Sammy's face. Her hair and nails were done to
perfection. She had spent two hours on her make-up. Starr knew
she was not beautiful, but tonight she presented a stunning appearance. Men were reacting as she had intended them to. But she was
more depressed than she could ever remember being.

"Could we sit down, Sammy?" she asked.

Sammy looked across the sea of churning white-clothed bodies and then back to Starr. "Looks like we'll be standing for awhile, Babe," he screamed back at her.

Starr wished she had never told Sammy that "Babe" was sometimes used as a term of endearment in OldAge.

Purple, red and orange lights were flashing from the walls and ceiling. People were bumping and jostling them as they went to and from the dance floor. But there was no place left to stand. Starr wondered why the club was so full of smoke, until she saw thin streams of it rising from vents in the floor. *What's next,* she thought, *acid baths from the ceiling? What a choice I have. The dream or this nightmare.*

A waitress with a bald head and some fake horns came by carrying a red tray. On it were stacks of tiny white wafers. Sammy placed his right hand under the tray, took two wafers and handed one to Starr. Along with him, she placed the wafer on her tongue and felt it immediately dissolve. Starr felt herself moving away from her surroundings, but not far enough, she thought. She had heard that the drug's effect depended on the personality of the user. Sammy, she noticed, was jumping straight up and down like he was on a trampoline.

There was an electronic drumroll and the music and the people stopped. What was left was the wavering, high-pitched moaning that was grating on Starr's nerves. Curtains opened, revealing a small stage with a raised white altar. Starr knew what was coming.

A giant of a man in a leathery black suit that wrinkled and folded over his entire body walked heavily onto the stage. His head was covered by a square iron helmet that rested on his shoulders, and he wore massive iron boots that threatened to crash through the floor of the stage with each step.

As he raised his arms, Starr noticed that his hands were not visible under the suit. It covered the ends of his arms as it would the ends of posts or beams.

"Greetings from the Dark Kingdom," the man said in a voice that sounded like shattering glass. "Tonight, we shall awaken to higher realities and attain ascendent levels of consciousness."

"Let's go, Sammy," Starr yelled. "I've seen this all before."

Sammy looked at her with a puzzled expression, then his face brightened as he realized she didn't know. "No you haven't. The City passed an ordinance this morning. It's legal now. This is gonna be the real thing, Babe."

"I'm not up to it tonight," she said as she walked away.

A nude girl about eight years old was being led onto the stage by two black-haired women in white robes. She had long, tangled brown hair and her soft eyes were huge with astonishment, terror and betrayal. When she saw the man and the white altar, she began a hopeless struggle against the women who held her.

As Starr passed the giant in black, she looked up at the iron mask. Light seemed to be draining into the slits for the eyes and around the mouth ice crystals were forming as he breathed. She stopped and Sammy bumped her from behind. Starr walked on, thinking it was the drug that had caused this. As they left she heard the terrible screaming of the child.

Sitting next to Sammy in the carrier on the way home, Starr watched the couples strolling along the sidewalks. She hated the sidebelts and was thankful they were installed only in a small central section of the City. She enjoyed seeing the differing gaits of the men and women and always felt better about herself when she walked somewhere. It seemed such a healthy and wholesome thing to do.

Starr dreaded the inevitable confrontation with Sammy at the door of her apartment. *What a night,* she thought. *After this the dream can't be so bad. But it was.*

The door slammed loudly behind her as Starr stalked into her apartment. "That man has got to be part octopus," she said out loud. "Why do I do this to myself?"

She took off her boots and belt, then stripped off the silk jumpsuit, carried them into the bathroom, and dumped the whole pile down the trash chute. "That's much better," she said. "Never again, Sammy Chi. Never, never again!"

But she knew the problem was not Sammy Chi. He was no worse than most men she knew. In fact, he was probably a cut above the average, even if he did have eight arms. No, the problem was Starr Omega and she didn't know what to do about it.

Starr showered and put on her heavy cotton robe and thick cotton socks. Then she went into the kitchen area and brewed a cup of herbal tea. Turning on her reading lamp, she stretched out in her recliner. She had paid a small fortune for the chair and knew it was more than worth it every time she ran her fingers over the soft brown leather. Taking her textbook, *Early Cinema in OldAge America,* from the table, she opened it to chapter twelve, *Romance—The Deadliest Form of Heart Disease.*

The text concerned itself primarily with the aftermath of romantic courtship: financial problems, unwanted and abused children, wife beating and divorce. There was precious little film footage in the archives, as anything other than interior scenes and selected shots of cities was prohibited, but Starr was fascinated by the ancient customs.

The bringing of flowers was her favorite. She often imagined some well-mannered (manners seemed important then) and gentle young man showing up at her door dressed in an old fashioned coat and tie and handing her a bouquet of red roses. She would put them in water in a porcelain vase. Then, the two of them would sit on a sofa in the parlor and talk. They would speak of poetry, music, and art, and of their families.

"And how are your mother and father?" he would say, taking her hand in his and smiling.

"Very well, thank you. And yours?"

"Fine, thank you." he would reply. "And your aunt Martha? I trust she's feeling better."

Starr tried to remember her mother and father, but their images were indistinct and so very far away. She seemed to recall a certain fragrance and a softness that was her mother, and the sound of her voice humming a simple sweet melody and the steady soothing motion of the rocking chair. Her father was gentle with strong hands lifting her higher and higher and swinging her around and around as she giggled and shrieked.

Nights in her bedroom were mommy and daddy kneeling by her as she lay snuggled in the cool sheets and warm blankets. Their voices were so beautiful and close as they talked—as they talked with someone they knew very well. Their love for her was like the warmth and softness of her bed. Her mother's song and her father's laugh folded around her and carried her safely through the long night.

The long night. Starr laid the text on the table next to her chair. What would carry her through this night—and the nights that lay before her like sworn enemies marshalling their dark forces? How would she ever endure those long, long nights to come?

There was a dreadful sobbing in the room and Starr sat up to realize it was coming from deep inside her chest. Tears were dropping slowly from her cheeks and sparkling in the light of the lamp as they fell on her trembling hands. After a time it stopped and she curled herself in the chair and waited for the dream.

The next morning Starr was at the stove watching the bacon wrinkle and pop in the frying pan as she breathed in deeply the heady aroma. She thought again of her parents. Her Caretaker had told her that they had "reached untenable positions of social maladjustment." She was all too familiar with the consequences for those residents of the City who distinguished themselves in this fashion.

How different her life would have been had she remained with her parents? She was taken from them when she was five, only because they hid her. Children were routinely taken into the custody of the City when they were two, as parents were not deemed suitable to rear them. The Caretaker system had been in effect for generations and was regarded as the most effective means of producing responsible, conforming citizens. It was designed to mitigate, if not eliminate, counterproductive emotions such as tenderness, empathy and love.

It might be nice to visit them once in a while. Some of her friends did that, although not often, and most of them never mentioned their parents. The sound of her mother's song was coming to her as she forcibly thrust it from her mind. *Not now,* she thought. *This is not the time for that. This is the time:*

To prepare a face to meet the faces that you meet—

She looked at the bacon. It was burned black and brittle. An acrid smoke was rising from the skillet. She scraped the bacon into the trash and tossed the skillet into the sink. Then she went into the bathroom, got into the shower and turned the water on as hot as she could stand it.

✦   ✦   ✦

Sheila Phi paced her office and waited for Starr. She would stop occasionally and stare at her portrait of Gertrude Stein. She loved the strong German face and the thick beautiful hair and the lovely dark eyes. If she could have been anyone in history it would have been Gertrude Stein. Stein had not only a portion of fame, having associated with Hemingway and other noted writers of the 1920's, she also had a succession of nubile and talented young proteges who lived with her.

However, Sheila Phi had no talent for writing (Some would say, "Neither did Gertrude Stein.") and became a history professor instead, because of her remarkable memory and because she loved any era but the present.

As all offices are, this one was a cloudy reflection of its occupant. Other than the portrait, there was a small bookcase with volumes that were never opened (all her reading was done on the monitor), a hard straight-backed chair, and a desk with an artificial rose in a squat plastic vase.

Starr was late—this was out of character for her. Sheila Phi noted this and pulled up other relevant information from the storage banks in her brain. Lately Starr's appearance was somewhat unkempt. Her hair tended to disarray and there was seldom any makeup. The brow wrinkled frequently and there was a hint of dark circles under the eyes.

This information was assimilated and processed by the computer inside Sheila Phi's skull, and the printout contained one word—vulnerability.

Sheila Phi had been pressing Starr for a decision for months now and today could be the culmination of those bouts of verbal fencing. She had students more attractive and maybe one or two more intelligent, but there was something different (and she hated that word) about Starr Omega, something that refused to be constrained by the rigid environment she lived in. Today could be the day Sheila Phi got her decision about the *Loving Friends* contract. She looked once more at the broad peasant face of Gertrude Stein.

The Caretaker System provided the ideal soil for the growth of Sheila Phi's garden of dark flowers. She had been an unlovely child and developed cunning at an early age. She was short with stubby fingers and a tendency toward overweight which she learned to control as an adult. Her right eye had a cast to it and her nose was short and pointed and tilted downward. The widely-spaced eyes were as vacant as a cat's, until she wanted something. Then they were whatever she told them to be.

Boys either avoided her or made fun of her and she came to regard men as emotional and intellectual inferiors. She made academics her god and all her pleasure depended on his benevolence. Relegated to the company of females, she developed a barter system for sexual favors. She planned to employ this system today as she sat in her hard chair behind the plastic rose.

This scene had its equivalent in the natural world in the way a hyena would patiently await the collapse of a young Thompson's Gazelle wounded by the lions.

Starr dreaded today's appointment with her advisor in the Department of History more than ever. Sheila Phi had been putting pressure on her for some time now to enter into a six month's contract with her, and she could make it extremely difficult for Starr to complete her dissertation if she were so inclined.

Starr thought of the mica glint in the eyes and the rigid, controlled movements of the body as she stood outside the door of the office. She knocked once.

Inside, Sheila Phi smelled the blood from the wounds of Starr Omega. "Come in," she said.

"Good morning, Omega," Sheila Phi said. "Have a seat."

" Thank you."

"You're not looking well. Something troubling you?"

"No, nothing," Starr said, avoiding those eyes that seemed to see inside her. "A little problem sleeping. That's all."

Sheila Phi got to her feet and walked slowly around the desk. She stood directly behind Starr's chair. "Sometimes loneliness siphons away our sleep," she said. "Sensitive girls like you need someone to share the long nights with."

Starr felt the hard stubby fingers pressing into the flesh of her shoulders and stroking the sides of her neck. Her stomach became queasy and her body involuntarily stiffened and pulled away. "That's not the problem. I still haven't come up with anything for my dissertation. Maybe that's it."

"Well, to business then," Sheila Phi said as she returned to her chair. "As we've discussed in the past, the relationship between student and advisor must of necessity be open and intimate to achieve maximum results. This is, of course, epitomized in the Loving Friends contract where symbiosis flourishes. The advisor as well as the student must grow to produce optimum gains."

"Yes, I see the wisdom of that," Starr said, but my apartment is ideally located for school, as well as my work, and I was on that waiting list for such a long time."

Sheila Phi left her chair and began pacing the office floor. "Some things are more essential to one's career than geographic proximity, Omega." She stopped in front of Gertrude Stein's portrait.

"Perhaps you're right, but I'm sure that you're aware of the hardship this would entail."

Sheila Phi looked at Starr, then at the portrait. "What do you know of hardship, Omega?"

Starr assumed the question was academic and made no attempt to respond.

Sheila Phi was still looking at the portrait. "Gertrude Stein knew true hardship. Can you imagine the humiliation she suffered, an enlightened woman, in the age in which she lived?"

Starr remained silent.

"What a handsome woman," Sheila Phi said. "And such talent. Are you familiar with her work, Omega?"

Starr looked at the portrait and thought the expression accurately reflected Stein's writing, painfully constipated. "Somewhat," she said.

As Starr left Sheila Phi's office, she felt her life closing in on her. She had managed to postpone the Loving Friends contract temporarily, but eventually she would have to accept it or leave her studies, and the thought of either was unbearable.

She considered the events of the last few days and knew the stress was fast approaching her level of tolerance. *I've got to come up with something to get me out of this mess, if it's only for a few months,* she thought.

Chapter Five

A WAY OUT

Starr walked the streets of the City of her birth. It seemed more like a prison now and her mind was formulating escape plans. The people she passed all wore the same complacent masks. None of them seemed unhappy, nor did they seem happy. Why hadn't this seemed unusual to her before now? The City was able to pleasure all the senses of its residents and did so liberally. In doing so, it created a lukewarm population with no sense of hot or cold.

Sheila Phi's stubby fingers were again stroking her neck and Starr felt her stomach going queasy. Pushing the memory from her mind, she let her thoughts turn to her last two assignments with the Department of Adjustment. She tried to sever her emotional reactions and examine them in the light of scientific detachment. There was no logical explanation for the behavior of Martha Epsilon and the man named Philemon. No wonder the City found it necessary to "relieve" them. They didn't respond normally to the Pleasure-Pain Principle that was the foundation of government.

After an hour, Starr found herself in front of the Department of Adjustment. She was not scheduled to work and decided to take advantage of the access the building afforded to the Dome Sled. A trip to the Fringe was just what she needed to get her mind off her problems. Maybe then she could get down to some rational, logic-based decision making. Starr thought of the one hundred and fifty foot vacuum tube that would catapult her from the Dome Sled Station to the loading platform at the roof of the Dome and almost changed her mind—and the course the rest of her life would take.

Starr shared the Dome Sled with nine other passengers. As always, she was content to enjoy the dizzying view of the City. *It should be cold,* she thought. Having been raised in the climate-controlled Dome, Starr had never experienced true cold, but now the stark angles and shadows of the City somehow had the look of winter. She could almost feel the touch of an Arctic wind.

The woman next to her was in an expansive mood and insisted on sharing "her reality" with Starr. Ignoring her proved to be a fruitless endeavor.

"I simply must share this with someone," she said above the jangle of her bracelets and chains. "I'll just explode if I don't."

Starr took a deep breath and leaned back on the bench. There was an urgency in the abrupt movements and wide eyes of the woman, but it was the underlying pathos that stirred something inside of Starr and caused her to listen.

"Well, after going off on tangents for years, I decided to get back to basics—the suspended pyramid and twelve crystal circle," she began excitedly.

Starr looked at the other eight passengers in front of them. None took any notice of the woman.

"And of course the special quartz crystal, given to me by the 'enlightened master,' taped to my 'third eye,' " she continued, tapping the middle of her forehead with her index finger.

"Enlightened master?" Starr asked. Immersed in her studies for so many years, she had never paid much attention to the plethora of spiritualists and religions that came and went like the latest fashions in clothing.

"Oh yes, Lord Krishnamurti, of the 'Higher Council of Universal Masters.' He introduced me to the 'Keys of Enoch.' "

"I'm afraid I don't understand what you're talking about," Starr replied.

The woman spread her arms wide, then dropped them and shook her head as if unable to measure the extent of Starr's ignorance. "It's gained favor again with all the enlightened," the woman said.

"What has?"

"The Keys of Enoch."

"I thought we were talking about the Universal Councils."

"Masters," the woman corrected. "Higher Council of Universal Masters."

Starr stared blankly at the woman.

"Surely you know they open the paths for us to be activated into a higher consciousness of light?"

"Ah—certainly," Starr replied, in the hope of thwarting another tirade by her unsolicited benefactor.

"Thank Freud!" the woman said. "I was beginning to think you were a complete spiritual illiterate."

"Hardly," Starr replied confidently. "What about these 'Keys of Eunuch?' "

"Enoch," the woman said. "Not these—it. It's a book."

"Oh yes," Starr said, trying to look interested. "I believe I remember it now."

"Well you certainly should," the woman said. "That is if you're interested in unlocking the mind-gates to the 'Spiritual Hierarchy of Light.' You are, aren't you?"

"Oh, yes," Starr replied, thinking that this trip was doing anything but clearing her mind.

"As you know then, the sixty-four keys to a complete cosmic synthesis of the spiritual and scientific realms will totally reconstitute the Earth and its peoples into a New World Order and . . . ."

"Excuse me," Starr said. "I thought we were talking about your getting back to basics. You know, the crystals."

"Yes, we were, but I get so excited at the thought of combining our New Age Spiritual Philosophy with Sacred Science to bring about the 'Second Genesis.' Just imagine, quantum physics, genetic engineering, holography, nuclear fusion technology and who knows what else, all perfectly meshed with the spiritual realm to create a Global Renaissance, a utopia."

Starr was totally confused, but she sensed that this woman was desperately seeking to fill some void in her life so she listened. Perhaps she also felt a certain kinship toward her.

"I can see you're a little confused," the woman continued. "So anyway, after I arranged the crystals, I sat directly beneath the pyramid—you know, in the 'crystal energy field.'"

Starr remained silent.

"You don't understand, do you?" the woman asked. "Let me refresh your memory. It amplifies 'higher vibrations' for receiving channeled thoughts from the spirit guides."

"Here's my station," Starr said, standing up. "I've certainly enjoyed our conversation."

"So have I. So have I. Maybe we could get together again. I'm being re-circuited into a whole new dimension of higher consciousness. You could join me."

"I'm afraid I'm a little busy these days," Starr replied as she stepped onto the platform. "Thanks anyway."

The woman's smile faded. "Surely," she said and looked directly into Starr's eyes as the sled pulled away.

Starr knew she would not soon forget the look in the woman's eyes and left the station in a gathering sadness.

The streets of the Fringe were literally bursting with the energy and excitement of the people. A small group to her left crowded around a bench where two men were seated playing music on trumpet and saxaphone. Everyone was clapping their hands and moving with the rhythm of the music.

Starr tried to push the woman from the Dome Sled out of her mind. *Why can't people just enjoy things the way they are,* she thought? *Why are they always reaching for something beyond themselves?*

As Starr stood there listening to the music, she noticed a boy of about ten tap dancing next to her. He had on shiny gold shoes, baggy purple pants and black shirt covered with gold sequins. When he saw he had gotten her attention, he stopped and bowed.

"You like my dancing?" he asked.

Starr was amused by his openness and innocence. "It's a thing of rare beauty," she replied. "You may very well be the next great star of the Sensories."

"Thank you, beautiful lady," he said, taking another bow. "You work for the government?"

"Yes I do," Starr replied. "How did you know? Are you a mind reader as well as a dancer?"

"I can just tell," he said. "I like your outfit. Especially those nylon boots."

"Why thank you. I like your clothes too."

"I bet I can tell you where you got those boots," the boy said as he began dancing again.

"I don't believe I understand you."

"It's simple. I can tell you where you got your boots. I can even tell you when you got them." The boy had stopped dancing and stood with his hands on his hips.

Starr was taken aback by his arrogant tone. "You most certainly cannot," she said.

"Wanna bet?"

Starr knew there were a hundred stores in the City that sold boots like hers. Even if he guessed the right one, he could never tell her when she got the boots.

"You scared, pretty lady?"

That was it! Starr prided herself on her intelligence and knew this child was no match for her, but decided that he needed to be taught a lesson. "No," she said. "I'm not."

The boy took a cheap gold bracelet from his pants pocket and held it out to her. "What you got to bet?" he asked. "Something good. This bracelet belonged to my grandmother."

Starr took a plain gold ring from her finger. It was very expensive, but she knew there was no chance of losing it. "How about this?" she asked.

The boy took it from her and examined it closely. "It'll do," he said, handing it back.

"You got your boots on your feet, on this street, right now," the boy said.

"What are you talking about?" Starr asked.

"I told you I could tell you where you got your boots and when," the boy replied.

"You made me believe you could tell me where I bought them," Starr protested.

"I can't make you believe anything, pretty lady," the boy said. "You just didn't listen."

Starr realized she had been outsmarted. She looked at the boy smiling up at her, hand outstretched. "You'd have been a great politician in OldAge," she said.

The boy looked puzzled, then smiled again as she handed him the ring, bowed gracefully and walked off into the crowd.

"What's your name?" Starr shouted as an afterthought.

"Pan," the boy called back over his shoulder.

Starr listened to the music for awhile before she continued on into the Fringe. She walked past a fire-eater on the next corner, watched a knife thrower for a few minutes and stopped at a small three-wheeled cart where a man was selling hot dogs. She counted all the calories as he placed the hot wiener on the soft, warm bun; thought of the cholesterol that would clog her arteries as he spooned on chili, onions and mustard, and forgot everything but how wonderful it tasted with the first bite.

Starr sat on a bench as she ate, and watched the people go by. She marvelled at their energy and animation. They all seemed so excited to be about their business, so eager to get to wherever it was they were going. In the Caretaker System, they were all warned against the enticing lifestyle of the Fringe. "They produce nothing, contribute nothing, think of nothing worthwhile," one of her teachers was fond of saying of the people who lived in the Fringe. They certainly seem to have a good time though, Starr mused.

After browsing through the shops and picking up a few trinkets, Starr found herself in front of the studio of the artist who was her personal favorite. She entered and saw him at work on a canvas in the rear of the small room.

"Well, well, if it isn't my favorite looker," he said, noticing her. "Make yourself at home."

Starr was watching the canvas come to life. "That's not fair, Jim. You know I'd buy all of your paintings I could afford if they weren't considered, ah . . . ."

"Subversive," he said, finishing the sentence for her. "We couldn't have that now, could we?"

"Exactly. The one I bought from the antique shop has put me under enough scrutiny."

Jim resumed his work while Starr watched, fascinated. A man stood at the edge of a wood under a huge tree that looked across an open field. In the distance, storm clouds were gathering in a dark swirling mass on the horizon, beginning to climb the sky. The wind was flattening the tall grass as it blew across the field toward the woods and the man, who looked inconsequential beneath the trees, appeared transfixed by the power and fury of the storm.

Some time later, Jim lay his brush down and washed his hands at a small sink. Starr hardly noticed him and continued to gaze at the painting, lost in the storm.

"How about some coffee?" Jim asked, pouring two cups at a table near the sink.

Starr came out of her trance. "Thank you," she replied. "It's a magnificent work."

"Hardly," Jim said, handing her the cup. "But it's not bad."

Starr looked back at the painting. "You really have some imagination," she said. Jim's face was toward her as he sipped his coffee, but his gaze had gone somewhere beyond her, beyond this room, beyond the City. Realization hit Starr like a physical impact. "You didn't create this scene!" she blurted out! "You painted it from memory!"

"I told you these paintings are for sale, not for discussion— even for exalted members of the hierarchy," he said absently, running his hands through the long straw-colored hair.

Starr looked into his stern face. "Have you really seen places like this?" she asked. "It's wondrous. What about the cloud of pollution that blocks out the sun? How did you get out of the City? Aren't the Primitives dangerous?"

The green eyes softened and Jim smiled. "My, my. Just look at you. I believe there's a woman's heart beating beneath those leather straps. Such passion."

Starr reddened and turned toward the painting. "It's just—just that I thought all of that was gone!"

Jim felt something come alive in Starr Omega that caused him to trust her. "Wait here," he said.

She watched him move to the front of the shop. He put the Closed sign on the door, locked it and pulled the blinds. Then he returned and arranged two chairs next to a floor lamp.

"Why the secrecy?" Starr asked after they were seated.

Jim leaned forward, his elbows on the arms of the chair, and rested his chin on his folded hands. "The earth is cleansing itself, healing itself, Ms. Starr Omega. That's the big secret. No one but the top echelon of our benevolent leaders and the Border Guards, of course, are supposed to know this most marvelous of all secrets."

"But the air—the water, they're poisonous!" Starr was incredulous. "The life span of the Primitives is only half of ours!"

"The air is pure. The water is clear and sparkling again," Jim said, leaning back with his arms resting loosely on the chair. "And the Primitives—only the strongest survived those terrible early years when everything you touched was poison. Now they're healthier and stronger than the best of us."

"Are you absolutely sure of this?" Starr was out of her chair, pacing back and forth.

Jim looked up at her and smiled again. "Omega, my dear, the greening of the Earth has begun."

"But why haven't we been told? Why are we still forbidden to leave the Dome?" Starr sat down, her mind reeling from this staggering knowledge. "It must be for our own protection. The criminals that have been banished would be a threat to our lives."

Jim looked at her evenly, without replying.

"That's it, isn't it? It's for our own good," Starr went on, not believing her words even as she spoke them.

"This is the place of death, the City." Jim said. "In the Fields, there's life."

"I can't believe that. I can't."

Jim reached over and took her hand. "The greening of the Earth has begun, Starr. Believe it."

"But why? Why would they hide this from the people? Why keep us inside the Dome away from the beauty and—and the freedom of the outside world? It doesn't make sense."

"History is your discipline, isn't it?"

"Yes," Starr answered. "Tell me why the Berlin Wall was built?"

Starr knew Jim didn't expect an answer. It was the key issue at the heart of every government. Freedom!

The revelation Starr had undergone was overwhelming to her. All her life she had believed everything outside the Dome to be alien and dangerous, placing her faith only in the City for safety. The City had been her refuge, her provider, her family since she had lost her parents. Now this world was gone, shattered, and she felt only loss and betrayal. How could she ever trust again?"

"Are you all right?" Jim asked.

His voice seemed to come from a great distance. She struggled from the fog that seemed to surround her. "Why did you tell me this? Why trust me?"

"I can't say for sure. You've been coming here for a good while, but this time something was different—something I can't put into words. I felt you needed to know this." Jim sipped his coffee and smiled at her. "Besides, if you tell anyone, we're both goners. You know that better than I do."

In her confusion, Starr's thoughts returned to Martha Epsilon. "I met a woman," she said. She couldn't bring herself to speak of the circumstances of the meeting. "She was very old and told me she was born in the Fields. She came to the City as a child, but all she could talk about were her beautiful green Fields. She wanted to go back there. Leave the City and go back there to die. What's so special about the place—that she would want to return after all those years?"

"I'm a painter, not a poet, Starr," Jim replied with that far off look in his eyes. "Maybe no one's words would be enough. It goes beyond the beauty of the land."

"There was something else about her, Jim."

He looked at her with a warmth in his eyes Starr had never seen before.

"She spoke of how beautiful the heavens were and she said a name—a name I've never heard before." Starr felt herself being drawn into something more powerful than anything she had ever felt and fought to control herself. "I believe she was a Crossbearer, one of those dissidents who cause so much trouble."

"They call themselves Christians," Jim said.

"But what was she talking about?"

"She saw the beauty beyond this earth"

"I don't understand," Starr replied disconcertedly.

"Nor do I, Starr Omega. Nor do I," Jim said as he returned to his easel. "But I know it's there."

"How do you know?"

"I've seen it in faces—and in lives."

Jim began to work on the painting and Starr remained in her chair, utterly perplexed. One thing she knew. She had to see the world outside the Dome! She had no idea how long she sat there, but before she told Jim goodbye, she determined how she would accomplish this thing that was now the driving force in her life.

✦　　　✦　　　✦

Bernard Alpha was stretched out on the cool, green grass in the shade of a willow listening to the sound of the children at play. He opened his eyes and saw how the sunlight touched the leaves above him with gold. The sound of water trickling over stones in the streambed came to him like soft music. He sighed deep in his throat, closed his eyes and was drifting, into a deep, dreamless . . . .

"Starr Omega here to see you, sir."

The sound hit him like an electric shock. He quickly replaced the black and white print, closed the desk drawer and locked it. "Yes, yes. Send her in."

Bernard watched Starr enter and take a chair. There was an intensity in her face and actions that he had never seen before. "I can't imagine what would bring you to this dreary place on your afternoon off, Starr. It must be urgent."

"Not exactly," Starr said, leaning forward in her chair, "but it could be exciting."

"If it excites you, Starr, it must be something truly cataclysmic," Bernard said. "Don't keep me in suspense."

"Well, I think I've come up with something that will kill two birds with one stone, to use an ancient phrase. It has to do with the Chr- -," Starr said, stumbling over the word. "Crossbearers."

Bernard had never seen Starr so animated. He noticed the flushed appearance of her face, then asked, "What about them?"

"As you know, I haven't decided on a subject for my dissertation yet," Starr replied. "I believe I can complete it on the 'Crossbearers' and render a service to the City at the same time."

"I'm intrigued, Starr," Bernard said. "Do go on."

Starr knew she must be cautious and choose her words precisely from this point on. "We all know this spurious philosophy is beginning to cause some problems in the Rim. For example, these people continue to congregate when they know this is expressly forbidden. Freud only knows what goes on at those meetings of theirs. There are rumors that the insidious effects of this—this blight have reached the Fringe and . . . ."

"Starr," Bernard interrupted her, "I'm quite familiar with the goings on in the City. Will you get to the point?"

"Yes sir. It seems that the stronghold of this—this . . . ."

"Christianity, I believe, is the word you're looking for, Starr," Bernard interjected.

"Yes, thank you." Starr was grateful he had used the word first. "The stronghold of this Christianity appears to be in the Fields. Word has it that even some of the Border Guards have fallen victim to its outrageous promises."

"That's quite correct," Bernard said. "The Border Guards are a different breed. Theirs is a profession that's been handed down from father to son for generations. Every precaution is taken to ensure their absolute loyalty to the City. Even so, some of them have succumbed to Christianity."

Starr had her opening. "This is precisely why I'm so excited about my project. If this disease can infect even the strongest of us, something must be done to eliminate it. In order to devise a cure, we must first discover what causes it. What I propose to do is to travel into the Fields, gather the essential facts and use them to implement a final solution to the problem."

Bernard saw the logic of Starr's proposal. He also saw the benefits for him if he were to sanction it and it proved successful. "How much do you know about the Fields?"

"Almost nothing," Starr lied.

"There are dangers, environmental and others, such as criminals that roam at will. The Border Guards can assist you in remediating them of course, but you will still be in some peril."

"It will be worth the risk if I can be of service to the City," Starr lied again.

"Have you cleared this with your advisor at the university?"

"Not yet," Starr said, trying to control her elation that things were going even better than she had expected. "I know that the White Tower must give approval for all trips outside the Dome. You're the proper authority to accomplish this."

"I can see you know your politics, Starr," Bernard said. "If I were to champion your cause in the White Tower, and persuade them to sanction it, that would override any objections you might encounter elsewhere. Most efficient."

"Thank you, sir."

"I'll take your proposal under advisement," Bernard said. "You'll hear from me soon."

"I appreciate your help, sir," Starr said, rising from her chair. As she left the office she saw that marvelous light streaming through the trees and felt its warmth on her like the caress of her mother. Her spirit soared within her as she walked through the fragrant, green Fields toward another life.

✦   ✦   ✦

The florescent light gleamed on Richard Xi's close-cropped white hair as he paced behind his desk. He reminded Bernard Alpha of the poet's description of another Richard, "clean favored and imperially slim."

"How do you know we can trust this Starr Omega?"

Bernard had been in the White Tower for thirty minutes and he couldn't wait to get out. After Starr had left his office, he arranged an appointment that evening with his friend, Richard Xi, in his office in the White Tower. He had known Richard for years (two of which were as Loving Friends), and knew he could persuade him to obtain the necessary approval. "You've read her file," he said. "On the same day last week she had two assignments who were Christians. She carried them out admirably."

Richard's eyes were dark as a ferret's as he looked at the monitor on his desk. "I also saw your notation of that date expressing some doubt as to her steadfastness in this area," he said.

"That was before the field assignment with the woman named Martha Epsilon," Bernard Alpha said with conviction. "The way she handled that erased all doubts as to her steadfastness, as you put it. It was her 'Rite of Passage' as a Reliever."

"I can certainly see the merit of her project," Richard Xi responded. "This Christianity business needs tending to and you've convinced me of her resoluteness. I'll see that the proper clearances are taken care of. I don't foresee any problems."

"You're a real friend, Richard," Bernard Alpha said as he rose to leave. "You won't be disappointed."

"I'm sure I won't, Bernard. You take care 'Old Friend.' "

As soon as the door closed, Richard Xi retrieved Bernard Alpha's personnel file from Central Records and typed the essence of their meeting in the form of a legal document. When he finished he looked at the screen and satisfied himself as to its accuracy. As an appendage he typed:

Respondent has agreed to accept full responsibility for the actions of his employee, Starr Omega. Should they go contrary to the best interests of the City—he is to be terminated immediately.

✦   ✦   ✦

Sweat and horse manure and sore muscles. This was what Starr remembered most as she readied herself for inspection on this final morning of her four week orientation at the Camp. It wasn't really a camp at all, but the Border Guards had called it that for as long as any of them could remember.

The Camp was a walled off area inside the Dome just north of the Main or Western Gate (the name the guards used). It contained a one-eighth mile jogging track, whose infield was used as a parade ground and physical training area; a gym, complete with exercise equipment, steam baths and four racquetball courts; an obstacle course; and a firing range. There were also stables for the horses and barracks for the men.

The guards lived with their families in an area very similar to base housing, located adjacent to the Camp. The barracks were used by new guards during their six months of Basic Training and there was one transition barracks for the Regulars who were going on and coming off duty. This arrangement made for convenience as well as a sense of unity for the guards and their families. It also gave the City control over this strategic and potentially dangerous body of men called Border Guards. Every guard on duty in the Fields knew his family remained under the watchful eyes of the Peacemakers.

"You're certainly a different girl from the one who showed up here four weeks ago. There's a little color in those cheeks and I do believe you've learned to stand up straight," Michael Kappa said as he walked around Starr, hands clasped behind his back. "Yes sir, you look downright healthy."

Starr did feel healthy for the first time in years, in spite of the aches and pains she had endured. Michael had been her personal instructor for the abbreviated training course and she had thought him a sadist for the first two weeks. Blonde and crew-cut, with eyes like gun metal, he reminded her of a Marine recruiting poster she had run across in her research. He had been relentless with her on the jogging track, the obstacle course and in the gym. Outside the Dome, she had ridden the horse until she could barely climb down from the saddle. Then there were the three days of wilderness survival—she didn't even want to think about that!

After a complete check of her horse and equipment, Michael returned to stand in front of her. "I guess you'll do, Starr Omega. You've come a long way in a short time," he said with a smile.

He actually smiled, Starr thought.

"I still think you should wear the standard Guard issue," he said, looking at her Levi's. "Some things never change do they? I expect they're durable enough though. At ease."

Starr took a deep breath and relaxed. Then she smiled back at Michael. "Have I been too much trouble?"

"You whined a little at first, but then so do most of the men. Actually it's been kind of interesting."

"Do you think I'll make it out there, Sergeant?"

"It's Michael now, Starr. Training's over," he replied. "I don't see why not. You've got plenty of rations, maps in your computer, a fine horse and you're in pretty good shape."

"I guess I'll be all right," Starr said, taking another deep breath.

Michael noticed the hint of a frown crossing her face. "Don't worry about the criminal element, Starr. Most of the Primitives are gentle, hard-working people. You may even grow to like some of them. Just don't attract attention to yourself before you get settled in one of the villages. You'll be fine then."

"I appreciate all you've done for me, Michael."

"Forget it. You've put me in the history books. No woman's ever graduated from here before."

"Do I detect a note of Chauvinism in this enlightened age of ours, Michael Kappa?" Starr said with feigned chagrin.

Michael smiled broadly. "Just a tad, maybe. By the way, your clearance came through this morning."

Starr was elated. "Oh Michael, that's wonderful! When do I leave?"

"Tonight."

Starr was visibly shaken. Now it was real. Tonight she would enter what most people thought of as a land of darkness and terror at the end of the world.

Michael stepped close to her and put his hands on her shoulders. "You're gonna do just fine out there, Starr. You've got what it takes," he said and put his arms around her.

Starr hugged him back and felt a strength and reassurance in his concern for her. She wondered what it must have been like to have grown up in a family and to have had a brother.

Part Two:

The Fields

Chapter Six

COLOR AND LIGHT

Holding the reins, Starr stood next to the palomino and watched the massive door of the Dome slide downward on its tracks and slam heavily into place. Putting her left foot into the stirrup, she swung into the saddle. She took a last look at the huge glowing bulk of the Dome that sloped up and away from her until it disappeared into the night sky. Then she turned her face toward the west and rode away toward the unknown.

The sound of the River came to Starr—a soft lapping of the waves on the mud bank. She had never seen a river except for a few scenes in the central files that had escaped the sensors, and she wished it was day so she could see this one. But she smelled it— smelled the cool, damp breath of it as she approached and saw the white mist that reached out from it all about her, as high as the horse's fetlocks.

"Who goes there?" a voice called out of the night.

"Starr Omega," she replied simply.

"We know of your journey." A man seemed to materialize twenty feet in front of her. He had on a rough brown jacket and pants of the same material tucked inside high-topped leather boots. A wide leather belt and leather straps that crossed his chest were laden with shells for the shotgun that hung on his right shoulder. "Follow me."

Starr dismounted and led the horse behind the man. When they reached the River, she saw a metal barge with a gangway leading up to it from the bank. The man motioned to her and she led the horse up through a gate in the railing that encircled the barge. She saw the man walk to a pole that stood in a concrete slab near the gangway and pull a lever up. There was a sudden jerk and a shuddering; then the sound of pulleys creaking and the barge began moving slowly toward the opposite shore of the River.

The waves slapped against the hull and there was a shriek of metal as the cable scraped against it. The horse neighed and shook his head, but Starr rubbed his neck and spoke softly to him and he settled down. The mist had thickened on the River and time and distance seemed to lose meaning. The shoreline appeared abruptly and the barge slid to a stop on the muddy bottom.

The gangway, which was on the opposite end from where she had boarded, lowered automatically and Starr led the horse carefully onto the bank. Then, as the gangway raised, the barge slowly backed into the River and was lost in the mist. Starr led the horse up a slope, feeling the grass brush against her boots. She paused at the top and bent down to feel the cool grass with her hands as the night wind blew unfamiliar fragrances to her.

The horse began grazing and Starr stood up and looked back across the River toward the only life she had ever known, as slaves must have done when they were freed from the plantations. Leading the horse down the slope, she felt an ill-defined fear in her breast, but there was also something deeper and stronger there; a kind of hunger, a longing—for what, she didn't know.

At the top of a second slope, a voice came from a speaker inside one of two black columns in front of her. "When this message is completed, you will have ten seconds to pass between the columns. Do not hesitate! A prosperous journey and safe return to the City, Starr Omega." A harsh buzzing sounded the end of the message.

Starr hurried through the laser fence and mounted the horse. As she rode, she reached behind her into the saddlebag for the computer. She flipped the cover open and the familiar glow seemed to comfort her. After calling up the section map for the area she was riding through, she decided to follow the creek south of her that ran almost due west.

Riding through the night, she listened to the sound of the creek and the wind blowing through the trees on its bank. There were frogs croaking, the cries of night birds and animals rustling in the underbrush. It was a continual source of fascination for Starr, and she had no trouble staying awake.

Around 2:00 in the morning she decided to give the horse a rest and stopped beneath a willow on the bank of the creek. She gathered some limbs for a small fire and lay with her back against the tree, watching the flames flicker in the breeze and the bright red glow of the coals.

Sleep had just begun to take her when the thunderous roar of a shotgun blast shook the night. Starr was fully awake and standing with her back against the tree when twenty yards in front of her a tongue of flame appeared and the shotgun roared again. She ran to the horse, who was rearing and snorting, and grabbed the reins.

A tall man dressed like the one she had seen at the River appeared at the edge of the circle of light. A large dark horse stood behind him, apparently undisturbed by the sound of the shots. The man had sandy hair and was almost bald on top, but the back and sides grew down to his shoulders. His beard was reddish blonde and was almost as wild as the look in his eyes. He held the shotgun in his right hand, pointing it at the earth.

"Starr Omega, I presume," he said as he smiled with his mouth and his eyes.

Starr was dumbstruck. She held onto the neck of the horse to keep from falling down.

"I heard that somewhere a long time ago—or maybe I read it. Anyway, I liked the sound of it. *I presume.* It has a certain ring to it, doesn't it?"

Starr was coming back from sheer terror to ordinary fear. "Why did you fire that awful gun?"

"This?" the man said, holding the shotgun out to her like an offering. "Why, I like the sound of it too. Tends to liven up a dull evening on the prairie, don't you think?"

Starr could think of nothing else to say.

The man led his horse over to Starr's and tied him to the sapling. Then he stepped to the fire and dropped his rucksack on the ground along with two dead rabbits he had been holding in his left hand. He built up the fire with some limbs she had gathered earlier and picked up the two rabbits. Pointing to them, he said, "Saw them in the edge of your firelight. Makes their little eyes glow red just like the coals in the fire."

Starr seemed unable to let go of the horse. "Who are you?" she asked. "What do you want?"

"Name's Will Sigma," he replied, as he pulled a long thick-bladed knife from a sheath at his belt.

Starr gasped.

The man laughed a deep rumbling laugh that made his eyes smile again. "And what I want is to eat these two lovelies, he said, walking the few feet to the River.

Starr felt the fear leave her. *He's had enough chances to harm me if that's what he intended,* she thought. She walked over to the creek bank where Will Sigma was kneeling and cleaning the rabbits.

He looked over his shoulder at her. "You're welcome to join me," he said with a deep voice.

She looked at his bloody hands and made a face.

Will laughed again. "Not with the cleaning of 'em, girl. With the eating of 'em."

Starr sat on the ground, watching him skewer the rabbits on a limb he had cut with one stroke of the big knife, then roast them over the fire. He had added salt and pepper and she thought she had never tasted anything so delicious.

When the meal was finished, Will threw the scraps into the River and made coffee in a small drip pot he took from the rucksack. Starr held the cup in both hands and smelled the rich aroma as the night sounds began to die out around them.

"What do you do out here?" she asked Will.

"Have a whale of a good time mostly," he said as he sipped the steaming coffee.

Starr smiled and thought that she had never seen anyone who enjoyed the simple fact of being alive as this man did. His presence seemed to brighten the night the way the fire did. *Does this wild open country do that to people?*

"I took this season's Quota Charts out to the villages in my sector. I'm on my way back to the City," he said.

"Will they let you stay there for awhile?" Starr asked.

"Not if I can help it," he said. "I can't breathe in that place and the food." He made a face and spat on the ground.

Starr looked at the shotgun and the knife. "What are these Primitives like?"

Will laughed again. "Not dangerous if that's what you mean. Most of 'em anyway. Some of 'em plunder their way through life though, like they would anywhere they were put down. There's a certain type of man who'd rather die than work for a living."

"I've heard they're mostly criminals and people who tried to overthrow the City government. The misfits of society."

"*Misfits.* I guess that pretty well describes them. They certainly don't fit in that place you come from." Will stretched his long legs and leaned back on his elbows.

"I shouldn't have any problem with them then?" Starr asked.

Will looked at her and his face was serious. "Some people change after they're out there for awhile."

"What do you mean?"

"It's hard to say exactly. Some of these primitives have insane ideas. They say you should love your enemies. Can you imagine that? They treat everybody pretty much the same. No big shots. I know you can't imagine that!"

Starr took the computer out of her saddlebag and began taking notes. "What else?"

"Well, once or twice a week they all get together and sing and somebody will talk to the others for awhile. And—other things that are hard to explain."

"Try to tell me about these—other things," Starr said, looking up from her computer.

"You'll see that for yourself," he said. "Everything is done in families. They raise their own children, live together, work together, eat together—everything."

"Go on."

"Can't do it, little girl. Got to get my report in. You ought to know how stuffy they can be if you're late with anything. Enjoyed your hospitality though."

Will washed the coffee pot and cups in the creek and packed them in his rucksack. Then he climbed on his horse that was tied next to Starr's. "You'll do all right out here," he said.

"Thanks for the meal," Starr said. "It was wonderful. You're a nice man."

"There's some who might disagree with you," Will said. "Don't get taken in by them Primitives, Starr Omega. *Love your enemies.* Can you imagine that?"

After Will Sigma was gone, Starr watched the embers dying in the fire and felt a strange sort of emptiness. The breeze was softening with the approach of morning and she decided to be on her way. She saddled the horse and rode away from the approaching sun.

Starr came to the top of a long rise and halted the horse. The sun was rising behind her and the first streaks of light broke over the horizon and swept down across the long gradual slope of the valley spread out before her. The tall wet grass seemed to ignite with a green-gold flame as the sunlight struck it, and, as far as she could see, it billowed and glistened in the morning breeze like a sea of fire and ice.

The colors were so vivid and brilliant they hurt Starr's eyes and made her dizzy. She closed her eyes and let the horse take her down the slope, leaving a wake behind him in the dew-wet grass. The words of Martha Epsilon came back to her, "the Fields. The beautiful green Fields where I was born." Starr opened her eyes and was dazzled by the waving glistening greenness around her. *This is what she meant,* Starr thought. *Now I understand what she meant.*

Starr thought of an old movie she had run across in the archives. It was about a little girl who was caught up in a tornado in this very part of the country and taken to a magical kingdom. The first part was in black and white, but when she reached the kingdom, everything was alive with glorious color. Starr felt she had lived in a black and white world until the sun rose on this day.

The smooth gait of the horse took them through the endless rolling fields of green with occasional streams and stands of huge trees. The sky was a cobalt ceiling curving from green horizon to green horizon. Puffy white clouds followed their shadows across the land like balloons being towed by invisible strings.

At the top of another rise, Starr saw three men plowing the green land into straight dark furrows. As she rode down toward them, one man left his horse and plow and walked toward the shade of a tree that towered alone in the midst of the plowed field. Starr followed him on the horse.

As Starr approached the man, she saw that he wore heavy boots, green work pants and a white cotton shirt. "Good day to you," she said formally.

The man turned quickly and looked up at her. "Oh, hello there," he said. "I'm afraid I didn't notice you. I sometimes have a tendency to get lost in the work."

"I'm sorry. I didn't mean to startle you."

"Think nothing of it. It's good to see a new face out here." He dipped water from a wooden bucket with what looked like some sort of a wooden cup with a long hollow handle. "Have some. It's very good," he said as he offered it to her.

Starr stepped down from the saddle and walked over to the shade of the tree where the man stood. She took the dipper and drank the sweet cool water. "Thank you," she said.

The man dipped again and walked over to the foot of the tall tree. He sat on the leafy ground between two roots that extended from the base of the tree like the arms of a chair. "Rest with me," he said. "You look like you've ridden a long way."

Starr sat in the cool shade under the tree and looked out across the grassy fields where the men were turning them from green to a rich dark earth color with their horses and plows. The wind sent gentle ripples across the surface of the grass and set the leaves rustling in the crown of the tree.

The man drank slowly with great sighs of pleasure. He was very dark with a small thin nose and brown liquid eyes. "My name is Obadiah," he said. "Call me Obie."

"All right, Obie." Starr said smiling at the small man. "I'm Starr Omega."

He extended his hand and she took it awkwardly as he gave it a gentle shake.

"Could you tell me what that is you're drinking from?" Starr asked, pointing at the dipper in his hand. "I don't believe I've ever seen anything like it."

He held it up in his thin hard-looking hands. "It's a gourd. We cut 'em, dry 'em and make dippers out of 'em."

Starr took it and ran her hands over its smooth, hard lightness. "It's lovely," she said. "Like a piece of sculpture."

"It's yours."

Starr was shocked. No one had ever given her anything without expecting something in return. "I couldn't," she said, handing the gourd back to him.

There was a hurt look on Obie's face. "Keep it," he said. "As a token of friendship."

"Friendship." she said, then added, "I'm doing research for a paper I'm writing. "Could you tell me where the closest village is?"

"That's easy," Obie said as he stood up. "The one I live in." He pointed due west.

"Is it very far?" Starr asked.

"You stop for the night and you'll reach it before dark tomorrow," he replied. "You could travel back with us but we stay out three or four days when we work the land."

Starr thought of asking him about the "religion" she had heard of among the primitives, but didn't want to put anyone on the defensive. Better to just wait and see for herself. "Thank you for the gift, Obie," she said.

"You're very welcome," he replied and walked toward his horse and plow in the green, ever darkening fields.

Starr rode for the rest of the day through the same kind of country. She never tired of the wonderful wild beauty of the land. She saw deer once or twice in the wooded areas near the streams and watched a hawk circling between the earth and the clouds, riding the thermals and never moving his wings.

She made camp at the crest of a hill, deciding not to build a fire. She ate some of the awful-tasting dried food that she had brought with her from the City, while the horse grazed on the abundant grass. As the night wind whispered across the hills, she lay back to rest and was paralyzed by the unexpected, majestic beauty of the night skies. She realized she had never looked up in the excitement of the first night. The great black dome of heaven was covered with thousands and thousands of bright twinkling stars and the shining of the planets. The clarity was such that she felt she could reach up and pluck one from the sky. She could have lain there all night and looked at them, but there was work to be done.

Starr opened the computer and wrote of the first day's activities and observations in the formal and stilted language of academia. Then she took a yellow pencil and a small tablet with a thick brown cover from her inside jacket pocket and began to write.

✦   ✦   ✦

The countryside is beautiful beyond belief. The air and water are pure as far as I can tell (Why the Dome?)

Met a Border Guard the first night. An exciting, entertaining character. Shot and cooked rabbits that tasted better than any restaurant food. Loves being in the Fields. Would never return to the City under any circumstances.

On the first day I saw men plowing the fields with horses. Met one named Obadiah (Obie). Very kind and gentle. Gave me a gourd as a present. (Is this a common practice?) Also gave me water. Giving may be a prevalent custom.

Should reach Obie's village tomorrow morning.

People fascinating. Land pristine and lovely.

Danger—Possibility of insidious effects from this
(Philosophy? Religion?) practiced by the Primitives.

Horse has performed admirably.

Chapter Seven

STORM

Awakening at first light, Starr realized she had gone to sleep while writing and slept the night through without taking a pill. *What an incredible sensation!* she thought. *I'm beginning to like this place in spite of myself.* The dry breakfast packet she ate put a damper on the morning, but she soon forgot it as the glowing rim of the eastern sky gave way to the dazzling blue and green beauty of the day.

Prairie flowers were as high as the flanks of the horse and flowed in waves of amber and blue across the gentle roll of the land. Starr rode all morning as if in a dream, stopping only to water the horse at an occasional tree-bordered stream that wandered through the Fields. As the day wore on, clouds began building on the western horizon and she watched them climbing slowly toward the sun.

Toward evening, Starr came to a rocky outcrop that dropped off fifty feet to a small valley below. Two hundred yards to the north, a steep path wound down to the valley floor. As she reached the last steep incline at the bottom of the path, a long black snake slithered from under a rock ledge startling the horse. He reared, throwing her to the hard-packed ground, and bolted away down the valley.

Starr lay on the ground in a daze. Bright flashes of color whirled in her head like a windless cyclone, and the colors were the pain that she felt as she lay on the path in the fading light.

Her head was throbbing and her left hip was stiff and painful as she awoke. She saw first the warm steady shine of the evening star and watched it wink out as the clouds moved toward her. Then the wind came sighing through the tops of the trees and the first heavy raindrops hit, shocking her with their stinging coldness.

Life in the climate-controlled Dome had not prepared Starr for the capricious turns of nature. She struggled to her feet and looked about. To her left was a dark area in the wall of the canyon. She walked stiffly toward it with her hip aching and pain radiating from the small lump at the back of her head.

The ceiling of the cave was high enough that Starr could not touch it with her hands. It was ten feet wide and six feet deep and there was a stack of firewood against the left wall. She placed some of the wood in a shallow pit, toward the rear of the cave, that was blackened from the fires of those who had been here before her. There were twelve matches left in the waterproof cylinder she carried in her coat pocket. She laid it on the stone floor of the cave and cut a small pile of shavings with her belt knife. They ignited with the first match and she added more until she had a small flame going. Adding broken twigs and larger pieces of wood, she soon had a respectable fire.

The rain sounded like a waterfall out in the darkness and the inconstant wind blew a cold spray through the mouth of the cave. Starr sat on the damp floor leaning back against the rough stone and watched flickering shadows play across smoke-blackened walls.

No! The City had not prepared her for this: this thundering darkness, this howling wind that seemed to have a life of its own as it snapped at the flames of her small fire like some enraged and formless beast. She huddled close to the fire's warmth. This was nothing like the open fields and sunlight and flowers. This was dampness and cold and decay. *Like a tomb,* she thought.

Most of all, Starr was not prepared for this singular and unrelenting aloneness. She had lived all her life in the company of others; the privacy of her apartment had become an obsession with her. Now she would give anything for the sound of a human voice. She felt she was alone, hurtling through space on a planet devoid of life, except for her own.

Then it hit her. Hit her with a sudden, brutal clarity: *This is death! This is what death is like! This total and unbearable aloneness. This suffocating darkness and the formless beast living in it, living on the pain of death. And there is no end to death—there is only eternal terror and pain and darkness.*

She suddenly knew with absolute certainty there was no endless recycling of the soul into body after reincarnated body. There was an eternity out there, but this life was the only one she would have to face it with. There was only one Starr Omega and some part of her would be alive somewhere forever after this life was over.

She thought of Philemon and of Martha Epsilon. How could they face this terrible empty darkness knowing there would be no other life in some other body? Where does such calmness and peace come from? Only with the most potent drugs had Starr seen anything approaching this and then only temporarily.

Lost in thought, it was some time before Starr realized the sound in the storm was the neighing of a horse. She was about to rise when a span of darkness deeper than the night loomed outside the mouth of the cave. A man stood at the edge of the firelight, then stepped out of the rain, his bulk filling the mouth of the cave. A heart-stopping fear washed over her when she saw him in the light.

His shaggy dark head nearly touched the ceiling of the cave and the heavy beard that grew almost to his eyes was matted and filthy. He wore a coarse black robe that hung below his knees, touching the heavy boots that were caked with mud. Water was dripping from his clothes to the floor of the cave and the smell that came from him was like the last stages of some terrible rotting disease.

But the eyes were the worst! They were lifeless and cold and appeared to be covered with an opaque film, like a reptile. He glanced at Starr as though she were no more than an insect and stepped to the fire to warm himself. She scuffled backwards and sat huddled against the far wall.

The man held his hands over the fire and Starr noticed the skin under the dark hair was stained and grimy, the long nails caked with dirt. He hawked up a great gob of yellow phlegm and spat it hissing into the fire. Squatting down, he pulled a bone with some scraps of meat and gristle clinging to it from inside his coat and began gnawing on it. So great was her fear of this man, Starr wished for the aloneness of the storm and the night. She gathered the remnants of her courage and said in a rasping voice she hardly recognized as her own, "What do you want?"

The man continued to gnaw on the bone.

"What do you want?" she asked again more strongly.

The man never looked up from his eating. "You make a lot of noise for a dead woman."

His words were messengers from the nether world that struck Starr with disbelief, sending a numbness crawling over her body like a swarm of hideous spiders. She felt herself being drawn into a dark pit and fought against it. If she lost consciousness, she knew that she would never awaken.

Starr decided to try one more time. "Please don't hurt me. I'll give you everything I have."

The man threw the bone into the darkness and looked at Starr. In the flat, dull saurian eyes she saw her life wink out like the evening star before the storm.

"It's already mine," he said.

The man stood and pulled a knife from under his cloak. It was as long as his forearm and glinted coldly in the light of the fire. Starr saw scenes of her life flashing past. She saw Martha Epsilon as her head moved slowly to the side when she fell asleep. Then the man was standing above her and the knife in the grimy hand with its black nails was moving toward her.

"Oh, God—help me!" Starr screamed, though she didn't realize what she was saying.

The actions that occurred next were almost simultaneous; only later was Starr able to piece them together. There was a blur of motion and a dull cracking sound as the bones in the hand that held the knife were shattered. The knife clattered to the stone floor and the man in the black cloak bellowed in pain and rage.

Another man stood in the cave now, facing the man with the crushed hand. He was as tall, but had none of the bulk of the man he faced. A staff of polished oak five feet long and the size of a woman's wrist was balanced lightly in his hands. A leopard moves toward his prey as he moved when he circled to his right, coming between Starr and the man with the crushed hand. Starr saw his broad shoulders in the gray cloak and the sheen of his long black hair as she scrambled to her feet and stood against the wall behind him.

The man in the black cloak looked at his long knife lying by the fire, but the man who moved like a great cat pointed his oak staff at the bearded face and moved it slowly back and forth.

Then the man with the crushed hand held it with his good one and backed out of the cave. "The hand will heal," he said and disappeared like a dark vapor into the rain and the howling wind.

The tall man in the gray cloak turned and faced Starr. She looked into his dark blue eyes and saw him smile. "My name is David," he said. "You don't have to be afraid now."

And Starr knew that she would never have to be afraid with this man as relief washed over her like the rain. She stepped to him and the fear broke loose in deep gasping sobs that rose from her chest. He put his arms around her, and blindly, without thought, she clung to him until the fear drained from her. She stayed there in the comfort of his arms for a long time, and she wept like a small child.

After she was taken from her parents, Starr discarded her dependency as she had the toys of her abbreviated childhood. She came to develop a certain pride in her self-sufficiency and kept a carefully measured distance from the lives of others. She was not a people-hater, but determined during her first years in the Caretaker system that nothing was worth the pain she had felt with the loss of her mother and father.

Standing in the arms of David, Starr sensed a battle beginning behind the wall she had built around herself. Years of self-discipline told her to break away, to stand apart, that no good could come of this. The warmth of his arms around her and the feeling deep within her breast told her something utterly different.

The years of her life seemed to flow backward as Starr searched them for some spark of meaning, some moment of true happiness. She felt she had been all her life a gourd, dry and useless, never knowing it until now—now as she was filled with a clear sweet water. She longed to let go, to release the aching burden of the years, to give that part of herself that was dying. She could not! The wall was built strongly and well during all the long nights.

David felt Starr's body tensing in his embrace, felt her hands pressing against his chest, but he didn't feel the dark anguish of her soul as she pushed him away.

While Starr sat watching the fire, David disappeared into the night and returned five minutes later with a canvas bag over his shoulder. He took two blankets from the bag and laid them by the wall where Starr sat. Then he took a skillet and several packets wrapped in oilcloth and placed them next to the fire. In a short time he had some red meat simmering in a gravy on the fire.

The smell of the food was intoxicating to Starr. She lay back on the blankets, luxuriating in the warmth and safety she felt with this man. David handed her a tin plate of meat and brown bread along with a metal knife and a fork carved from wood. Then he served his plate and sat with her on the blankets.

The food was even better than Will's. As she ate, Starr found herself staring at a white scar that cut through the tan skin along David's left cheek. It extended from just below the eye directly down the prominent cheekbone to the corner of the mouth. It reminded her of the Prussian dueling scars she had seen in the old texts while doing reasearch on Adolph Hitler.

"It's a gift from your uninvited house guest," he said, looking up. "I'll always remember him fondly for it. His name is Abbadon and there aren't many around like him, thank God."

"I'm sorry. I didn't mean to stare," Starr said. "Why did you allow him to leave?"

"He was helpless."

This made no sense to Starr. She looked at Abbadon's knife laying next to the fire and decided to change the subject. "I had another meal very much like this last night," she said. (Was it only last night?) "It was prepared by a man named Will."

"I know him. He's a good man," David said as he looked up from his food.

Starr looked into the steady blue eyes that seemed to reveal the man. How can he say this of one of his captors? she thought. "Do people out here eat like this all the time?" she asked.

"On the move we do. It's much better in the villages," he said.
"What do you eat?"

Starr handed him one of the food packets. "This was prepared
for my journey. It has all the nutrition necessary to sustain one,"
Starr said formally.

David opened the packet and tasted the green pasty substance
inside. "It also has the smell and taste necessary to make one lose
his supper," he said, handing the packet back.

"Food is required for the maintenance of the body," Starr replied defensively. "We derive pleasure in ways you never dreamed
of."

David finished his meal, set the plate aside and leaned back
on the blankets. "Such as?" he asked.

Starr took a small plastic box from her inside coat pocket, slid
the top open and offered it to David. "Try one of these and you'll
find out," she said.

David looked at the thin white wafers inside the box. "What
are they?" he asked.

"They make you feel good."

"I already feel good."

Starr pushed the box at him insistently. "Try one. What are
you afraid of?"

"Nothing I can think of right now," he replied.

"Look. I'll show you," Starr said. "It'll heighten your pleasure" She took one of the wafers and placed it on her tongue.

David watched her with curiosity.

Starr felt the drug rush through her system and saw David
getting smaller and smaller as she lifted above him. She seemed to
be drifting outward into the darkness and, by a supreme effort,
willed herself back beside him on the blankets. Starr felt there was
a great gulf between her and David and she desperately wanted to
cross it, desperately wanted to be where there was contentment and

peace, but she didn't know how. She felt her will go and began quietly weeping.

David put his arm around her and lay her head against his shoulder. "There, there. It's all right," he said. "A person can stand just so much pleasure."

Starr awakened in the dead of night. David lay next to her on the blanket, breathing deeply in his sleep. She marvelled that he had made no advances toward her, but expected it soon. In fact, as she looked at his lean tanned face with its dueling scar, she was excited at the prospect. *He's merely a Primitive,* she thought. *How can I possibly have these feelings about him?*

The storm was over and she heard the ticking sound of the rain dripping in the trees. In the distance, frogs were croaking and the cicadas were droning their nocturnal symphony. The air was fresh and cool and sweet. Starr felt that the coming of Abbadon was something out of a nightmare, something that could never truly happen in this clean, wonderful land.

Starr smiled in the dark and stretched herself in the warm blankets. "Are you all right now?" she heard David say.

"I'm just fine," she answered.

David stood up and put more wood on the fire. He smiled down at Starr as he stoked it, and the coals sparked and glowed brightly. "I'm glad," he said.

He lay back down and Starr turned slowly toward him, determined to put him in his place when he reached for her. As she waited, she saw him turn away from her and he was soon asleep.

What's the matter with him? she thought. *What's the matter with me?*

The morning came to Starr with the sound of birdsong and the rich smell of coffee brewing. She sat up and yawned, surprised that she had rested so well with only a blanket between her and the stone floor of the cave. The sun was sparkling in the wet trees and on the long grass down the valley.

David handed her a tin cup of coffee and she held it in both hands, sipping it slowly. "How do you manage to get coffee out here?" she asked. "It's hard enough to come by in the City."

"We have a few contacts," he replied, looking out of the cave at the bright morning.

Starr looked at David as he sat wrapped in the plain gray cloak he had dried by the fire. There was something regal in his relaxed, confident posture. "You haven't asked me why I'm out here in the Fields," she said. "Aren't you interested?"

"You'll tell me if you want me to know," he said, looking at her with the rumor of a smile on his face.

"I'm doing reasearch for my doctorate degree," she said. "Are you familiar with that?"

"Somewhat."

It struck Starr that this was the same reply she had made to Sheila Phi's question about the work of Gertrude Stein. "No matter. A man named Obie told me there was a village near here. That's where I'm going. Are you familiar with it?"

"It's called Haven," he replied. "That's where I live. We'll be there by noon."

David had set their dishes outside in the rain after supper and he now dried them and put everything away in his canvas bag. "I'll go get my horse," he said. "By the way, he had some company during the night. A palomino."

Starr's face brightened as she followed him outside. Twenty yards down from the cave, there was a shallow overhang in the cliff with two oaks growing at the edge, their limbs spreading over it forming a natural shelter. Starr's palomino stood next to the chestnut stallion belonging to David.

www.gapines.org
Neva Lomason Memorial

Checkout Receipt

You checked out the following items:

1. **Beyond the river**
   Barcode: 31057903328774
   Due: 10/23/2018
2. **Wind from the wilderness**
   Barcode: 31057000143050
   Due: 10/23/2018

Total Amount Owed: $0.00

GRL-HQ 10/9/2018 11:30 AM

"He came in during the night," David said. "Doesn't seem to be in any hurry to leave."

Starr ran to the horse, spoke to him and patted his neck. "I didn't realize how attached to him I'd become," she said. "It's the first time I've been around an animal."

As they rode through the open countryside, Starr became intrigued with what kind of place the village would be. "Will there be a place for me to stay?" she asked David. "I have Credits."

"What would we use them for?"

"I hadn't considered that, I guess."

"Don't worry. We'll find a place for you." David reassured her. "You'll have to work though."

"What kind of work?"

"Whatever you can do," he said. "Everyone does some kind of work in Haven."

As they rode, the day warmed and David tied his cloak behind his saddle. Starr took off her coat and put it in her saddlebag. The sky was a rinsed blue after the rain and perfectly clear. A wind was freshening from the west and the long grass was billowing and glistening in the morning sun.

At the top of a rise, Starr noticed what looked like a gigantic pile of rubble several miles to the north across the open fields. "What's that?" she asked, pointing to the north.

"What's left of a city. You do know they destroyed all the cities inside the laser wall, don't you?"

Starr knew, but she had never seen any pictures—could never have imagined such complete destruction. "I guess I'd forgotten," she said, looking away from the ruined city.

"The government of the City didn't want us to have any of the modern conveniences: electricity, running water, no machinery of any kind. They even tried to destroy all the books. Thought it would people their "Gulag System" with sub-humans, beasts of burden incapable of rational thought. I find it has proven a blessing for us."

"In what way?" Starr asked.

"It's difficult to explain and it hasn't been in every way—medical care for instance is pitifully inadequate. But there are things more important than medical care."

Starr pondered on this man David and what she might expect in his village. He was strong enough to defeat a man like Abbadon, who could easily handle anyone in the Peacemakers. Yet he had let this man live for no good reason she could think of. He was gentle and considerate with her and didn't try to press his advantage during the night. She tried to imagine Sammy Chi in the same situation—then blocked it from her mind.

David never considered using drugs and he seemed to have limitless courage without them. Starr knew he had no opportunity for a formal education, yet he appeared in some ways more educated than she. She decided to look further into this enigma. As she watched his relaxed, controlled movement astride the stallion, she thought of something Will had said of some of the Primitives. She couldn't speak for the rest, but David would most assuredly be a "misfit" in the City.

They had come to a small river and crossed it at a shallow place with a rocky bottom. Far to the north, she could see where it joined a much larger river. North of the crossing, the land began to rise and became a high bluff with its apex where the rivers joined. The entire area, bordered on the east and north by the two rivers, was heavily forested with towering oaks, smaller trees and various kinds of shrubs.

They followed a path through the trees that ran close to the rising bluff that looked down on the smaller river. Gradually the forest began to open up and the underbrush and smaller trees had been cleared. Starr saw several columns of smoke rising in the distance.

Soon they were riding alongside acres of vegetable gardens in the open land on the west side of the path. On the east side, among the open trees, were pens holding various types of livestock. People working in the gardens and tending the stock waved and shouted greetings to them.

Farther along, among the largest trees, were the houses made of logs. They brought to mind the American frontier she had seen pictures of in her research. The first sound Starr heard as they rode into Haven was the laughter of the children.

Chapter Eight

HAVEN

David brought Starr straight to his parent's house, which lay on the outer rim of the village itself. "We're in time for the evening meal," he said, then guiding her up the steps that led to the snug log cabin. He opened the door calling out, "We have a visitor."

As the family came to greet them, Starr felt very strange, almost as if she had been plucked out of the world she had known and set down in another. A tall, sturdy man of about 50 dressed in rough work clothing came to stand before them, observing Starr with dark blue eyes. There was a light in them she had seen before, in much different surroundings.

"This is Starr Omega," David said. "She's come to do a study of the Fields. I thought it would be good if she stayed with us for a time."

"We're glad to have you in our home, Daughter."

Starr looked up at Caleb, David's father, who was smiling as he spoke, and the formal greeting she intended did not come. The word "daughter" caught at her somehow, and she faltered slightly before answering. "Why, thank you—" she began, but could not find the right words. She had learned how to handle social communication in the City, but there was something in Caleb's smile and eyes that made those skills obsolete.

The woman by Caleb's side saw her embarrassment, and said, "I'm Sarah, my dear. You've had a hard trip. Let me show you where you'll sleep. David, get her things." She led Starr up a set of steep, ladder-like stairs, talking cheerfully all the way. When Starr stepped into the room, she found herself facing a young woman. "This is our daughter, Miriam," Sarah said, then gave Starr's name to the girl. "Supper will be ready in half an hour."

As her mother left, Miriam said, "It's good to have you, Starr. Why don't you take that bed by the window. You can put your things in that chest."

"I hope I won't be a bother, Miriam," Starr said uncertainly. She looked around, adding, "This is a wonderful room." It was a large room, with a ceiling that sloped overhead. Everything was wood, the rafters, the floor, the walls, and the smell of the wood was pleasant. Walking over to the window to look outside, she was delighted to see a pasture where a large number of black and white cows grazed lazily, the wobbly-legged calves staggering after their mothers. They were in a valley, and the dark green outlines of the mountains framed the scene. Turning to face the girl who was watching her, she said, "I don't think I'll be here very long. I'll try not to be a bother."

Miriam smiled, and as she did, Starr saw the strong family resemblance she had to David. She was tall, willowy, and her lustrous black hair fell past her shoulders to her waist. There was a directness in her gaze and a quiet peace in her demeanor that gave Starr confidence. She thought *This will be helpful. I can get close to this girl—get a genuine reading on the mentality of these people.* Aloud she said, "I owe your brother my life . . . ."

Miriam listened as Starr related her narrow escape from the man called Abbadon, then nodded. "You were fortunate. He's a very wicked man."

"I was very lucky David came when he did.

A slight smile tugged at the edges of Miriam's lips. "Lucky? I think it was more than that, Starr." At that moment David called from downstairs, and Starr went quickly to get her things. When she returned and was putting them away in the small chest, she asked, "What did you mean by David's coming when he did was more than lucky?"

Miriam was standing by the window looking out on the fields. When she turned, a slanting ray of sunshine fell across her, heightening the planes of her face. There was a moment's pause as she seemed to think about the question, then she turned to face Starr. "I mean that life is more than just good luck or bad luck," she said quietly. "When people play cards I suppose it's just chance or luck that gives them a good hand. But life's not a game of cards. When something happens to us, there's meaning in it."

Her calm assurance piqued Starr, for it had long been her conviction that life was a matter of chance. Closing the drawer, she sat down on the narrow bed, then remarked, "I believe in cause-and-effect, Miriam. If I'm standing on the edge of a cliff and choose to jump off, I'll be killed. But the choice lies in my hands. I'm responsible for what I do. I guess," she said slowly, "I believe every person makes his own life by what he chooses to do."

"But you didn't *decide* to be killed by Abbadon, did you? It was something beyond your choice, wasn't it?"

"Well—that's true, of course, but—"

"Do you know how large the Fields are, Starr? And do you know that David doesn't hunt in that area at this time of the year? Just think for one moment, here you are in a place where my brother wouldn't ordinarily be, and at the exact instant when that beast attacked you, he suddenly steps in to save you. What if he had been a mile away, or half a mile? What if he had stopped to cook a meal so that he arrived half an hour later? What if it had been a man less strong than David who could never have defeated

Abbadon?" Miriam shook her head, saying quietly, "Some say it takes too much faith to believe that things happen to us for a purpose. But to me, it takes too much faith to believe that the 'right' man just 'happened' to be at the spot at exactly the 'right' time to save your life."

Starr stared at Miriam, trying to find a logical answer, but none came. Finally she said, "So you believe we're controlled by some power. That we're nothing but puppets?"

"No, not like that," Miriam said quickly. "But we aren't alone. Our lives have meaning. I heard of one scientist who said, "Life is like an onion. You peel it off layer after layer, and when you get to the center—there's nothing there!" I don't believe that."

Starr asked cautiously, "And this—this power that you believe in, that brought David to save me, I suppose you mean the stars?" In the city practically everyone believed in astronomy. One chose an astronomer with as much care as one chose a personal physician. Starr herself paid little heed to the charts her own astronomer gave her, but most of her friends obeyed the signs rigidly.

Miriam gave her an even look, saying, "No. The stars were *created*. How can anything that is itself created have power over human life? But the One who made the stars, He's the one who brought David to help you, Starr Omega." Then she turned, saying, "I'll call you when the meal is ready."

For a few minutes Starr sat on the bed, thinking of what Miriam had said. How was it? *The One who made the stars, He's the one who brought David to help you.* Such a thing went against everything she had been taught all her life, and she rose swiftly in an effort to shake off the effect of Miriam's words. Removing her clothing, she was delighted to find a shower in the small bathroom that adjoined the room. There was no hot water, but she delighted in the cool water that ran down her body, and seemed to sluice away not only the dust and sweat but also some of the tension that had been building up in her since she had left the city.

After drying off with a rough towel, she put on clean clothing: fresh underwear, a pair of denim jodphurs, a red-and-white plaid shirt and clean white boot socks. Her boots were muddy, but would have to do until she had time to clean them, and just as she slipped them on, she heard Miriam call. "Starr? Supper's ready."

"I'll be right there!" she called, then paused just long enough to give her thick hair a quick brushing. Her cheeks, she noticed, were already filled with color from the short time she'd had under the sun, and she saw that excitement brightened her eyes. *You're on your way!* she said silently, then descended the stairway quickly.

Miriam was waiting for her, a smile on her face. "Come along and meet your family, Starr." Her choice of words gave Starr the same peculiar feeling she'd had when Caleb had called her "daughter," and she wondered why such a thing should be. In the City, no one called another "daughter," and the word "family" had become almost archaic.

Entering a large room on the left of the hall, she found herself at a long pine table loaded with food. The fragrance of fresh bread had come to her on her way down, and she stared in unbelief at the plates of meat, the bowls of steaming vegetables and the platters with fresh brown bread.

"This is Starr Omega," Caleb announced. "She'll be with the family for a time. Starr these are our sons, Joshua and Timothy—who like to be called Josh and Tim."

"I'm glad to meet you both." Josh, she saw, was much like his mother, having her small frame and brown eyes. Then she turned to Tim and shock ran along her nerves. *He has Down's Syndrome! And he must be at least twelve or thirteen.* She managed to smile pleasantly as they sat down, but the shock persisted. She had never seen a child as old as Tim with Down's Syndrome. In the City they were Relieved as soon as a final diagnosis was made. There had been cases, of course, of mothers hiding their babies for a time, but they were always discovered. Starr suddenly remembered her instructor, the Chief Reliever, speaking on this subject. *You will encounter resistance from parents, but you must get across to them that it is much kinder to Relieve the child at the earliest possible age. In the end the child must die, and it is better for the state, the parent and the afflicted one for Relief to come as quickly as possible.*

"Sit down, all of you," Sarah said, her voice breaking into Starr's thoughts. Starr took the place between David and Miriam, and when they were all seated, Caleb said, "Tim, would you like to give thanks for the food?"

"Yes!" A glow of pleasure came to the boy's face, and at once he bowed his head. Starr gazed around the table, startled and confused. Then David turned to smile at her, at the same time holding out his hand. She took it without thinking, noting that the others were all joining hands. She reached out with her left hand which was clasped firmly by Miriam. Tim said in a thin, clear tenor, "Thank you God for this food . . . ."

As the boy spoke, Starr was acutely conscious of the intimacy of the moment. Both her hands were held firmly in the warm, firm hands of David and Miriam, and she seemed suddenly to become a part of the small group. She had eaten with groups all her life, but always before there was in her the sense of firm isolation. *You are there—and I am here.* Now the sense of *otherness* had somehow been dissolved. She felt that those in the circle around the table had absorbed her. She was bound together with them by living flesh— and something more than that which she could not identify.

And it frightened her! Starr had carried on a secret battle all her life to maintain a sense of self. Even as a child she had been aware that almost everything in her world sought to draw her into the whole. She had read once an old fable written by one of the OldAge writers, a man called Bram Stoker. It had dealt with vampires, horrible creatures that lived off the life blood of others. And once someone was bitten by one of these, he also became one of the "living dead," as Bram Stoker, the author, called them.

The tale had almost crippled Starr, and for years she felt that something was trying to get at her, to suck her life away—and she suffered nightmares that she had lost herself, had become one of the living dead. But in later years, she had somehow come to realize that the "vampires" of her world were not bat-like creatures as in the tale, but were the agents of her society. The government itself was some sort of life-draining creature, always seeking to break down the secret place in her where that part of her that was *other* than all others were, and to destroy it, or rather, to *absorb* her into itself.

It was this constant attempt of her world to destroy her secret self, to make her part of the whole, that had driven her to take every means at her command to avoid such a fate. She had retreated to her own apartment as a haven from the pressures which, like a mighty maelstrom, sought to suck her into the maw of the City. Her resistance to forming any sort of close personal relationship with others had its source in this fear of being lost, of becoming just a number in a system. Yet, ironically, her loyalty to the City was unabated, for it was the only life she knew.

And now, as she sat there holding hands and listening to the boy give thanks to his God, she was shocked to realize that she *was* being drawn into something! Something in the intimacy of the moment, the warm atmosphere of the small group pulled at her. And for the first time in years she felt a strong desire to let down her resistance, to let herself flow into whatever it was that held this family together.

But she had a lifetime habit of resistance to such things, having seen that the reason people wanted you to "join" them was that they wanted something you had. There was something predatory in the groups she had been exposed to, as well as in the graspings of Sheila Phi, who wanted Starr to satisfy her own greedy hungers.

Suddenly she realized that in her struggle to resist the force that drew her toward those at the table, she had tightened her grip—so much that when Tim said, "Amen!" she opened her eyes to see David casting a glance at her, and was aware that her wrists and fingers were weak with the strain of the effort she had put into them. She glanced quickly at Miriam, and saw both surprise and a trace of pity in the girl's dark blue eyes. Quickly she took her hands away, shocked at the intensity of the emotion that had seized her.

"Well, now, everyone eat up," Caleb said loudly. He winked at the rest of them saying, "Your mother's a terrible cook, but no matter! We'll make the best of it." Picking up a long knife, he skillfully cut off a large slice of meat, saying, to Starr with a gleam of humor in his dark eyes, "Let's have your plate, Daughter, before these gluttons eat everything!"

Starr stared at the huge slice of venison, thinking, *That's one person's ration of meat for a week!* David began spooning vegetables on her plate, making a mound of steamy potatoes, tender carrots, and green peas. She took the slice of fresh bread from the platter, and dipped into a large bowl of creamy yellow butter—real butter, which she had never tasted in her entire life. *I'll never be able to eat that synthetic butter again!* she thought.

The talk ran around the table, mostly about the work that had gone on that day. No one pressured Starr to enter in—she didn't know that Caleb had warned the others, "Let the girl talk when she pleases. Don't pester her!" She listened with interest as Josh told how one of the cows had produced a new calf, and Tim related how he had found 19 guinea eggs that morning—"More than anyone ever found before!" he said proudly.

The food seemed to melt in Starr's mouth, and finally she had to say, "No thank you," when Miriam urged her to try the yellow squash. "I've never had such a wonderful meal!"

"You can't quit now!" Caleb said. "Sarah, didn't you open a jar of those blackberries we canned last summer? I do believe I saw a cobbler on the stove, didn't I?"

"Yes, indeed!" Sarah rose and went to the kitchen, coming back at once with a large bowl which she set on the table. Taking a spoon, she broke the firm brown crust, and steam rose, a delicious fragrance filling the room. "Company first," she announced firmly as Josh reached for the first bowl she filled to the brim with berries and crust. "Put a little cream on that, dear," she said to Starr.

The cream was so thick it wouldn't pour, so Starr ladled out a dollop with a spoon over the succulent berries. She took a tentative bite, and her eyes flew open. It was the first natural fruit she'd ever tasted, totally unlike the hard little affairs from the City Greenhouse that passed for berries. "Oh, this is wonderful!" she exclaimed.

Tim laughed at her. "You've got a white moustache!" he said.

"Never mind what she's got, Tim," Sarah said. "If I know you, you'll have cream up to your eyebrows before you're finished!"

After dessert was finished, Caleb said, "A special treat tonight. Coffee for all." As his wife brought an ancient enameled pot and filled their mugs with the rich, black coffee, Caleb said, "Everything else on the table came from our own land. But coffee won't grow in this country."

To Starr his statement was a revelation. To think of growing all the food she had seen on the large table! The thought of the green globs of paste-like substance she'd forced herself to eat so often at restaurants in the City came to her, and she thought, *It would have been better if I'd never had this meal. I'll remember it every time I have to eat that tasteless food back home!*

After the meal, Starr insisted on helping with the clean up, and her offer was taken without any protests. "I'll do the washing if you'll do the drying," she said, and soon she and Miriam were busy with the dishes. There was something about working with the young woman that broke down inhibitions, and by the time they were finished and went into the large den, Starr felt very comfortable with her.

David and his father were arguing about the best way to clear new land for the crops. It was, Starr noted, a very amiable argument, for though each man was certain his method was right, each would listen as the other presented his case.

"That's enough talk about your old crops," Sarah said firmly. "You'll bore Starr to death with all that!"

Caleb said at once, "Right you are, wife!" The whole family, Starr saw, had gravitated into the room, and now Caleb asked, "Well, what shall it be?"

"Games!" Tim shouted at once, and everyone laughed. Caleb said, "You and your games! Well, just one or two."

At once Tim chose a simple game that involved thinking of items of the same sort that began with certain letters. He explained it to Starr in excited tones. "I say 'The minister's cat is a curious cat while we clap our hands, and then you have to call the cat something that begins with a *c*."

"You mean," Starr smiled at the boy's excitement, "I would say, 'The minister's cat is a clever cat?' "

"That's right!" Tim nodded furiously, "You're real smart! Now, I'll start it off, and you can be after me, Starr!"

Tim began the simple rhythm game, Starr making notes in her mind that she would later put into her computer. *Simple people. Play a game that goes far back into antiquity. Check origin of game—was played as far back as 18th century, OldAge.*

For nearly an hour, the family played the games that Tim chose, then Josh groaned, "Enough games for tonight. Let's have some music!"

"Good!" Caleb said, and going to a cabinet on the wall, reached inside and brought back two instruments—one was a violin and the other a stringed instrument that struck a chord of memory in Starr's mind. As Josh took it and placed it in front of him, then took out two round sticks with felted knobs, it came to her: *A dulcimer! Used by mountain people before the end.* She watched with interest as the two began tuning their instruments. Finally Caleb nodded, "Here we go, Josh." He began playing a lively tune on the violin, and the clear notes from the dulcimer made a lovely harmony. It was a rollicking song, and at once the others joined in singing. Their voices blended, and Starr sat back, delighted with the performance. They sang song after song, and clearly they had spent many evenings gathered in this room singing the songs.

Sarah was the best singer, her clear contralto rising sweetly to fill the cabin. When the jolly songs had been sung, Tim said, "Sing the one about the poor man, Mother!"

"No, it's too sad!" Josh protested, but Sarah gave Tim a smile and a wink. Then she lifted her voice and sang a song that was, Starr realized, older than any of her research. Caleb and Josh did not accompany her, and as the woman's voice filled the room, Starr was amazed at the pathos and emotion that Sarah put into the ancient ballad:

"In Scarlet town, where I was born,
There was a fair maid dwelling,
Made every youth cry *Well-a-way!*
Her name was Barbara Allan."

All in the merry month of May,
When green buds they were swelling,
Young Jemmy Grove on his death-bed lay,
For love of Barbara Allan.

"Oh, 'tis I'm sick, and very, very sick,
And 'tis a' for Barbara Allan;"
"O the better for me ye's never be
Tho your heart's blood were spilling."

He turned his face unto the wall,
And death was with him dealing:
"Adieu, adieu, my dear friends all,
And be kind to Barbara Allan."

And slowly, slowly rose she up,
And slowly, slowly left him,
And sighing said she could not stay,
Since death of life had reft him.

"O mother, mother, make my bed!
O make it saft and narrow!
Since my love died for me today,
I'll die for him tomorrow."

As the sweet voice reached the end then paused, a silence fell over the room. And Starr felt the power of the song in a way she had never felt before over any music. Tears welled up into her eyes, and she blinked them away angrily, not understanding the sadness that had come to her. The music of the City was composed by computers, and had become so sophisticated that one could buy a program, feed information into it by simple commands:

THEME—SEX IS WONDERFUL;

STYLE—WALTZ TIME;

INSTRUMENTS—STRINGS.

The computer would whirr briefly, then out would come a song exactly as prescribed by the commands.

But none of the songs from her computer had stirred Starr as this one had, and she knew instinctively that this was music that had come out of life! Somewhere in the dim, distant past, there had been a young man who had died for love of his sweetheart. All was lost over the years, except the scrap of a ballad, but that scrap had made the tragedy last for generations.

"Why are you crying, Starr?" Tim asked suddenly.

"Oh, I don't know, Tim," Starr tried to smile. "I guess I just feel sorry for the young man."

"So do I!" Tim nodded seriously. Then he asked, "Father, why do I like a sad song?"

Caleb looked fondly at the boy, thinking about the question. "I think we'd get tired of nothing but happy songs, Son," he said. "Life has its sorrows, you know. And we need to be reminded that they're going to come to us."

"Well, *I* don't have any sorrows!" Tim smiled happily, looking around the room. "We have a good time, don't we, Mother?"

Starr did not miss the quick glance that Sarah threw at her husband, and was certain that the mother's eyes were misty with unshed tears, but she covered it up by laughing and getting to her feet. "Yes, thank the Lord, we do have a good time. Now, it's time for a little from the Book, and then to bed."

Starr saw that they were all looking to the father, and she watched as he opened a thick book that Sarah passed him from a shelf containing a few books. This was not a book in the ordinary sense, but a loose-leaf notebook, thick with well worn pages. Caleb shuffled through the pages, found a place, then began to read:

"Though I speak with the tongues of men and of angels, and have not love, I am become as a sounding brass or a tinkling cymbal . . . ."

He was, Star realized, a fine reader, his voice deep and clear, and it was also evident that he knew the passage he read by heart, for he would often look around the room without missing a word.

And it was a beautiful passage, though Starr did not recognize it. It spoke of how love was the most important thing in all the world, and then it listed the characteristics of genuine love: how that it was never jealous and always rejoiced when others were blessed. And love never grew angry or bitter when a person was treated badly. As Caleb read on, Starr felt a strange longing growing in her heart. It was something that she had felt before to some extent, but now it came almost like a pang. She leaned her head back, eyes closed, and the longing grew until it was a pang sharper than anything she had ever felt.

Yet—she realized that she did not even know what it was that she was longing for! Yet it was there, keener and more demanding than a physical desire for food or drink. She felt like a fool, sitting there almost sick with desire for something she could not even name!

Suddenly a fragment of memory came to her, tantalizing and vague as an almost forgotten tune that slipped around the edges of the mind. What was it? Something she had read—about just such a feeling. She had learned long ago that to throw her mind into a search for such things was useless. Better to relax, to think not of the mystery that lay just outside the rim of her consciousness, but to wait—"

And then it came, with a clarity so sharp that she could almost see the black words on the white paper. A seer from England! What was his name? Yes! Lewis, that was it! C.S. Lewis! Now it all came to her, the words of the man so long dead. Words she had read in a book, that told of Lewis' experience with just such a longing as gripped her. He had related how that he had seen a glimpse of beauty while still a boy, that it dominated all his life. He told how he had spent years trying to find that beauty—and had failed completely. He called the emotion, the longing for beauty or truth by it's German name, *sehnsucht,* Starr remembered. She let the memory flow into her, then it came to her. Lewis had found that beauty no place but in God! That was the reason, she realized at once, that the works of C.S. Lewis were on the Index, forbidden to publish or to possess! Only her position as remedial historian had brought her to the text of the man, and now she knew exactly what he had felt!

". . . For now we see through a glass, darkly; but then, face to face: now I know in part; but then shall I know even as also I am known. And now abideth faith, hope, love, these three; but the greatest of these is love."

A small chorus of "Amens" went around the room, and without a pause, Caleb began to pray. Starr instinctively bowed her head and closed her eyes. It was a simple prayer, not long. Caleb thanked his God for all the goodness he and his family had received, asked protection from the dangers that might lie ahead—and closed by saying, "Thank you for delivering our guest from harm. Be near to her, Lord, even in her heart." And then he said, "In the name of Jesus Christ we ask these things. Amen!"

Once again the family said "Amen," and then Sarah said, "To bed with you Tim, and the rest of you, as well!"

Starr rose and feeling Caleb's eyes on her, said, "Goodnight. And thank you for your hospitality."

"God be with you, Daughter," Caleb nodded. And when Miriam had led Starr up the stairs and the others had gone to their own rooms, he said, "There's a child with a heavy spirit, Sarah."

"Yes. But she felt the hand of the Lord tonight. I saw it in her eyes. Come, we'll pray for her. I feel that she has a dark way to tread."

Caleb stared at his wife, for he had long known that she had a sense for such things. The two of them joined hands, and offered a fervent prayer for the young woman who had come into their lives.

Upstairs the two young women got undressed and ready for bed. "Would it bother you if I did a little work before we turn the light out, Miriam?" Starr asked.

"Not at all. I want to read for awhile myself."

Star took out her small journal and yellow pencil. But she soon discovered that she could not begin. Usually words flowed from her, but the day had been so strange that she could not put her feelings into cold words. Shaking her head with a stubborn motion, she determined to write down *facts,* leaving her emotions out of it:

My first contact with Primitive family. They are friendly and hospitable, very much so! Can they be this open with every visitor? It seems too good to be true. As time goes on, in all probability I will discover they have their angers and jealousies just as other people.

The boy Tim came as a shock. They must know that he is doomed! There is little medical knowledge here, but they must have seen other children afflicted with Down's Syndrome. They are especially gentle and tender with the boy, and he seems happy. But it is a disturbing factor! The State knows best, of course, and has laid out the principles of Relief so that suffering will be alleviated. Yet—they are all so—!

They are extremely religious. And the worst sort of religion, that of the Crossbearer. It came as a shock to hear the head of the family pronounce the name of Jesus quite openly. In the City he would not last long! He might survive in the Fringe, but even there the most flagrant cases of this primitive superstition does not go unnoticed by the leaders in the City!

During the course of the evening, while the father was reading from some ancient text, I was stricken by some sort of emotional disturbance. No doubt it was the result of my terrible fright with the man called Abbadon. I had thought myself more stable than to fall into such a tragic state, for I have always prided myself on keeping my emotions under firm control, but tonight, as Caleb read about love—"

Here Starr broke off suddenly, panic stricken, for even the memory of the words Caleb read caused the longing to rise in her breast! She closed the notebook hurriedly, put it in the locked section of her bag, then lay down on the bed, trembling despite herself.

"Good night, Starr," Miriam said quietly, looking up from her book. "Tomorrow I'll show you around the village, if you like."

"Yes, thank you," Starr said quickly. She rolled over, pulling the cover over her, but sleep did not come easily. She lay there until Miriam finished her reading, turned the lamp down, and went to bed. It was very quiet in the attic room, and soon Starr heard the even breathing of the other girl.

Finally she grew calm, and the last thought that came to her before she drifted off was a phrase from Caleb's book: ". . . the greatest of these is love."

Chapter Nine

A TRIP TO THE MARKET

The soft sound of Miriam's voice drew Starr out of sleep, but she made no sign of awakening. On her first morning, she had been alarmed when the voice of the girl had wakened her. For a moment she had been completely disoriented, not knowing where she was. Tense with fear, she lay there ready to leap out of bed and defend herself—then memory came flooding back, and she glanced across the room to see in the dim light that the girl was kneeling beside her bed.

This was the sixth morning of her visit, and Starr lay quietly under the warm coverlet until Miriam finally rose and slipped quietly from the room. As soon as the door closed, Starr arose, put on the wool robe Miriam had given her, then lit the oil lamp on the table. It cast a golden gleam over the room as she quickly pulled her computer from her pack and began her daily report. Morning, she had discovered, was the best time for this. The women were preparing breakfast and the men were taking care of early chores. The days were so full that by bedtime she was ready to go to sleep at once. She had discovered that the fresh air, vigorous exercise, and delicious food were better for making one sleep than the Morpheus Capsules she had brought along in her kit. Nor had she needed any other of the drugs she had brought, not even the Uplifter pill that she had assumed was necessary each day to get her to a working pitch. For most of her life Starr had taken pills to sleep, to heighten her mental processes, and to blot out the fears and anxieties that lay under the surface of her consciousness.

Sitting down on the bed with the VoiceWriter in her hand, she was struck by the thought *Why don't I need all the drugs I've used for years?* It was a disturbing question, somehow, and she shook it off quickly as she began speaking into the VoiceWriter.

"Sixth day of Starr Omega Investigation. Subject: Familial patterns of Primitives."

"Most common social structure in the village called Haven is the nuclear family, consisting of father, mother and one or more children. Basic power flow begins with father, the strong authority. Archaic submission patterns exist in wife and children. According to all modern sociological research, such a pattern of male dominance should produce extreme tensions. Even in OldWorld's primitive structures, toward the end progressive groups, such as Women's Lib, Gay Power and the ACLU, had managed to eradicate the older religious and mythological concepts of marriage. It is to be noted that the misery and unhappiness that have proven to result from such archaic structures are well hidden by the dwellers of the Fields . . . ."

Starr paused, shut the VoiceWriter off, and picked up her notebook. Slowly she wrote: *Why are they so happy? I know it must be some sort of self-hypnosis! They do everything that our finest scholars and social workers have proven to be evil—yet they seem so content!* She jammed her pencil so hard on the exclamation point that it snapped, and with a gesture of frustration, she suddenly thrust the tablet and pencil back into the kit, shoved it into a drawer, then began to get ready for breakfast. But as she brushed her hair, the enigma of Caleb and his family kept gnawing at her.

There was, for example, the matter of Caleb's father, Amos. Ever since she had been taken to meet him on the second day of her visit, she had been haunted by his face. Caleb had said cheerfully to her after supper, "I'd like you to meet my father, Starr." She had agreed and followed him upstairs. "He's feeling very well today," Caleb had informed her, opening the door, and following her into the small room with a tall window that looked down onto the front yard. The sunlight had blinded her momentarily, and she had stood there blinking as Caleb had said, "Well, now, Father, you have a visitor! This is Starr."

As her eyes grew accustomed to the glare of sunlight, Starr had looked for Caleb's father, but no one was in the room—at least not that she had seen at first. Then she realized that a man was in the bed beside the window, a small man, shrunken by age until he made only a slight outline under the cover. His face was shrunken as well, so that there was a skull-like quality about it, but the eyes that looked at her were alive. His lips were thin and seamed, and when he spoke Starr had to strain to catch his words. "Welcome . . .!"

Starr had swallowed, then nodded, forcing herself to speak normally. "I'm glad to meet you, sir." That was all she had been able to manage, but Caleb had kept the conversation going, telling his father what Starr had been doing, throwing in bits of news about the farm and the family. As he had talked, Starr had sat there, looking at the ancient face and slowly gotten over her shock. The man was the oldest human being she had ever seen, for in her world no one would be permitted to live so long past usefulness. As a Reliever she had been assigned to many who were no longer able to maintain their level of usefulness; some of them had been rather painful cases. One woman came to her mind, a middle-aged woman who had been signed over to the Department of Concern by her son. *She's not able to keep up any more* he had informed Starr, and the mother's eyes had dulled as she was told that her family had assigned her to be Relieved.

And yet, Starr remembered, that woman had been much stronger than Caleb's father! What amazed her most, however, was the gentle care and love that the old man received. He was almost helpless most of the time, and the family all took part in caring for him. He was, she found, much like a new infant, having to be bathed and fed special food. Yet there was no complaint from any of them, even Josh, who was very impatient with most things.

After that first visit, Starr had become intrigued with the situation, for it was something totally foreign to her experience. She visited with the old man more than once. Sometimes he just slept, but at times he became almost animated, speaking of the old days. She had heard that it had been that way with elderly people before they were Relieved—that the days long gone were more real and vivid to them than the present. David had spoken of that once, as the two of them had sat beside Amos. "He can remember almost everything that happened thirty or forty years ago," he had said thoughtfully, "but he sometimes can't remember anything about what happened this morning."

As Starr finished brushing her hair, she suddenly thought, "I wonder if he could have known my parents?" The thought came unexpectedly, and for a few seconds, she sat there staring in the mirror. She had found herself thinking more about her parents lately, perhaps because she knew that they had been sentenced to the Fields. Always she had tried not to think of them. A Psychologist had warned her when she was only a child, "It is not healthy for you to think of them. They were Heretics and the City became your family to save you from them. Banish them from your mind. If you cannot do so, we have medication to remediate the problem."

Starr had resisted medication, suppressing all thoughts of her parents when the Examiner tested her at regular intervals for soundness of mind. But now, the City seemed far away. Almost every night since she had been with David's family, seeing the closeness of the father and mother with their children, Starr's long-buried memories had begun to surface. Sometimes it was in the form of dreams which came just before dawn. The dreams were frightening, yet strangely alluring. In one of them she saw herself as a little girl sitting on the shoulders of a tall man with black hair. There was a woman by his side. The three of them were walking beside a small stream. The man had taken her from his shoulders, and the woman had removed her shoes and stockings so she could wade in the pool. The water had been cool. In the dream all of them had laughed when Starr almost fell into the water. She could remember few details, but the man had a kind face and a black patch over one eye. He had a terrible scar on the right side of his face. The woman was beautiful, and in some of the dreams she sang a song to Starr—something about a lamb. One thing that made this dream somewhat frightening to Starr was the fact that she wore something that had belonged to her parents—a small gold pin in the shape of a lamb. She had not worn it for years, knowing that if anyone knew of it, she would not be allowed to keep it.

Suddenly, she reached back into the kit, removed a small leather case and drew from it the tiny pin. It was a simple piece of jewelry, of little value. But as she held it she realized for the first time how much she treasured it. It was the only link to her past—to her parents. With a defiant gesture she suddenly pinned the brooch over her left breast. She had worn it a few times, when she was a child. But it was always when she was alone. Now, as a woman, she wore it for the first time. It seemed to glow in the rosy light of dawn that pierced the window.

Starr left the room, her face intent as a vague plan began to form in her mind. By the time she got downstairs, she knew what she would do. Saying nothing to any of the family, Starr smiled and spoke cheerfully to the others. When the meal was over she said, "Let me take your father's breakfast to him this morning, Caleb."

Caleb looked at her with surprise, saying, "Well, he's not a very neat eater, you understand."

"Oh, that doesn't matter," she answered quickly. "I want to help, and I'm not as quick as Miriam. If he's feeling well, I'll sit and talk with him awhile." She quickly made the fine mush with the butter and a little salt as she'd seen Miriam do several times. Then she filled a cup with hot milk and made her way back to Amos' room.

"Good morning," she said cheerfully as she entered. "I'm your new maid, Amos. Let me help you sit up . . . ." She saw at once that he was alert, the old eyes bright as a bird's? She kept up a busy chatter while she sat beside him and fed him small portions from a pewter spoon. After he had eaten all he wanted, she cleaned his face, put the tray aside, and asked, "May I visit with you awhile?"

"Yes, of course," he nodded, his thin lips trembling slightly. "You are—" he said, then his eyes clouded. "I forget—!"

"I'm Starr," she said, and waited until his eyes gleamed with recognition. "I've been thinking of the past," she said casually. "What it must have been like in those days. I suppose it was very hard?"

Her question caught his interest, and at once he began speaking of the past. "Yes, it was hard," he nodded, "There was nothing easy about the Fields when the first of us came. The land had to be cleared by oxen. At first we had to live in caves . . . ." He rambled on, sometimes getting the present and the past confused, but out of the patchwork recitation a picture began to emerge. Starr had always had an analytic mind, but at the same time was able to see things in vivid images. As the old man spoke, she saw a ragged group of outcasts cut off from the civilized world and forced to struggle mightily for bare survival in a hostile and dangerous world.

Starr leaned forward, her eyes wide as Amos spoke of the fierce battles with wild animals that had begun to proliferate as the earth renewed itself. She was horrified as he spoke casually of one of his children being dragged off by a band of marauding wolves, the child's frantic screams being heard throughout the night. "There was nothing we could do," Amos said slowly, his eyes turned bitter over the tragedy that had taken place long before Starr was born. "If I had gone outside I might have been killed as well. Then the others would have fallen to the pack." He stared at her, his eyes opaque, yet filled with grief. Then he smiled suddenly, his entire countenance lighting up. "But God was faithful," he whispered. "He brought us through the flood and through the fire. Blessed be the name of our God!"

Once again the longing that had been coming to Starr flooded her. She could do nothing but sit and listen as Amos spoke of the goodness of his God. His simple faith was alien to all that she had accepted as true and, though she let none of it show in her eyes, conflict in her breast raged.

Finally, seeing that the old man was tiring Starr asked, "Did you ever know a man with one eye and a terrible scar on his face who was exiled from the City? It must have been about twenty years ago? He and his wife?"

"There were so many," Amos muttered, then he cocked his head to one side, a thought coming to him. "But—yes! There *was* such a man!"

Starr said nothing, for she had learned that to press people was to interfere with their memory. Patiently she sat there, while he searched through his past. He was like a shopper, going through a large box filled with all sorts of things, looking for one specific item, and discarding all the rest. "He was a very large man with reddish hair—no, wait, that was Thaddeus, not him. But he did have one eye, I remember that very well!" He nodded emphatically, demanding, "Do you know how I can remember that? Because he was such a strong fellow! Why, he had more strength than three men!"

"Really? What was his name?"

Amos stared at her, his eyes going blank. "Name? Why, I can't recall. Was it James something? No, not that. An unusual name—never heard it before."

Starr asked casually, "Was it something like Jason?"

"Jason!" A light burned in the old man's eyes, and he nodded proudly. "Yes! That was it—Jason!" He peered at her curiously. "You couldn't have known him. You're too young."

Starr said tightly, "He—I think he was my father." Then she had to ask, "Is he still living?"

"Oh, my, I have no idea!"

"Do you know where I might find him? Or someone who could tell me about him and his wife?"

"No! No! You don't want to be looking into that!"

"But why not?"

"Because he was sent to the Badlands, him and his wife!" The thought seemed to distress the old man, and he slipped down in the bed, closing his eyes.

Starr leaned forward, knowing that she might never get another chance to discover anything from Amos. He had been more lucid than she had ever seen him, and it was unlikely that he would even remember what he had told her. "Please! Help me, Amos! I must find them!"

The ancient eyes opened and she saw that he was struggling with something. Finally he whispered so faintly that she had to put her ear almost to his lips to catch his words: "Assad! He will know!"

"Assad?" she asked, but he had dropped off abruptly in the way of the very old and the very young. She pulled the cover over Amos, stood to her feet and whispered, "Assad!" Then she picked up the tray and left the room.

"You stayed a long time," Miriam said as she entered the kitchen. "Was he awake much?"

"Yes. He was telling me about the old days."

"He's one of the few who remember them. David and I would like to make a book from what he's told us."

Starr exclaimed, "Oh, I'd love to read it, Miriam!"

"Of course. It's all in my sorry handwriting—mine and David's. It's in the bookshelf by my bed—the one in a green notebook. Help yourself, Starr."

Just then David came in, "I'm going to the market. Anybody who wants to go better get cracking!"

Starr, urged by Miriam, went outside to find the wagon loaded with vegetables. "Climb aboard, woman," David smiled at her, holding out his hand. "You're like all the rest, I see. Can't resist a trip to shop." His strong hand closed on hers, and she was pulled bodily up into the wagon. She fell against him, then pulled back at once, moving to the far side of the seat. He gave her a quick look, "Where are the others?"

"They're not going. But your mother gave me a list of things to bring back."

David spoke to the team and they started off at a brisk trot. As they moved down the dusty road David asked, "How was Grandfather this morning?" He listened as she gave her report, then nodded. "I'm glad you spent some time with him. When he is up to it, he likes to talk about the old days."

Starr hesitated, then made a quick decision. "He really was a help to me, David. Part of my job here involves looking up a few people. And your grandfather gave me a clue about the one I need to see most."

"Oh? Who is it?"

"A man named Jason. He came here about twenty years ago, but your grandfather remembered him." When she saw the name meant nothing to David, she added in a casual tone, "Your grandfather said I could find out where he was now from a man named Assad."

David stiffened and turned to fix her with his eyes. "Assad? I only know of one—and you wouldn't be interested in meeting up with him, Starr."

"Oh, I suppose I'll have to, David. Part of my job." Starr was reluctant to tell her secret to anyone, but she could see that David was going to be difficult. "He's in the Badlands, your grandfather said. I think I'll go over there next week."

"That's not the best idea," David shot back. "Remember your friend Abbadon? That's his home territory. And to give you an idea of what sort of place it is, they consider Abbadon a pansy!"

Starr's heart sank, but she said stubbornly, "I have clearance to go to any section of the Fields, David."

"You think a piece of paper means anything to that crowd? Starr, even the Border Guards are afraid to go there. They won't ever go alone. Always take a troop, and be well-armed." He glanced at her, his eyes serious. "They'd take you, use you up, and knock you in the head when they were finished!"

The rough edge of his voice, as well as the raw warning about the place, silenced Starr momentarily. She sat quietly in the seat, noting the rich fields of green grain waving in the breeze. All the time she was aware that no matter what David said she was going to make the attempt to find her parents. Nothing further was said about the matter.

Soon they reached the village square which was humming like a beehive. Starr had been there twice earlier in the week, but it had been almost empty. Now there was a teeming mass of people, all of them seemingly wearing the brightest colors available. The square looked to her like a kaleidoscope with the colorful shirts of the men and the dresses of the women constantly in motion. Booths of every sort were set up and a babble of voices filled the air as the vendors called out loudly to entice customers. David found a place to hitch the team and then helped her down. "Got your list?"

"Yes, but I don't have any of your money."

You won't need much," he said. "That's why we brought the vegetables."

For the next hour Starr had a wonderful—and confusing time. When she found an article at one of the booths, a large iron pot that Sarah had listed, she was astonished at what followed. Seeing her hesitate, David whispered, "I'll give you a quick lesson in how to get a bargain." He sauntered up to a booth, picked up a pot and looked at it with a frown, then tossed it down saying, "Thaddeus, that's the worst piece of work I've ever seen! I knew your creativity would suffer when your dear old father died!"

The vendor, a chunky black-eyed man with a bristling moustache that seemed to quiver with rage, shouted at him, "You pig-farmer! You wouldn't know good iron work from a potato!" Snatching up the pot, he began pointing out the fine qualities of the piece. When he had finished David said, "I feel sorry for you Thaddeus, but because I liked your father and promised him to try and keep you from starving, I'll give you two bushels of the finest, sweetest carrots ever dug."

The moustache twitched and Thaddeus laughed scornfully, "You can't get rid of those stringy old carrots, so you want my family to try to digest them, is that it? Two bushels, ha!" He pulled at his hair, "David, because you're young and not likely to do well with that sorry farm, I'm going to do you the favor of letting you take this splendid, hand-crafted piece of work home with you for your dear mother—for only ten bushels of your withered carrots."

Starr stood there amazed as the two fought back and forth. She had never bargained for anything in her life. When she wanted something, if she had the Credits she would simply thrust her hand out, allowed the machine to read her number—that was it. After what seemed like a long and angry battle between the two men, David finally agreed to deliver seven bushels of carrots to the home of Thaddeus in exchange for the pot.

"See you at the Ecclesia in the morning, Thad," David said with a smile as he tucked the pot under his arm.

"Of course, and give my best to your family, David," the vendor smiled at both of them, then turned away to begin shouting at another customer.

"Now, you can do the rest of the shopping," David said with a faint smile. "Here's a list of the stuff in the wagon. Don't let yourself get cheated."

Starr opened her mouth, but before she could object, David turned and disappeared into the milling crowd. Feeling helpless and afraid, Starr wandered around the market. Finally she said to herself, *This won't do! What are you afraid of? Just march over there and start shouting!*

And it worked! She haggled with a young woman who almost screamed when she made an offer of five ripe melons for a bright silk scarf. But Starr held her own and got the scarf for only six melons! She had no idea if she had gotten a bargain, but it had been exciting. She lost herself for the next three hours, bidding, arguing, walking away then allowing herself to be called back.

David found Starr, and after looking at the pile of goods he whistled, "What a stack of plunder! You didn't get all this for that wagon load of vegetables?"

"Yes! It was fun, David! I've never had such a good time!"

David looked down at her, noting the color in her cheeks, the brightness of her gray eyes. She was wearing one of Miriam's dresses, and it was the first time he had seen her in anything other than jeans and boots. The dress was a bright green, with a white bodice, and, since she was larger than Miriam, it fit her snugly at the hips and breast. He wanted to say, "You look beautiful." But instead, he held the words back, "If a visit to a market is the best time you've ever had, you must have had a real dull life, Starr."

Starr saw admiration in David's eyes. It was what she had seen in the eyes of many men, and learned to dread it. But Starr wanted to please him. When he said nothing except, "Let's walk around for awhile," she was disappointed in.

They spent another hour at the market, then David delivered the vegetables to the different vendors. They were about to get in the wagon, when a man came running up to say, "David, tell Miriam I'll be by tonight."

He stared at Starr, "That's Saul Thomas. He wants to marry my sister."

Starr looked surprised. "He's much older than she is, isn't he?"

"Sure. He's got a lot of competition, but he's the richest of all her suitors." The thought somehow displeased him and he said, "He's one of the leaders at the Ecclesia. That means a lot."

"I don't think I understand the Ecclesia. What is it, David?"

"It's those of us who follow Jesus, Starr." He saw her look of perplexity, "You'll know more about it after tomorrow. That's when we meet. Will you come?"

Starr hesitated, aware that two forces were at work in her. Part of her wanted to go, the other part didn't. But it was for this she had come. So, she nodded, saying, "I'd like to go very much."

"Fine." They came to a shallow creek a few minutes later, and he stopped to give the horses a rest and allow them to drink. Tall trees shaded the crossing and as the horses snorted and pawed the water, they sat there until he turned to her. "You know something?"

"What?"

"You look very nice today."

The compliment caught Starr off-guard. Her cheeks suddenly grew warm. She lifted a hand to one to conceal the color, "Thank you."

"As a matter of fact, you look so nice that I'm going to break a promise I made to my mother."

Starr stared at him in bewilderment.

"I promised mother I'd never kiss a young woman on our first buggy ride," David continued. "But you look so fresh and pretty, I'm going to make an exception."

David pulled her close, and before she could resist, placed his lips firmly on hers. Starr found herself responding to the kiss, adding her own pressure. As the kiss continued, she found herself disquieted at the feelings that rose within her.

Finally, David drew back, and a smile pulled at the corners of his lips. "You mustn't expect such favors *every* time I take you to town, Starr!"

Then Starr realized that David was teasing her, and pulled back. She tried to be angry, but the sight of his amused smile made that impossible. She laughed suddenly, determined not to let him get the better of her. "I can see you've had lots of practice. But I'll take the matter up with Sarah."

David became uneasy, "I—I don't think that would be such a good idea. Mother is—a little old-fashioned."

He suddenly looked like a young boy caught with his hand in the cookie jar. This delighted Starr. "Yes, I think your mother should know what her son is up to. I'll talk to her as soon as we get home."

David looked uneasy, then he caught a glimpse of the smile that was pulling at her lips. "Well, if I'm going to be whipped, I might as well give her a good reason!"

He reached for Starr as she drew back laughing. "No, I won't be a party to corrupting your promises to your mother. Now, get those horses moving!"

The incident had lightened their moods, and they laughed at little things on the rest of the trip. But just as they pulled into the yard, Starr said, "David, I enjoyed the day." She was feeling happier than she could remember, and impulsively leaned over and kissed his cheek. "Thank you, David!"

He stared at her, touched his lips, then said with a gleam of humor in his dark eyes, "Well, let's go give Mother the bad news!"

"Maybe we'll wait until next market day," she said, smiling up at him. Then they both laughed and got out of the wagon. Starr felt secure in some strange way and the thought of his strength gave her a strong pleasure—which for some reason, disturbed her.

Chapter Ten

LIGHT OF THE WORLD

Starr sat on a fallen tree high above the River looking out over the dark expanse of water toward the light-rimmed east. As the thin glowing band grew wider and brighter it seemed to her that she was inside some monstrous beast whose jaws were being pried apart to let the light shine in darkness.

A different dream had come to her during the night and she awakened with a terrible longing, an aching deep inside her, for which there seemed to be no cause nor cure. She could remember little of the dream (wandering in a place shrouded in heavy fog; circles of light with hands reaching out to her that vanished as she tried to grasp them) but it had left its mark.

The morning wind was sighing through the tops of the tall pines on the bluff. Starr drew the light blanket around her against the chill and watched the glow in the eastern sky change from red to a pale pink. The stars slowly faded as the sun slipped the bonds of night and rose from the earth, turning the sky white as bone. The surface of the River ruffled in the wind, dancing and sparkling as if to celebrate the new day.

"The Light of the World."

Starr turned quickly around. "David, you startled me!"

"Sorry," he said, sitting beside her. "I was watching the sunrise. Guess I was thinking out loud."

"What was that you said?"

"The Light of the World," he replied. "It's from the Bible. That's one of the many names for Jesus."

Starr watched the sun as it grew brighter; scattered trees lay their long shadows down across the prairie. As light touched the tall grass dewdrops glittered like millions of jewels reaching to the far horizon.

"Are you all right?" David asked.

"It's so beautiful," she said, pointing down across the River where light was pouring into the land. "Is that what He's really like, this man you call the Light of the World?"

"In a way He is, but no one can truly describe Him. You have to see Him with your spirit—know Him with your heart."

"It's all so confusing." Starr rose and walked to the edge of the bluff.

David followed and stood beside her, seeing the breeze catch her hair, swirling it in a dark cloud about her head and shoulders. Her brow was furrowed in thought as David's eyes saw in her the face of a child. "The wise are confounded and the children understand," he said.

"What's that from?" Starr asked, turning to face him.

"From me," he replied. "It's how you come to a knowledge of God's word. More than that," he continued, "it's how you come to know God. Jesus said, if we don't become as little children we can't see the Kingdom of Heaven."

"I'm not going to think about this anymore now," she said, shaking her head slowly. "I'll go insane if I do."

David put his arm around her and they stood together on the high bluff overlooking the River. Behind them were the sounds of the village coming to life and before them lay the paths they would choose as they journeyed through life.

"Well I have to get to work," David said. "You coming?"

"David?"

"Yes."

"David, I have to go look for my parents. I'll never have any peace if I don't do everything I can to find them."

She had spoken of her parents earlier, but David had not expected this. He frowned down at her. "You're going into the Badlands? You wouldn't make it through the first day in that place."

"I don't think I'll make it anywhere if I don't try to find them, David."

He could see there would be no changing her mind. "I'll speak to my father. Arrangements have to be made. We'll leave at sunrise tomorrow."

✦   ✦   ✦

As Starr came down the stairs she saw David packing his knapsack for their journey. There was smoked meat, dried fruit, brown bread and other supplies. Starr's saddlebags lay unopened on the table.

"Good morning," David greeted her while continuing to pack. "You ready for our big adventure?"

Sleep still clouded Starr's mind. *How can he be so cheerful this early in the morning?* she thought. "I'd better be, hadn't I, since the whole thing was my idea?"

"Here," David said, smiling as Starr rubbed her eyes with both hands, "put some of this stuff in your saddlebags."

Starr packed the remaining supplies and greeted Sarah as she came into the room with a steaming platter of scrambled eggs, smoked ham and hot buttered biscuits. David cleared the table and the three of them sat down to breakfast.

"Where's your husband?" Starr asked.

"Oh, he left hours ago. Had to take some men to begin clearing one of the new fields. It's a long way off. I expect he'll be gone for three or four days," she replied. "I hope you two children won't be gone much longer than that.

"David sliced a generous portion of ham and speared it with his fork. "She's like an old mother hen, Starr. Always worried about something happening to one of her brood."

"Oh David, that's not true," Sarah admonished him quickly. "I just like having the family together, that's all."

"Well, you don't have to worry about Starr and me. She's been trained by the Border Guards," David said. "Men like Abbadon tremble at the very mention of her name."

Starr had a mental picture of Abbadon's hulking, smelly presence. He had his knife in one hand and a huge piece of greasy meat in the other. A voice called out, "Starr Omega" and he began trembling uncontrollably, slinking away from the sound of her name.

She smiled slightly, then wider and finally laughed out loud. David and Sarah had joined in, and after a few giggles and chuckles, they sat around the breakfast table smiling and content, and it was as if they had known each other for years.

"You never know what's going to strike somebody as funny, do you?" David asked.

"He doesn't seem nearly so dreadful now," Starr said. "I may actually laugh at that creature if I ever see him again." And she meant it. Somehow laughter had healed the wound Abbadon had inflicted in her soul, and the consuming fear she had carried with her since their encounter had vanished.

"I wouldn't advise that," David warned. "Abbadon isn't known for his sense of humor."

They finished breakfast and went outside to ready the horses for their journey. It was still dark and the full moon bathed them in a gossamer light as it settled in the western sky. They finished their work and mounted the horses just as Sarah came out the back door and headed toward the stables. She walked between the horses and David leaned over and kissed her on the cheek.

Starr was surprised when Sarah turned toward her, but she followed David's example, and kissed his mother on the cheek. How strange and yet how comfortable she was beginning to feel with these people. *And how easily I'm adapting to their customs,* she thought. *Next thing you know they'll have me giving thanks at the table.*

Sarah reached up and took David's hand in her own, then Starr's. "Heavenly Father, we praise you for another day you've given us. Bless these children, protect them on their journey and return them safely to us. We thank you for your angels that will keep them in all their ways."

Starr felt a stirring in the air and a small chill down her back. She quickly opened her eyes and saw the bowed heads of David and Sarah. She felt the warmth of Sarah's hand. Then Starr gazed heavenward at the vast scattering of stars: cold, silent, remote.

Soon David and Starr were riding in moonlight through the pasture where the cattle were still bunched together and the calves close to their mothers. This was the last hour of darkness. Then they entered a forest, following a path through the towering pines and underbrush until sunrise when it met the open rolling hill country. Two doves flew by in front of David and Starr, the early sunlight silvering their wings as they sped toward the small stream at the bottom of the hill. "Light of the World" flashed across Starr's mind like the silvered wings of the doves.

All morning they rode with the sun warming their backs. The mountains across the River appeared to be getting smaller and the rolling land they rode through became a dry, rocky plain. At noon they stopped under a solitary tree on the bank of the River to eat their lunch.

"When we cross the River the country and the people will be different than what you've seen so far," David said, eating some of the dried peaches.

"Worse than Abaddon?" Starr asked.

"Probably not, only more of them. I don't want you to ever be separated from me, not even for a short time." David told her solemnly. "You may not think it's important, but take my word for it. Things can happen very quickly out here."

After eating and resting they crossed the River at a ford upstream where the water was swift but deep enough to reach their stirrups. As they rode, Starr noticed a dead tree on the opposite bank. It was wide as a barn and a hundred feet tall—its dead limbs barren and black against the bright sky. Vultures sat silent and still on the highest branches, somewhat like statues adorning an alien house of worship.

David noticed Starr staring up at them. "Our welcoming committee," he said. "They got the job because they're the friendliest looking things in this part of the country."

Starr looked at him with a puzzled expression.

"See that one at the very end of the highest limb," David said, pointing to it. "That one's a prize winner—sweetest smile."

Starr laughed softly. *Humor is an art I must learn. It seems to take the sting out of life.*

David and Starr continued on the north bank of the River until they reached a dam that formed a vast lake. David stopped at a coppice near the shore and dismounted. "We'll spend the night here," he said, unsaddling his horse. "It'll be dark soon."

David took the canteens to the lake and filled them. When he returned Starr was unpacking the food and blankets. "Aren't you going to make a fire?" she asked.

"Not in this country," he answered. "Out here a flame might attract some big, cantankerous moths."

"Moths!" Starr said, then realized what he meant. *I'll catch on eventually I guess.*

At the edge of the trees David and Starr sat on the blanket they had spread over a bed of leaves. As they ate smoked ham and bread they watched the sun as it painted the western sky with streaks of peach, violet and pink. As the sun sank into the lake it seemed to set the horizon aflame and turn the water into blood.

"What was it like out here, David, when everything was poisoned and dying?" Starr asked. "Does anyone know?"

"Some of the tales have been passed along. They're not very pretty," he said.

"I've studied the history of how it came about: pollution from industry and automobiles; depletion of the Ozone Layer; destruction of the last remaining rain forests. That seemed to be the final blow. Even the scientists leading the reform movements didn't expect what happened. It came too suddenly and the extent of it was far beyond anything they had imagined."

David was looking out over the lake at the last of the light. The first star appeared in the sky. "It all sounds so bare and sterile when you tell it like that; those histories written inside the Domes," he said, turning toward her.

"Tell me the stories of your people, David."

"I'd hear them talking about it as a boy—those old tales that were passed down through the years." David's voice was growing softer like a whispering in the trees. "The thing I remember most was the burning rain. They say when it touched the skin it was like liquid fire and made terrible blisters that wouldn't heal. After it rained, the little sunlight that came through those poison clouds made the trees and plants smoke and burn. The earth was blackened.

"Sometimes the clouds would settle to the earth and wherever that happened the people would . . ." David stopped. The sound of frogs croaking came to them from the lake and the crickets provided counterpoint from the grass along the shore like a miniature string section. "I don't think I want to talk about this anymore, Starr," he said. "I might say some things you wouldn't want to hear."

"No. I want to hear."

"As you know, the New Age or New World Order governments were ruling the country—the earth! When the Domes were built, there was no room for all the people. The helpless were either killed or forced outside to die. Old people, children like Tim, the sick and the cripples were treated worse than animals. And of course the Christians were the first to go." David looked at Starr. "I don't mean to condemn you," he said. "Those were desperate times. I'm sure your government would never condone such things now."

Starr determined then not to talk about the government of the City, especially her occupation. *How could he ever understand the enlightenment of the civilized mind?* "Yes, those were desperate times," she said confidently, but there was a tightness in her chest that she couldn't explain.

"Why don't we talk about something more pleasant?" David asked, rising from the blankets. "I need to stretch my legs after being in that saddle all day. We could take a walk along the lake."

"Sounds great," Starr replied. "May I ask you one last question? No more after this. Promise."

"Let's go," he answered and walked away.

Starr caught up to him. "How did the people out here survive the bad water and air?"

"Caves," David answered, striding briskly along the shore.

"Caves?" Starr asked, trying to keep up. "What do you mean?"

"Up in the mountains. The air was cleaner. There were underground pools and streams."

"What did they eat?"

"Food!" David said as he stopped and turned around. "Look, I don't have all the answers. No one does. But I can tell you this. People can be very creative when their lives depend on it."

Starr decided to drop the subject; they walked together in silence. It was a beautiful night. The moon lay down a path of light acoss the surface of the lake and the waves plopped softly along the shoreline.

"David, I'm sorry if I brought back bad memories for you," Starr said contritely.

"Forget it. Maybe it's best to remember to keep the memory of the horror alive so it will never happen again," he said. "Let's hope man has learned from this."

"Where will we go tomorrow?"

"The first village. It's a two hour ride."

✦   ✦   ✦

They traveled the north shore of the lake and the first thing Starr noticed shortly after the village came into sight was the smell of the pigpens. "What's that awful smell?" she asked, holding a scarf over her face.

"This is the village of the Pigkeepers," David replied. "It supplies the whole region around here with pork."

"How do they stand the smell?"

"Pigs can get used to anything I guess," David replied.

"What do you mean?"

"Wait'll you meet the Pigkeepers. You'll find out."

They rode down the narrow, muddy road between acres of squealing, oinking, snorting pigs, hogs, sows and boars. The pens were alive with hundreds of them, all sizes and colors, lying down or moving about in a sea of mud. The racket was deafening.

A man, pulling a wooden wagon that held several large barrels, walked toward them. He was about Starr's height and weighed about three times as much. His baggy jacket and pants were dun-colored and a wide-brimmed felt hat was pulled down on his fore-head.

When they were fifty feet from the man it hit Starr like an invisible wall. Her stomach turned over and she thought she would vomit as she reined her horse. David looked at her with a slight smile on his face, then took a deep breath and rode toward the man. Even the horse began backing away and shook his head as if the stench were tormenting him.

Starr settled the horse down and watched as David spoke with the man at the wagon. Beyond them several children were playing in the streets. They looked as much like misshapen mudballs come to life as children. But they were running and squealing and teasing each other the same as any children would do. The village itself was a double row of identical sod houses lining both sides of the road. The grass of the sod walls had long since decayed and blown away. They were, in fact, mud houses with wooden roofs. Smoke curled from the roofs of most of the houses.

Two hundred yards north of the village was an immense, low-roofed building made of wood. From inside it came the shouts of men and the terrible shrill cries of the hogs. Dozens of black iron pots were smoking on fires in front of a series of large open doors facing to the south. Women and older children were moving about in regular patterns as if they had been doing it all their lives. The women and girls busied themselves around the pots, while boys led small groups of hogs into the building and pulled laden carts out of it toward the rows of pots.

Starr sat on her horse and held the scarf to her face, trying not to think of what was going on inside the building. She saw David take a packet of dried fruit from his knapsack and hand it to the man with the wagon. Then he turned his horse and headed back toward her while the man opened a narrow gate and pulled his wagon into an alleyway that ran between the pens.

"I think I may have found the man we're looking for," David said as he approached.

"David, please," Starr said through her scarf. "Let's get out of here before we discuss anything."

"This isn't so bad," he said.

Starr was astonished at his remark. "Are you demented? What could be worse than this?"

"Our next stop," he answered, pointing toward the north. "The village of the Dung Gatherers."

David saw Starr's eyes widen above the scarf. She turned the palomino and galloped out of the village at full speed. "Hold on!" David yelled, racing after her. "Starr, wait a minute will you?"

He caught up to her at a grove of trees near the edge of the lake where he grabbed the reins of the horse and pulled it to a stop.

"No! No! No!" she shrieked. "Absolutely not! I refuse to go to a place like that."

Starr had closed her eyes and was shaking her head. When David make no remark she stopped and glanced at him. A smile was slowly tugging at his lips.

"I mean it David!" she said sternly. "I'm not going there."

David was laughing now.

Starr realized what had happened. "You did it to me again, didn't you?" she said furiously.

David's head was thrown back and he was roaring with laughter now. He dismounted with some difficulty and sat under a tree.

"I don't see what's so funny about it," Starr said, getting down and walking over to him.

"You're absolutely right. It's not funny at all," he said with tears streaming down his face. Then he rolled over on his side and broke into another spasm of laughter.

"Well, if you're not going to take this seriously, we might as well go home," Starr snapped, sitting down under the tree. She was surprised at the way she used the word *home*.

David gained control of himself and sat up. "I'm serious now," he said. "I'm truly serious.

"Starr looked into David's eyes, still glistening with tears of laughter, and thought how much he looked like a little boy. "I guess it was sort of funny after all wasn't it?" she asked.

David looked back at her with a soft smile. "I didn't mean to make you mad," he said. "It's just that I've been worried that you might get hurt out here. I think I just needed a good laugh to break the tension. Works every time."

Chapter Eleven

A KISS AFTER DYING

On their way to the Badlands, David and Starr rode through the Sand Dunes north of the River. They had been formed thousands of years before by the winds picking up sand from dry river beds. As the wind was constantly changing the shape of the Dunes, there were no permanent landmarks to get one's bearings. Thus, many travelers wandered there until they died of thirst or exposure.

It was now mid-afternoon and Starr was covered by a fine layer of sand. She had followed David's example and tied a cloth about her face to protect her nose and mouth. She shielded her eyes with her left hand. Starr found herself blinking constantly. With the sun blotted out she had no sense of direction and she could barely see David a few feet in front of her. So, she closed her eyes and trusted her horse to follow David's.

"How much further?" Starr called out.

"It won't be long now. We're only touching the edge of the Dunes."

Thank God for that, she thought.

Starr closed her eyes again and let her mind drift with the easy motion of the horse. Something pulled her from her reverie and she suddenly realized the horse had stopped. Opening her eyes she quickly scanned the area in front, then on all sides. Nothing!

"David! David!" she cried, but her voice was lost in the storm. There was nothing but the dreadful moaning of the wind and the driving, blinding sand. She urged the horse ahead to try and catch up with him. *Surely he's missed me by now. He'll be coming back any second.* Panic was beginning to overtake her. Her breath was coming in shallow gasps and she couldn't control her thoughts.

Then she saw him! A man in a pale cloak riding an ivory-colored horse. *But he's going the wrong way! Directly toward the interior of the Dunes.* She shouted at him, but he was out of earshot. *I've got to stop him. He'll die in this storm if he keeps going.* She whirled her horse around but could gain no ground on the man in the pale cloak. In a few minutes time he was out of sight.

Starr was desperate now. *I'm too far into the Dunes for David to ever find me! I'll never get out of this place!* An overpowering fear took her and she quietly wept as she gave in to despair. She was choking and her eyes were filled with grit. Untying the cloth, she wiped her eyes and face.

"I told you not to get separated from me!"

Starr looked up. She felt unreal. *How could this be David?*

"What's the matter with you?" he demanded.

"Oh, David, I thought I was lost forever in this place."

"What are you talking about? I only missed you a few seconds ago. I thought you were right behind me."

"I got lost. I rode the wrong way," Starr said breathlessly. "I followed a man and he led me back to you."

"What man?"

"Didn't you see him? He was riding a light colored horse."

"I didn't see anyone." David said. "The Dunes can do strange things to your mind, Starr."

"He was real, David," she insisted. "If I hadn't followed him, I never would have found you."

"All right. Settle down. We'll talk about it later. Right now it's time to get out of this place."

An hour later they rode out of the Dunes into the Badlands. To their right, a towering sandstone butte ran northwest, disappearing into the purple shadows of the mountains. In the afternoon sun it glowed like a giant ember risen from the fiery depths of the earth. They turned west, riding into the sun through a dry rock-strewn plateau, thus avoiding the narrow twisting canyons that scarred its surface.

"Do you really think this man will know where my parents are?" Starr asked.

"I don't think the Pigkeeper was lying," David replied. "He's not sophisticated enough to learn that particular skill. But his information was old and may not be much help to us now."

"How could they possibly be alive after all these years in this awful place?" Starr asked.

"People are a lot more durable than you think, Starr," David said. And as an afterthought, "Your father must be a good man for them to exile him to this part of the Fields. Either that or he had to use this place as a refuge."

As they rode Starr gazed at the snow-capped peaks of the mountain range to the north. They were gleaming in the sunlight like cold fire. *There is beauty in all this desolation,* she thought.

Toward evening they came to a small gathering of huts. Their walls were made of stone and the roofs were rough-cut timbers sealed with pitch. In front of some of them fires were smoking in pits dug in the ground. Women wearing long drab-colored dresses and scarves or bonnets were cooking in black iron pots. Men in coarse trousers and jackets or slouched together in twos and threes strolled on what passed for a street.

David stopped his horse at the edge of the first hut. "Wait here," he told Starr, handing her his reins. He took the few steps over to the first fire and squatted next to a woman who with a wooden ladle was stirring a mixture of black beans and corn.

Starr heard him ask about the man named Assad. The woman with no teeth looked up from her cooking and smiled at him. "Why you want that little worm?"

"Information," David answered.

The woman turned back to her cooking. David took a silver coin from his jacket and began turning it over in his fingers. It glinted in the firelight and caught the woman's eye. Then she looked away, but it drew her head slowly back like a heavy winch. She pointed at a building on the opposite side of the street. David tossed the coin at her feet. Scooping it quickly into her hand, she dropped it into her apron.

"Stay here with the horses," David said, unbuckling the leather strap on his knapsack.

"I want to go with you," she insisted.

David reached into his knapsack, took out a wide-bladed knife with a bone handle, and slipped it inside his belt under the jacket. "Someone has to watch the horses."

"But I don't want . . . ."

"Do as you're told!" David barked, pulling his staff from its leather case alongside the saddle.

His words stabbed at her chest. She had seldom been spoken to like this, and never expected it from David.

David saw the pain in her face and took her hand in his, looking directly into her eyes. "I'm sorry," he said softly, but out here you have to do as I tell you. There may come a time when your life—both our lives will depend on it."

"I understand. I'll do better," she said shyly.

"This shouldn't take long," he explained. "If you hear me call you, bring the horses to the front of that building. If I'm not out by the time you get there—wait."

David turned and walked into the dusty street, slinging the staff over his left shoulder by its strap. The sun was sliding behind a low range of hills, casting an orange glow over the village. As darkness gathered, shadows flickered along the walls of the buildings in the smoky light. As she watched David walking among the fires, Starr remembered Martha's prayer about angels and wished there was something she could do to protect him.

Inside the makeshift saloon it was darker than the twilight David had just left. He stood at the door and let his eyes adjust to the gloom. A bar to the left was nothing more than a rough plank laid across two barrels. An oil lamp sat on it and another hung from the low ceiling. Two men stood at the bar drinking from pewter mugs. Three more sat at a table in the opposite corner playing cards. They did not look like the type who would enjoy family picnics.

David walked to the near end of the bar while keeping the five men in his line of vision.

"What'll it be?" the bartender asked.

"Assad," David replied and saw the eyes of a small man at the table dart toward him.

Assad lived by his wits and missed little that went on about him. He had watched from the door of the saloon as David tossed the silver coin to the woman. He talked about it with the men who sat with him. Their plan was to relieve David of the burden of any additional coins he might be carrying.

The bartender made no reply to David, but glanced at the table in the corner and then walked to the other end of the bar.

David observed the small man in the dark robe. The sharp angles of his face were shadowed under the hood and his dark eyes had a malignant glint. His companions were "bookends" owned by a giant with a morbid sense of humor. Both had wiry red hair that curled like Medusa's about their heads. Even their eyes had a reddish tint to them. They wore filthy black jackets that matched the color of their teeth perfectly.

"I'm looking for a man and a woman," David said flatly, staring down at the small man. "I was told you might be able to help me."

Assad smiled at the "bookends." "Helping isn't exactly my line of work. Maybe you should find the nearest priest." The three of them thought this exceedingly funny.

When they finished laughing, David produced a gold coin from his jacket and held it between thumb and forefinger, three feet from Assad's face.

"What I know is worth more than that," he responded as his right eye twitched almost imperceptibly.

David sensed it was coming and now he knew when.

Some men are born with that combination of speed and power that are as rare as the cardinal virtues—David was such a man. Had he been born in OldAge, he could have excelled in any sport—but he was not. He was born in an age where survival, rather than touchdowns and home runs, made timing and quick reflexes essential. What he excelled at was staying alive.

A thin-bladed knife appeared in the hand of the man nearest him. David stepped back with his left foot, the right hand reaching across his body to grip the staff three quarters of the way down. His left arm pulled free of the staff's leather strap as the hand reached behind his back and found the bone handle of the knife.

The thin-bladed knife was aimed at David's heart as the man holding it lunged forward. David uncoiled from his crouched position, pivoting on the balls of his feet as his right shoulder turned with the arm following through, whipping the staff around with a backhand motion. It exploded against the side of the man's head one inch above his right ear, crushing the skull like an eggshell. He dropped like a side of beef. Less than a second had lapsed since he pulled his knife.

David's left arm continued around from behind his back and forward, hand gripping the knife, wrist bent inward. The second man was on his feet, swinging a heavy short-handled axe toward David's chest with his right hand. At that moment, David flicked the knife with a vicious motion of his forearm and wrist, his body continuing around away from the path of the axe. He hit the floor, catching himself on his left hand and spinning to put his back to the wall, the staff held in front of him. Two seconds had lapsed.

Blood was seeping through David's jacket where the axe had grazed his left shoulder. The man who had thrown it stood perfectly erect, eyes bulging as he gripped the handle of David's knife with both hands and tried to pull it from his throat. A gurgling sound came from his open mouth and red froth bubbled down his chin as he collapsed across the table.

Assad was frozen to his chair. He was not the type of man to do his own dirty work. David had counted on that. The two men at the bar returned to their conversation.

David picked up his gold coin from the floor and stood before Assad. "I believe you have some information for me," he said evenly.

Starr almost shouted for joy when she saw David leave the saloon and walk across the street toward her in the last of the light. "Did you find out where my parents are?"

"Assad knew them, but . . . ."

"David, your shoulder!" Starr interrupted him.

"Let's get out of here now," he said, mounting his horse. "We'll fix it later."

As they rode away from the village, David continued. "Assad hasn't seen them in years. He told me there's a man close by who may know something."

"Do you think he was telling the truth?" Starr asked eagerly.

"I believe he was," David answered. "This one time anyway."

They stopped outside the village at a small stream that meandered along the base of a hill. Starr watched as David cleaned and stitched the wound himself. "How can you stand to do that to yourself?" she asked, horrified at the sight.

"No doctors—no hospitals out here. You do what you have to. Everyone carries a first aid kit with them when they travel."

Starr was obviously shaken at what had happened. The violence of the City was usually clandestine, but the rawness of this world dismayed her. "David, what happened back in the village?" Starr asked. "I mean—was anyone else hurt?"

David had finished the stitching and was putting the needle and thin coil of gut away. "Yes," he said and his face mirrored the anguish in his voice. "Sometimes there's no way to avoid it."

Starr sensed that satisfying her curiosity was not worth what it would cost David to talk about it. "Thank you for helping me look for my parents, David," she said sincerely. "This has been a whole new experience for me out here in the Fields—people helping each other and expecting nothing for it."

David looked at Starr with a quick smile. "That must be some place you live in, that City," he said, swinging into the saddle.

As they rode up the hillside on a winding path, a night breeze was rustling the leaves of the stunted oaks. In the distance an owl was calling. It was time for the hunt to begin so he lifted from his treetop with a silent, deadly power.

"Who is this man who knows my parents?" Starr asked.

"His name is Lazarus. Assad seemed to think he was exiled from the City years ago."

Around a sharp turn of the path they came to the cabin abruptly. It was built like those in the village, only smaller. The single front window was glowing with a dull yellow light. A thin stream of smoke drifted upward from the chimney.

The door opened inward and Lazarus appeared like something out of a dream. He had a long full beard and shoulder length hair. Both were white, the same color his robe had been years ago when it was new. He was nimbused by the lamplight from behind him and his expression was that of someone listening to ethereal music. Starr thought of sixteenth-century paintings she had seen of men who had been labeled by the church as "saints."

"Welcome to my home," he said with one hand on the door and the other outstretched toward them.

"Do you know him?" Starr asked quietly.

"Never laid eyes on him before."

They sat on leather-backed chairs before the fireplace. Lazarus lay propped up on pillows on his narrow bed against the wall. The only other furniture was a crudely made table and a wooden chest that sat in the opposite corner. The single room was warm and cleaner than Starr had expected.

In the light of the lantern that hung from the ceiling David could see the sallow color of Lazarus' face and the pale eyes that were clouded with pain. "How long before you go home?" David asked him.

Lazarus' eyes took on a far away look, a longing to break free of mortality. "God knows," he replied wearily.

Starr was puzzled. "This isn't your home?"

Lazarus looked at David, who made no response, then back to Starr. "I'm dying, child," he said in a kindly voice. "David means my eternal home."

Again Starr was mystified by the way these people regarded death—like it was no more than opening the front door of a house and going outside. "I'm sorry," she said awkwardly.

"Oh, don't be, child! I've grown weary of my role as stranger and pilgrim. I long to be with my own."

David noticed Starr shifting about uneasily in her chair and asked Lazarus about her parents. Starr relaxed as the conversation changed direction.

"I knew them in the City before we were all banished to the Fields," Lazarus responded, his eyes lost in memory. His face turned to Starr. "Your father was one of the first leaders of the Christian Movement. The City Fathers branded us 'Disciples of Treason.' They spent two years looking for your father. He and your mother were both sent to the Relievers, but at the last minute the City Fathers were afraid this would make martyrs of your parents, so they banished them instead."

"What are these 'Relievers?' " David asked.

Lazarus told him. "It's their ultimate method of control," he said, finishing his explanation. "Anyone considered a threat can be declared a dissident and executed."

"That's barbaric!" he exclaimed. "I thought they were more civilized than that."

Starr was visibly shaken.

"I'm sorry," David said to her. "I know you can't control what your government does."

Lazarus explained that he had not seen Starr's parents for many years. He believed they were still living in one of the villages in this remote part of the Fields. David and Starr visited with him for a while longer, saying they would make camp outside and leave early in the morning. Lazarus prayed for them to have a safe journey and that Starr would be able to locate her parents.

The fires in the village below were dying out one by one as Starr made beds of pine boughs and leaves. David had built a fire and was preparing their first hot meal since leaving Haven. After eating, David and Starr treated themselves to cups of coffee.

Starr was agonizing over David's reaction to the "Relievers." She had come to believe that it was an honorable profession and that she was making a contribution to her fellow citizens in the City. "Our worlds are so different," she said.

David sipped his coffee thoughtfully. "How else could it be, between slave and master?"

"Why do you talk like this?" Starr lamented.

"Because that's how it is. You think we chose to come out here?"

"But you and I haven't been like that. Like slave and master. I won't listen to this anymore," Starr said, resting her head in her hands. "I'm not like that. Let's talk about something else."

David lay back on his blanket, looking up at the night sky. Starr fought against the emotions that were tearing at her. How could she remain loyal to the City and feel so strongly attracted to this "Primitive" and his way of life. She looked at him lying next to her and the words were spoken as if by someone else. "David?"

His eyes were closed. "Hmm," he said, stretching his lean frame and turning his back to her.

"David, is there anyone—" she paused. "Anyone special in your life?"

"Dozens," he said without turning around.

"I'm serious, David."

He turned over, sat up and rested his arms on his bent knees. "What's this all about?" he asked.

"I'm—I'm interested in the customs of your people, relationships between men and women, courtship patterns. It's for the research I'm doing."

"You first," David said with a tomcat smile.

"We don't have courtship."

"What do you have?"

"If two people consent, they sign a 'Loving Friends Contract,' " Starr said with a trace of arrogance.

"What in the world is that?"

"They live together for a specified period of time, not to exceed six months. Under certain conditions, it can be extended if they both agree."

David was appalled and it showed on his face. "That's barba . . . That's very interesting," he replied calmly and lay back down.

"Well?" Starr asked indignantly.

"Well, what?" David teased her.

"What are your customs?"

David got up and walked to the brow of the hill. "Ah yes, our customs. I'm afraid they're painfully boring next to yours."

Starr walked over to him. The moon had risen, casting its pale light on the winding stream below. Starr thought it looked like a silver necklace shining at the base of the hill. "I'd like to hear about them," she said. "For my research."

David looked down at her upturned face in the moonlight. "If a man and woman have affection for one another, courtship can follow. The man begins by . . . ."

"Only the man can initiate it?" Starr interrupted.

"I'm afraid so. It's his choice." David paused thoughtfully. "At least we like to think it is."

"What's next?" Starr asked a little too eagerly.

"He asks the father's permission to see her. Then he'll bring her flowers or a gift. They go for walks, have picnics, go to family gatherings, sit in the parlor and talk—any number of things."

Starr was thinking of flowers—flowers and sitting in a parlor with David.

"Starr, are you listening to me?"

"Yes, yes, go ahead."

"Well, if things work, courtship can lead to marriage and a family."

"How long are these marriage contracts for?"

"Life."

Surprisingly this didn't shock Starr, although she knew logically it should have. She had the warmest feeling in her breast—warm and yet somehow cold, for she was beginning to tremble.

"Are you all right?" David asked, taking both her shoulders in his hands.

Starr felt weak. She moved close to David and pressed against him, holding his waist. His arms went around her with a gentle strength. Starr was frightened at the feelings welling up inside her. She tilted her head back and traced the scar on his face with her finger. She felt his hands caressing her back, her neck and touching her face. She was on tiptoe now and his lips were touching hers with a warmth that moved like a current slowly through her body and returned to the place where they were joined as one person, one breath, one life.

"No!" something seemed to scream deep inside Starr. This can't be. Not with this—Primitive. "I shouldn't have done that. Forgive me," she said and turned away.

"Of course."

That moment would return to them again and again for the rest of their lives. The time they stood together on the hilltop in that wild land with the moonlight streaming through the trees and their lives were indelibly changed.

Chapter Twelve

A NEW LIFE

At dawn a rain began to fall, causing Starr to awaken with a start. The sudden miniature thunder of the fat drops on the roof pulled her out of a sound sleep, and for one instant panic claimed her. Wildly she looked across the room half expecting to find Miriam awake, but the dark-haired girl was sleeping peacefully. Then she sat up, staring at the rain falling in thin silvery lines. The drops that struck the window ran crazily down, some meeting others in an abrupt joining.

Starr lay back, listening to the drumming on the roof close to her head. It was the first time she'd lain and listened to the rain, and as was true with so many experiences she'd had since coming to the Fields, she was filled with a faint sense of regret. The opaque Dome that enclosed the City had served to protect the population from the deadly air and water produced by the Greenhouse Effect years ago—but now it screened the things she had found most beautiful. Open skies, running brooks, the rumpled soil, and the activity of bird and beast had become a delight to her. Now the sight of the rain falling aslant and the patter of drops on the roof brought pleasure to her. *I'll miss it all!* she thought, then suddenly felt that she was betraying her way of life.

Closing her eyes, Starr settled herself under the blanket. Soon the sound of the rain brought sleep again. When she awoke,

Miriam was gone. Starr could hear the faint sounds from below—the women speaking quietly, the noise of dishes and pans floating up the stairs. Throwing back the cover she arose, washed her face and dressed. Then she took the VoiceWriter from her case, but hesitated slightly before she began her report. After she'd gathered her thoughts she pressed the switch and began.

"Starr Omega. Report Number 26 to Remedial History Section. Attention Emmett Tau. Subject—Mystic and Romantic Tendencies of Primitives. This report will give instances of actual behavior patterns resulting from those mystical and romantic strains delineated in Report Number 23. Basically, this element (which seems to be inherent in some of the subjects) is most clearly seen in two areas—religion and courtship. The religious activities will be dealt with in Report Number 27, while this report will document the 'romantic' element that makes up the character of the primitive psyche."

Starr pushed the *Pause* button, then walked over to the window. For a few moments she stood there watching the rain as she organized her thoughts. Then she activated the VoiceWriter and said in a flat voice, "The mystical strain that evidences itself in courtship patterns is not easy to isolate, though the results are evident. The primitives believe in something which they call 'falling in love.' This phenomena is almost unknown in the modern world, but its roots go back to ancient times. Basically 'falling in love' is antithetical to the reasonable and logical processes which exist among the civilized today. On the surface the phenomena can be observed when a male and a female begin to turn from others and find pleasure in each other's company. In the City this occurs, of course, but enlightened people base this on personal need, and are not bound by any commitment other than a Loving Friends agreement. Basically, in the City the individual entering into this sort of contract is saying, 'I need you and will do whatever I have to do to

get you.' Hard as it is to believe (and even more difficult to understand!) the Primitives who have 'fallen in love' are saying, 'I want
you to have something.' Obviously, this cannot be true, for all modern scientific study by our sociologists indicate that human behavior is totally self-centered, and much of our educational processes
are devoted to teaching individuals to get *what they want and need*
from others, no matter what must be done to the other individual."

Here Starr paused momentarily, thinking of a couple she had
met on a field trip. David had taken her to a small cottage seven or
eight miles from the village, saying just before they got off their
horses, "I think you'll find this couple interesting." Luke, the husband, was tall, strong and about twenty years old. He had married
a girl, a year his junior, named Dorene. Starr had heard that Dorene
was one of the most beautiful girls in the village and sought after
by many young men. But she had chosen Luke, and they had married. Only six months after their wedding, their small house caught
fire, and though Luke had escaped with only minor burns, Dorene
had been terribly scarred. David had taken Starr to their home, and
the sight of Dorene's twisted, ravaged face and claw-like hands had
repelled her. Starr saw that she was expecting a child very soon,
and had kept the revulsion from her expression by an effort. She
had been shocked when the ruddy handsome Luke had put his arm
around his wife's waist and kissed her scarred cheek. When they
had left the cottage, Starr asked, "How can he bear it, David? She's
hideous!" He had given her a strange look, then said, "Love is not
love which alters when it alteration finds." He said no more than
that, but Starr guessed his meaning. "You mean," she had asked
with a puzzled frown, "that love doesn't change when something
bad happens to the other person?" He nodded, but the whole affair
haunted Starr. She considered putting the story into her report, but
was certain that her superiors would never believe it.

For half an hour Starr spoke clearly and concisely, letting no emotion register in her voice. A memory flashed through her mind as she told how a young man with a bouquet of flowers had come to call on Miriam. She recalled how she had run across such things before in her research, and was aware that something in the simple action appealed to her. Quickly she said, "It is my theory at this point that such behavior has its roots in a certain body of primitive literature which has somehow survived in the Fields. This literature consists of poetry, especially that of a medieval poet called Shakespeare, and stories called 'Novels' most of which date back to the last period of OldAge. Such material has long been eradicated from the City—except for those copies which are peddled by pornographers—but they do exist in the Fields.

"One of the most popular of these I located in the small collection of the family I am staying with. There was no cover, so the title and the author are lost. The story concerns a man with the strange name of *Rhett* and a young woman with the equally bizarre name of *Scarlett*. The action takes place in the distant pre-industrial past of OldWorld, and is almost completely devoid of logic. What it does contain is the strange—magnetism or attraction that Scarlett possesses. Young males are drawn to her like moths to a candle flame; they apparently possess no more sense! She treats all her *suitors,* as they are called, like dirt; which doesn't seem to bother them at all. They keep coming back to her, unable to resist the powerful force that she exudes. The character called Rhett is different from the other males—and in some ways is just as attractive to females as is Scarlett to males. It is a long book, concerned with some civil struggle, but basically deals with the phenomenon that centers on the relationship of Rhett and Scarlett. She is obviously a very silly young girl, and the book never explains how a man as powerful and handsome as Rhett is willing to put up with her—this is where *falling in love* finds its expression. Logically, they should not become involved. But they cannot seem to help themselves."

Starr paused again, then continued: "From my study of these 'romantic' works, it seems to me that 'falling in love' is somewhat like a virus. The subject in this condition, when in the presence of his or her lover, is described as being short of breath, flushed in the face, stricken by a heart that beats abnormally fast and hands and limbs that tremble unaccountably. The classic symptoms of a virus! However, those who 'fall in love' react as though this experience is the epitome of human existence, for when they are separated from their lover, they go into a psychological and emotional pit of despair. This despair is quite illogical, for there is no shortage of available mates. Why these primitive people, on losing a partner, cannot simply move on to another is a subject that defies the logical mind. End of report. Starr Omega."

She pushed the button abruptly when she heard Miriam's voice calling her down to breakfast. Stowing the VoiceWriter back into her case, Starr left the room to take her place at the table beside Timmy. "Hello, Starr," he said with a bright smile. "I wish my hair was curly like yours."

Starr laughed and ran her hand through his straight black hair. "Maybe I'll give you a permanent, Timmy," she said.

"A permanent what?" he asked in surprise.

"Oh, that's something that makes your hair curly."

"Do *you* have one?" he demanded.

"Oh, no. Mine just grows this way. But I think we'd better not make your hair curly. I think it looks nice the way it is."

"All right," he answered agreeably. Then he picked up a biscuit and bit off a mouthful. "Will you read to me some more today?"

"I will if David and I get back in time. He's going to take me to see some people."

"Can I go, too?"

David had been sitting back watching the two. "Not this time, Timmy, but tomorrow after the service, Starr will take you down to the pond if it isn't raining."

"Oh, that'll be good!" He launched out on a rambling tale of how he and David had caught a turtle in the pond; and the grown-ups made no attempt to interrupt. Once again Starr was struck by the obvious love the other members of the family had for Timmy. She wondered, but not for the first time, if they realized that he would not be with them for long. *They must know. Surely there have been other Down's Syndrome children born here.* But she said nothing, and after breakfast David said, "Let's get on our way, Starr."

"Don't be late, David," his mother said. "You don't want to tire Starr out."

"Oh, David is quite entertaining on the buggy rides we take," Starr said innocently, but with a gleam in her grey eyes. "He always—"

"Time to go!" David broke in hurriedly, and taking Starr's arm he almost pulled her out of the room. "We have lots of chores to do."

When they were in the wagon, she asked impishly, "I didn't have a chance to tell your mother about how you behave on buggy rides."

"Never mind that!" he said hastily. "I told you, Mother is pretty old fashioned. Why, she's told me lots of times that she never kissed any man but my father—and him only *after* they were married!"

"Oh? I wonder why you fell into such bad habits?" Starr teased him lightly as they drove along the muddy road, enjoying the sheepish look on his face. Finally she asked, "Where are we going today?"

"As I told you, we have quite a few members of the Ecclesia who need visiting. Some of them are widows, some are elderly or sick. The men of the Ecclesia visit them pretty often. See that they have firewood, fix anything that's broken—things like that."

Starr remained silent for a time, then said softly, "I think that's nice."

"Nice? Well, I guess so. Never thought of it that way."

It was a fine day, the sun coming out to warm the earth, sending its beams over the pools standing in the fields. The road was muddy, and the hooves of the horses splattered the red mud over the buggy, including some that came to adorn Starr's face. David observed that she looked better with it, and then let her have his big handkerchief to wipe it off.

They spent all morning visiting, most of the stops were at the homes of elderly people. Everyone greeted David with warmth, and all were curious about Starr. With the frank curiosity of old age several of them asked, "Is this your sweetheart, David?" At first Starr was nonplussed and felt her cheeks redden, but David laughed at her. "No, this is my old aunt here on a visit," he would say. Once he said, "No, she's looking for a husband, but she told me right out that I wasn't handsome enough for her." The shrunken old lady he said this to had stared at Starr with displeasure, saying pertly, "Well, you're just too choosy, Missy! This boy is fine looking enough for you or anybody else."

"See?" David had said as they were back in the wagon. "You're too choosy. I'm fine looking enough for any young woman."

"Too bad *you* think so!" Starr retorted, but glancing at him, she thought, *Well, he is good looking! And he doesn't know it, not really.*

A little after noon they stopped and David pulled a basket out of the back of the buggy. "Nice place for lunch over there," he said. Hopping down he reached up his hand. At first Starr thought he wanted her to hand him something—then realized that he was waiting to help her down. No one did such things as that in the City. Women were proud of their independence and would have taken such a gesture as an insult. But as she put her hand in his she discovered that the act made her feel—womanly was the only word for it. "Thank you, Rhett," she smiled up at him.

"Who?"

"Oh, just a name," she said quickly. "Let's eat over there." She ran to a large tree that had fallen, and soon the two were sitting on it eating their lunch. As always, she tore into the food as if she were starving. David grinned at her as she chewed and swallowed the thick beef sandwiches, popping hard-boiled eggs into her mouth like peanuts. "Want mine, too?"

"Oh, this is so good!" she exclaimed, ignoring his teasing. "What's in the little wrappers?"

"Fried pies."

Starr opened one of the packages and her mouth watered as a delicious smell came to her. "I thought you *baked* pies."

"Sometimes you do," he answered. "Sometimes you fry them in grease." Watching her taste the pie, then begin to eat it with huge enjoyment, David said, "I better eat mine or you'll take it away from me." He watched her eat two of the pies, then added, "I don't see how you stay so trim. As much as you eat you should be as fat as old Jezebel." Jezebel was the huge sow that came grunting to the fence for handouts. David gave her a close inspection, then shook his head. "No. You've got a much better figure than Jezebel. At least, that's what Jonah Logan told me."

"He didn't say that!"

Jonah Logan was a young friend of David's who had come to the house several times lately to visit. He was shy, but Starr knew that he liked her. "Not exactly. He said you were very pretty and asked if he could come calling on you." David carefully ate the last of his fried pie, then dusted his hands regretfully. "I told him he couldn't."

Starr's head jerked around to face him. "You told him *what?*"

Ignoring her indignant outburst, he said calmly, "I told him you went around kissing men in buggies. He's a fine lad, and I don't want him to pick up your City ways."

Starr's jaw dropped, and she began sputtering. "Why, you—!"

David shook his head. "Jonah's going to marry Beulah Wright. She's been in love with him since they were ten years old."

"Well, is he in love with *her?*"

"Not yet, but he will be."

"Oh? He will be? And how do you know that, may I ask?"

David began stuffing the remains of the lunch into the basket. When he was finished, he looked at her and said evenly, "God gave me assurance that he would. Come on, we've got a lot of visits to make."

His reply silenced Starr for some time. Only after they had made three more visits, and he announced that they had only one more stop, did she bring up the subject. "You say *God* told you that Jonah and Beulah would get married? What did He sound like— God I mean?"

David said easily, "Starr, God doesn't speak to us with a voice. He's a spirit. He can use any method He wants, but with me it's like an *inner* voice. And usually when God speaks to me, it's something I've been thinking and praying about. For example, I'd been worried about Jonah and Beulah. He's a little flighty, you know. Apt to be impressed by flashy women." She glared at him, but he ignored her. "So I began praying for them, and after a time I began to get this assurance. Can't really explain it, but I'd been in doubt—and then for no reason, I just began to *know* that Jonah would wake up to what a fine girl Beulah is."

"Maybe you just *thought* that yourself, David."

"I doubt it. Nothing to make me think it. Jonah hasn't changed. He's still running around after young women. Still doesn't give Beulah a thought. No reason why I *should* know he going to marry her. But he is."

Starr asked after a long silence, "Did you ever feel that God had spoken to you—and find out you were wrong?"

"Sure."

His ready assent caught her off guard. "Didn't that—make you *doubt?*"

"A little, I guess. But the longer I serve Jesus, the better I know what He wants." He seemed to be struggling with words, and suddenly turned to her, his dark eyes intent. "Starr, the longer you're close to somebody, the better you know them. Isn't that so?"

Starr could only stare at him. Finally she whispered, "David, I don't know. I—I've never had anyone that I could really come close to."

David was shocked by her reply. He kept his eyes fixed on her, then shook his head. "That's not right," he said gently. "You've got to let people get close to you. We all have our little boundaries, Starr. Walls we build because we're afraid that if people get close they'll hurt us."

"Well, won't they?" she asked sharply.

"Some will, sure. But I'd rather get hurt than be a hermit and live alone."

His answer struck her hard, and he saw her lips tighten. "God never meant for us to be alone, Starr," he said gently. "He sets the solitary in families."

Starr had no answer for that, but changed the subject. After they had driven for two hours she asked, pointing across a pasture, "Isn't that where the girl who was burned lives?"

"Luke and Dorene," he said. "There's Luke—" He broke off abruptly; for the man had started running toward them. "Something's wrong," he said, and slapped the reins on the horses. Coming even with the man, he jerked the horses to an abrupt stop. "What's wrong, Luke?"

"It's the baby, David!" Luke cried. "It's coming early."

"I'll go for my mother!"

"No time!" Luke said, grasping David's arm. "She's afraid, David—and I guess I am, too!"

David leaped out of the wagon. "It's God's baby, Luke. I've heard Dorene say that many times. Well, God will help bring the child into the world. Better get back to her." Luke wheeled and ran to the house, and David said, "Come on, Starr!"

Looking down at the hand which David held to her, Starr was filled with apprehension. "I—I'll wait in the buggy."

But David reached up and lifted her out of the buggy as if she weighed no more than Sarah's kitten, Bobo. "Time to break down one of your little walls!" he said roughly.

"But, I don't know anything about birth!" she practically squalled, and even as he pulled her across the yard, a line from the book about Scarlett and Rhett almost spoke itself in her mind:

Miss Scarlett! I don't know nothing about birthin' no babies!

Suddenly he whirled and grasped her by the shoulders. His eyes burned into hers, and his voice grated, "You're a woman, aren't you? Or maybe not. I've been wondering a lot about you, Starr. Now I guess I'm going to find out. Are you just a machine taking notes and spitting them out? Or are you a real live woman?"

"That's not fair!"

"It never is! What do you want to do? Get in the buggy and ride off? Leave them alone?"

Starr tried to break free, but his grip was like steel. She pleaded then, "David, I can't help! We need a doctor!"

"Dorene needs love and someone to hold her. Someone to tell her she'll be all right. You can do that." Then seeing her expression, he suddenly loosed her. She almost fell, but he said, "No, I guess you can't. You don't know what love is. And you never will!"

His words cut into her, and anger welled up at once. Who was he to tell her she didn't know love! She whirled and ran away from the house. A small grove of trees bordered the cabin, and she moved toward it her pulse throbbing. But the silence of the tall trees did not stop the voice that kept ringing in her ears: *You don't know what love is. And you never will!*

She had entered the grove at a fast clip, anger raging through her; but it slowly ebbed, leaving her with a barren emptiness. The shadows of the towering trees made a gloomy sanctuary and the silence of the grove was broken only by a mournful cry of a bird, faint and far away. Finally she slowed her pace, then came a strange sense of loss. It was bitterness, she recognized at once, and then she understood that David's words had touched a raw spot that had been in her all the time; dormant and hidden even from her own consciousness. The sense of poignancy that came to her was like the plaintive cry of a violin she had once heard, a sound that had brought tears to her eyes, though she never understood why. She knew that David had spoken the truth.

"I *don't* know what love is!"

She started, for she had spoken aloud, and the sound of her voice in the silent glade sounded loud. Despair came to her and as she looked up, her eyes filled with burning tears, she cried out, "How could I know love?"

No answer came, and Starr stood there as the echoes of her voice faded. She remained motionless for so long that a small furry animal she'd never seen before came out of the underbrush, sniffing eagerly and grabbing green shoots. He came right up to her feet and almost touched her—then his entire body seemed to become electrified! He threw himself backward in a paroxysm of fear and tore across the vine-covered earth, scrambling with a desperate intensity to escape the Other Thing that had invaded his world.

The fear of the animal touched Starr and she whispered, "You're afraid, too, aren't you?" Then she lifted her head and the muscles of her jaw grew tense. Slowly she nodded, then turned and made her way back to the clearing. Without a pause Starr walked up to the cabin. The sound of a woman's voice crying in pain came to her. Starr hesitated for only a moment—then pushed the door open and entered.

Both men were standing beside the bed, and they both turned to stare at her. The woman's eyes were closed and her scarred lips were sealed as she pressed them together. Slowly she opened her eyes and looked at the newcomer. Fear was there, but more than that, a plea for help for someone to share the pain.

Starr moved across the floor, then dropped to her knees beside the bed. Taking the frightened girl's hand, she reached out with her other and pushed a strand of hair back from the pale forehead.

"You mustn't be afraid, Dorene," she said quietly. "You'll be all right—and so will your baby!

She spoke with a firm assurance that she didn't feel. But Dorene's hand clamped down on her own, and hope appeared in the pain-filled eyes. "I can't help it!" she whispered.

"We'll help you," Starr said gently, and even as she knelt there assuring the woman, her mind was busily reconstructing the pages of a book she had once read. A book that dealt with primitive medical techniques. And Chapter Seven had been entitled, "Childbirth."

Starr looked up and said, "Get some water boiling—and all the clean towels and cloths you can find—!"

✦   ✦   ✦

By the time David pulled the horses to a stop, the sun was breaking over the trees to the east. He silently admired the line of crimson light that traced the contours of the eastern hills, then turned to look down at Starr.

She was lying in the crook of his arm, her face pressed against his chest. "Starr——we're home," he said. Her long eyelashes fluttered, and then her eyes opened.

"It's morning!" she exclaimed. Then she realized that she was lying in the curve of his arm and quickly pulled away. Her limbs were stiff, and she stretched to relieve them. The memory of what had happened came rushing back to her. He watched her mobile lips move slightly into a smile, "It was like nothing I've ever seen, David," she murmured, her eyes bright with the memory.

"You did fine, Starr."

"Oh, I didn't do much," she added quickly. "I didn't want Dorene to know it, but I was more frightened than she was!"

"You sure didn't show it," he remarked. "A beautiful little girl."

Starr thought of the moment when she had cleaned the baby, noting with wonder the perfect fingernails, the completeness of the small body. She had never seen such a thing, and it had given her a sudden sense of despair to recognize that she had "relieved" many mothers of babies not much younger than the one she held in her arms.

And when she had placed the child in Dorene's arms, the sight of the smile on the ruined face took away all the ugliness of the scars. The miracle of birth had shaken her thinking about the meaning of life. She knew as she sat there with David, that no matter what else, she would never again be able to abort a child so long as she lived.

"Guess this is where I apologize." She looked up with a startled expression, finding him watching her with a serious look. "About what I said—that you never knew what love was," he explained. "I was wrong about that."

Starr could not speak for a moment, then she said slowly, "No, you were right, David. I don't know what love is."

"It's what brought you into the cabin to help Dorene when everything in you fought against it," he answered. "You didn't do it for money or recognition. You came to help Dorene in any way you could. And to tell the truth, if you think *you* were scared, you should know what Luke and I were feeling! We were absolutely paralyzed! Starr, if you hadn't been there I hate to think what would have happened!"

She merely shook her head. But as he helped her down from the buggy he asked, "Do you know what Dorene told Luke she wanted the baby named?"

"No. What was it?"

He held her for a moment as she came to ground. Then as she looked up at him, waiting for his answer, his broad lips curved in a pleased smile. "She named the baby *Starr*—which I thought was appropriate." Then he said gently, "Another little Starr for this world. Makes me feel very good. Come on, let's tell the family about it."

She smiled briefly, but her mind was filled with the image of the tiny baby resting on the bosom of the young woman with the scarred face—and of Luke, the strong, handsome one, looking at both of them with love and pride in his eyes.

Chapter Thirteen

AN UNWELCOME MESSAGE

Exhausted physically and emotionally after the crisis with the birth of Dorene's baby, Starr wanted desperately to fall into bed and rest. But this proved to be impossible, for she and David arrived just as the household was beginning to stir. Miriam and her mother were finishing the cooking, and soon the room was humming with the sound of talk around the breakfast table. David and Starr were kept busy answering questions about the new baby and the parents. The young couple were good friends of Caleb and his family.

David minimized his own efforts by saying, "It's a good thing Starr was there! Luke and I were useless, but Starr knew just what to do."

Starr was uncomfortable with the admiration she saw on the faces around the table. "Oh, Dorene is the one who did all the hard things," she said quickly. Starr had finished her eggs and bacon, but when she said, "I think I'll rest for awhile," Timmy protested.

"You said you'd go to the Meeting with me today! Aw, you can sleep anytime."

Starr started to shake off his pleas, but there was such disappointment on his face that she hadn't the heart. "I guess I can sleep later," she surrendered, and went at once to shower and change clothes. Miriam came in just as she was getting dressed, and taking a look at her said, "We usually wear dresses to the Meeting, Starr. I know you don't have one, but you can wear this one if you like. We're about the same size."

Starr took the dress at once, not wanting to violate any local code. Slipping into it, she took a quick look in the mirror and was pleased at what she saw. The dress was a simple gown, light blue with a finely wrought collar of white lace. It clung to her figure, and she said, "What a nice dress, Miriam!"

"Oh, it's just one I made myself. It looks nice on you, Starr." She herself was wearing a light brown frock with a full skirt that swept her ankles. As she brushed her hair, she spoke about the new baby, and it seemed to Starr that she was somewhat envious. "I can't wait until I get married and have children, can you, Starr?" She ran the brush down her thick mane of glossy black hair, not noticing that Starr did not respond. "I'm going to be late starting my family. Most of my girl friends are already married." Putting down the brush and getting to her feet Miriam smiled ruefully, "I'll be married this year, though."

"Will it be Saul?" Starr asked.

"Oh, no!" The answer came quickly, and Miriam shook her head emphatically. "I'm not in love with him. Besides, he doesn't want a wife—he wants a mother for his two girls. And there are lots of women around who'd welcome the chance to marry him. Several widows would jump at the chance."

"Who will it be, Miriam?"

Miriam smiled at Starr, then said with a slight smile, "I'll marry Nathan."

"Has he asked you?"

"Not yet, but he will when I give him the sign."

Starr looked up with interest. "The sign? What's that?"

"Oh, you know, Starr!"

"No, I really don't."

Miriam gave Starr a strange look then said, "It's not any one thing. But when a girl wants to let a man know she approves of him, there are ways she can do it."

"Why not just say it?" Starr asked seriously.

"Oh, no! You have to be more subtle than that," Miriam protested. "You have to become very attentive to him. Smile at him more, and once in awhile when he helps you down from the buggy, you hold his hand a *little* longer than necessary. . . ."

Starr listened with astonishment as Miriam described the patterns of courtship, and finally when the girl was finished, Starr shook her head, getting to her feet with a short laugh. "It's very complicated, isn't it?"

Miriam suddenly bit her lip. "No, not really. I'm making it sound like it. But when a woman loves a man he'll be able to see it. How could he not?" Then she shook her head and laughed, "Well, the lessons on how to deal with men will have to continue when we get back. Come on, Starr. Mother hates to be late for the Meeting!"

❖　　　❖　　　❖

David pulled the buggy to a stop beside a long hitching rail. "That's where we have our Meetings," he said, nodding toward a single-story structure made of peeled logs. "We're a little late this morning."

He helped Starr down, then reached up and swung Timmy to the ground. "I want to hear you sing nice and loud this morning," he said putting his hand on the boy's shoulder. Then David led the way to the front of the rectangular building, followed closely by the rest of the family who had come in the wagon.

As Starr entered the building she looked around curiously. She saw a single room broken on both sides by three windows that admitted bright rays of light. The long seats were made of planed lumber, and most of them were already filled with people. "There are three seats down front," David whispered. Starr followed him reluctantly, for she would have preferred a less conspicuous place at the back of the room. She noticed the looks she received as they walked to the front and sat down. She tried to ignore them.

As soon as they were seated, Timmy whispered, "It's about time for the singing, Starr. That's my favorite part of the Meeting."

Even as he spoke, one of the men got up and stepped up on a low platform at the front. He said nothing, but lifted his voice and began singing in a clear tenor voice. At once he was joined by the entire congregation and the sound filled the room. Starr did not know the song and wondered if the group met to practice. Finally, she determined that they learned the songs by repetition. She sat there listening carefully to the words, looking down once in awhile at Timmy, whose face was rapt as he sang in a piping voice. The words were:

> *Make a joyful noise unto the Lord, all ye lands.*
> *Serve the Lord with gladness:*
> *Come before his presence with singing.*
> *Know ye that the Lord he is God:*
> *It is He that hath made us, and not we ourselves.*
> *We are his people, and the sheep of his pasture.*
> *Enter into his gates with thanksgiving and into his courts*
> *   with praise:*
> *Be thankful unto him, and bless his name.*
> *For the Lord is good; his mercy is everlasting;*
> *And his truth endureth to all generations.*

The song was sung several times, and soon Starr found that she could sing along with the others. She had a quick ear and a fine contralto voice. Timmy looked up at her, his eyes warm, whispering, "You sing *good,* Starr!"

The song service continued for an hour. There were no solos, which seemed strange to Starr, and the musical accompaniment consisted solely of a man and a woman who were on one side of the room playing guitars.

Perhaps it was the very *simplicity* of the music that touched Starr; she was accustomed in the City to highly complex and complicated forms of music. Here the music seemed an extension of the people who stood and lifted their songs with faces radiant and eyes filled with obvious joy. Most of them were poor people, wearing colorful but plain clothing. Starr had seen how hard they worked and how little they possessed. Why were they so joyful? A joy that filled the room in the form of song.

Her professors had taught her that religious emotion was simply a psychological response. *Learn how to push the right button in people's psyche* they had said, *and they'll respond. Just like Pavlov's dogs who drooled when a bell was rung.*

But something in Starr denied this, since there was no stimulus to cause these people to behave as they did. Some of them raised their hands in a simple gesture of longing, some clapped their hands when the song was fast, and many of them had faces stained with tears—tears of happiness rather than of sorrow.

As the service continued, Starr struggled to understand it—until something happened that was past *understanding.* The leader started a new song, the words simpler than the ones he had already sung:

> Jesus! Jesus! Jesus!
> How I praise the name of Jesus!
> Fairer than the Morning Star,
> He's everything to me!
> Jesus! Jesus! Jesus!
> He fills my deepest need,
> Only Jesus!

For no reason that she could comprehend, as the song went on, the word *Jesus* began to have a strange and disturbing effect on

Starr. The first indication she had was when her voice began to falter as she sang the song. Then, deep within her a poignant sorrow began to make itself known, and she could say that name no longer. All her life she had trained herself to keep any deeper emotions under careful control, and even as the sadness and voiceless grief grew stronger, she set her lips and kept her face stiffly fixed.

But she could not control one thing—the tears that rose unbidden to her eyes. Almost angrily she willed them away, but the singing continued softly, and every time the name Jesus sounded, it was like a small dagger into her heart. Fiercely she bit her lips to keep them from trembling, but the tears would not be controlled. To her horror she felt the hot drops running down her cheeks, and quickly she dashed them away, hoping no one had noticed.

But her hope was unfounded, for David had caught the motion, and without a word he took a handkerchief from his pocket and handed it to her. She took it and removed the tears, then tried to think of something else—anything to keep from breaking down in public!

Finally the song dwindled and fell away, and without a sign from anyone that she noticed, the people all sat down. Gratefully she sank into her seat, took a deep breath and determined that the emotion that had swept her would never be mentioned in an official report. She could imagine what a cold fish like Bernard Alpha would make of such a thing in one of his researchers!

She was fairly well under control when a man got up and faced the congregation. He was not impressive, being only slightly above medium height and having a plain round face. But there was something in his light blue eyes that caught her, a hint of some sort of inner fire that she had seen a few times—mostly in poets and artists.

But his voice! She had never heard such a voice in her life! It was not loud, but she knew that if he had chosen to lift it above the almost conversational level he used, it would have filled the small building like an enormous bell!

And yet—it was not the sort of voice used by professional politicians which overpower the hearer. No, it was really an intimate voice, warm and informal. The sort of voice one would stop reading to listen to. Without meaning to, Starr found herself listening to the man, and soon she was drawn into what he was actually saying. He began by saying, "The portion of the Book that I will read from this morning may seem strange to you, but it has been a comfort to believers for centuries . . . ." Then he explained that what he would read was part of a vision that God had given to a man named John after the death and resurrection of Jesus. He began reading from a book, and though the language was almost mystical, she found herself caught up in the imagery of it:

> *And I saw in the right hand of him that sat on the throne a book written within and on the backside, sealed with seven seals.*
>
> *And I saw a strong angel proclaiming with a loud voice, Who is worthy to open the book, and to loose the seals thereof?*
>
> *And no man in heaven, nor in earth, neither under the earth, was able to open the book, neither to look thereon.*
>
> *And I wept much, because no man was found worthy to open and to read the book, neither to look thereon.*

He paused, then looking out with compassion in his direct blue eyes, said, "He wept. Why? Because he wanted someone to help him—but he knew that no human being was able to help. That is the problem of all of us, even of kings and emperors. We long for something beyond what we have, but search as we may, we never find it. We search the philosophers and the thinkers of the past, and find that they did not have the answer, not even for themselves.

Many try to avoid the question, throwing themselves into pleasure, but they still weep inwardly. . . ."

As he continued to speak Starr had the frightening sensation that he was speaking directly to her! His eyes fell on her from time to time, and it took all her will to keep her gaze steady. *He knows!* she thought desperately. *He knows all about me!* The horrifying fear came that he would point his finger at her and lay bare all that she had managed to keep hidden from the eyes of others.

But he did no such thing. After he had spoken of the search that men and women made to find peace—which always failed— he said in a stronger voice, "But there is one who can open the book! Every book, even the book of your life which you've kept hidden from everyone! For the rest of the passage says:

> *And one of the elders saith unto me, Weep not: behold, the Lion of the tribe of Juda, the Root of David hath prevailed to open the book, and to loose the seven seals thereof.*
>
> *And I beheld, and, lo, in the midst of the throne, and of the four beasts, and in the midst of the elders, stood a Lamb as it had been slain, having seven horns and seven eyes, which are the seven spirits of God sent forth into all the earth.*
>
> *And he came and took the book out of the right hand of him that sat upon the throne.*
>
> *And when he had taken the book, the four beasts and the four and twenty elders fell down before the lamb, having every one of them harps, and golden vials full of odours, which are the prayers of the saints.*
>
> *And they sang a new song, saying, Thou art worthy to take the book, and to open the seals thereof: for thou wast slain, and hast been redeemed up to God by thy blood out of every kindred, and tongue, and people, and nation;*
>
> *And hast made us unto our God kings and priests: and we shall reign on the earth.*

Then the preacher lifted his hand toward heaven and raising his voice like a trumpet, he shouted, "Who was this one who alone could open the book? Jesus! Jesus Christ, the son of God!"

The congregation began to cry out, "Jesus!" and what Starr had felt before was nothing to the sudden surge of emotion that erupted in her! It was fear and joy and hope all at the same time, and she sat there, trembling in every nerve, knowing that she could no more stand to her feet than she could fly out of the window!

The preacher began to speak, and she heard him as if she were a long distance away. What she did hear was the name of Jesus, many times, and each time that name was spoken it was as if a sword pierced her heart. She did not understand the words that had been read, and only faintly did she grasp that the preacher was saying that this person, Jesus Christ, was God, and that somehow He wanted something from every man and woman.

She felt Timmy's hand touch hers, and grasped it blindly, not daring to look at him. She felt his other hand come to rest on hers, and somehow that gave her a great comfort.

Finally the voice ceased to speak, and she was able to stand to her feet with the others. Dimly she heard someone speaking a prayer of some kind. Then David was leading her outside. She was aware that a few people spoke to her, but she could never remember what she answered. She was able to come up with a smile and some sort of response, but it was a relief when she was alone with Timmy and David as they drove slowly back down the road toward the house.

Timmy chattered happily as the horses plodded along through the muddy track. David spoke from time to time, but Starr heard little of it. She was still shaken by the storm that had swept over her, leaving her drained and weak.

Finally they came into view of the house, and she looked up when David said, "I think you've got company, Starr."

Looking up quickly she saw a tall man lounging under a tree, his great stallion tied to a branch. When they got closer she said in surprise, "I know him. He's one of the Border Guards."

"Will Sigma," David nodded. "One of the better ones."

The guard waited until they all got out of the buggy, then pulled a piece of paper out of his tunic pocket. "Message from the City," he said without expression. His shaggy blond hair and eyes the color of flint made him look tough, but he stepped back after delivering the note.

Starr's hands trembled slightly as she fumbled with the envelope. A sense of foreboding seized her, and she saw that the note consisted of one line and a signature. When she read it, a sense of fear came over her, for it said what she had most dreaded to hear:

You will leave at once with the bearer of this message and report to me. Sheila Phi.

Chapter Fourteen

TO SEE JESUS

Looking out the window of Miriam's room, Starr was packing her saddlebags which were laid across the bed. She thought of the peaceful nights of drug-free sleep and of rising to a bright morning refreshed and eager for the day to begin. The times around the breakfast table with the family as they shared the delicious home-cooked meals before going their separate ways for the day, the lowing of the cattle coming across the evening meadows, and the sound of music and laughter in this home were things she could not bear to think of losing.

Below, Martha was preparing coffee and Starr could hear the conversation of David and Will Sigma as they sat around the table. It still surprised Starr that this family could treat even a Border Guard the same as they would an old friend who had come for a visit. As she finished packing and descended the narrow stairs, Timmy came running to her.

"Starr! Starr!" he said breathlessly. "You told me you'd take me to the pond if it wasn't raining. Remember?"

"I remember, Timmy," Starr said, rumpling his hair. "But something's come up and I have to go back to the City now." Starr looked at Will who was shifting uneasily in his chair.

Martha brought the coffee service to the table and began pouring the rich, steaming liquid into their cups. "I'm sure Mr.

Sigma has time to eat a piece of my blackberry cobbler," she said, looking at Will. "It'll be ready in a few minutes."

"I can't think of anything short of a firing squad that could keep me from it," Will said, smiling broadly. He looked at Timmy standing with his arm around Starr's waist, then nodded to Starr."

"Thank you, Will," Starr said as she left the room with Timmy holding tightly to her hand. "We won't be long."

The afternoon sun was pouring into the valley, filling it with pale gold light as Starr and Timmy walked hand in hand across the pasture toward the pond. Spindly-legged calves were frolicking and wobbling among the scattered trees, never straying far from their mothers. From the south came the distant dry rumble of thunderheads forming and Starr knew they would bring rain by evening. She had come to love the rain, to love its whisperings among the leaves of the trees and its cool breath through her window.

She remembered the first time she had seen the painting that hung in her apartment and believed that a world like this could never exist. She had found that world and now she was losing it. Timmy's hand was warm in hers, but what she felt was a stone cold aching in her breast. The land around her was green and growing and full of life—she saw only the stark barren towers of the City. *Oh, God, I can't go back there! To that dead place! I can't leave all this!*

"What's wrong, Starr?"

Timmy was pulling on her hand and Starr knew he had sensed her distress. "Nothing, Timmy. What could be wrong when I've got a friend like you?"

Timmy beamed up at her. "Watch what I can do," he said excitedly, collecting a few small stones from around the water's edge. Starr sat on a rough wooden bench under an ancient gum tree and watched while he tossed them into the pond. Near the far shore trout were feeding under overhanging willow branches, dimpling the surface of the water.

In her mind Starr was back in the City. She saw Philemon—Martha Epsilon as her head turned slowly to the side and she fell asleep, her face framed by the ragged white hair and faded blue shawl, beautiful in death—and others! Memory battered her heart until the pain flowed upward from her breast and coursed down her cheeks in hot rivulets. A massive silence engulfed her and she found herself gasping for breath. All she had valued, all she had longed for had come to nothing but loss and grief.

"Starr."

She heard Timmy's voice as if from a great distance, so great she could not reach him.

"Starr," Timmy called, walking over to her. "Why are you crying, Starr?"

Starr put both hands to her face and began wiping the tears away, unable to speak.

"I know what will make you happy," Timmy said softly. "I'll sing a song for you. It's the first song I ever learned."

Starr took a deep breath and managed to control her sobs. "I'd love to hear it, Timmy," she breathed.

"Mama taught it to me when I was real little."

Starr smiled and took both of Timmy's small hands in hers as he began to sing in a clear voice. The song of a Meadowlark came to her across the pond, a breeze rustled the leaves above them and set the water shimmering in the sunlight—as an old woman, Starr would remember every detail of the next moments with perfect clarity.

Jesus loves me this I know.

Starr looked into the face of this child who would be despised and rejected in her world and she saw the Wisdom of the Ages.

For the Bible tells me so.

In the weakness of the child she saw a power greater than any she knew existed.

Little ones to Him belong.

She saw peace—perfect and eternal.

They are weak, but he is strong.

Starr closed her eyes and a silent cry rose from the depths of her soul. Oh God, help me! I'm sorry! Have mercy on me!

Yes, Jesus loves me.

She sat there listening to the simple song, and when Timmy finished, he looked up into her face. "Starr, do you know what?"

"No, what?"

"When I was real little, I cried, just like you."

"Did you, Timmy?"

"Sure!" His eyes were open and trusting, and he was very serious. "I wanted to have Jesus in my heart—like Poppa and Momma and David."

Starr asked, "What did you do, Timmy?"

"I asked Jesus to come into my heart!"

She waited, but he obviously felt he had given her the answer. She hesitated, then asked, "What did you say?"

"I said, 'Jesus, I don't like the way I am. I want you to make me happy, like Momma and Poppa. So come on into my heart.' " Beaming up at her, he nodded with absolute assurance. "That's what you've got to do, Starr."

"But, Timmy, that's too easy!"

"Sure it's easy! If it was *hard,* I couldn't have done it!"

His words came to Starr like a blow! She suddenly realized that she was hearing the absolute truth about Jesus. She had assumed from what she had heard at the Ecclesia and from the members, that what they did was do the best they could. But that had never rung true to her. She knew full well that her best was not good enough for God. And she knew as well that her life had been very wrong, filled with things that were totally contrary to all that she had seen and heard in the Fields. No matter that they were accepted in the City—she *knew* there was such a thing as right and wrong!

Her problem had been one of understanding. Over and over she had asked herself the question *How can a man who died centuries ago bring anything to me?* But she knew from her observation of the members of the Ecclesia that those who followed Jesus Christ were different. But *how* to make it work—that had been her downfall.

She sat there beside Timmy, everything in her saying no! to what was happening. *If I did become a follower of Jesus, I'd lose everything!* she thought. And she flinched from the thought of being an outcast. *But how can I go back? How can I face life in the City, when the only real happiness I've ever known has been in the time I've been here? And how can just asking Jesus to come into my heart make any difference?*

Her mind whirled—yet deep within her spirit something was pulling at her. She felt very certain that the decision she faced was not one which she could reverse, and it frightened her—and yet—it frightened her worse to think that she might pass by the only reality she'd ever known.

"Come on, Starr," Timmy urged, pulling at her hand. "It ain't hard. Just tell Jesus to come in and fix you up."

Starr knew that it was her "moment of truth," as the old seers had called it. And with a sense of desperation, she closed her eyes, and feeling very foolish said huskily, "Jesus, I ask you to come into my heart. Cleanse me from all that's dark and wrong—and make me as innocent as this child!"

She opened her eyes—and saw the face of Jesus! How could she know this Jesus—see him in the face of a child? How could His love flow through her like warm oil—healing every wound—

bearing every sorrow—cleansing all sin? How could there be such a pure love, accepting her completely in spite of all she had done, demanding nothing in return? She knew she would never be alone again behind her wall.

Starr remembered as a child when her father would toss her high into the air and she would fall, it seemed forever, before he caught her. Now she let go of her life completely and fell into the arms of One who would hold her forever. She was never able to explain or even understand what happened to her that day. In all the years to come, she would speak of it as "The day I saw Jesus."

Timmy finished the song and looked at the tears streaming down Starr's face. "You're all right now, Starr," he laughed. "Those are happy tears."

Starr remembered the words David had spoken to her that morning on the bluff. *The wise are confounded and the children understand.* "You're right, Timmy. Your song has made me very happy."

"That's because it's about Jesus," Timmy said, clapping his hands. "He's my best friend."

David was saddling Starr's horse when he saw Starr and Timmy walking up from the pond to the house. Martha was waiting for them on the back porch. She spoke with Starr for a moment, then hugged her goodbye. Timmy did the same and Martha took him inside the house. As Starr walked along the path from the house to the barn, David could tell there was something different about her. When she took his hand and looked up into his face, he knew what had happened.

"I don't know how it happened, but you truly are part of our family now, Starr Omega," he said, taking both her hands in his and smiling warmly down at her.

"I'm so happy, David! The world seems different now."

"It's because you've been changed, Starr—by the presence of Jesus Christ living in you. The emotion you feel may fade, but His love never will. This is truly the beginning of your life. You need to remember, though, others will be angered at this change in you. It happens to every Christian. But we endure through the strength that we have in Jesus. We can't do it ourselves."

"Oh David, how can I leave you! How can I ever live without you!"

David drew her close to him as she circled his waist with her arms and pressed her face to his chest. "There can be no goodbyes for us, Starr," he said, brushing her soft hair with his lips. "We'll be together again. But for now, you must go."

"I can't, David! I can't!"

David touched her chin with his fingertips and turned her face up toward him. "I'll come to you, Starr. I promise."

"But how?"

"I don't know yet. But I will," he assured her. "For now remember—you have a friend who will never leave you or forsake you."

Starr became quiet. She was confused and afraid, yet in the deepest part of her being there was strength and a sense of peace she had never felt before.

"We can't always understand why things happen to us, Starr," David continued. "But the Bible tells us 'that all things work together for good to them that love God, to them who are the called according to his purpose.' Now let's go. Will's waiting for us."

"Think of me, David," Starr said as she touched his face and looked into his dark blue eyes.

"You're part of me, Starr. Part of my life." He kissed both her cheeks softly, then her lips. "Being apart won't ever change that."

Starr had no words for what she felt. She couldn't bear the thought of leaving David and the life she had found here. The City and all she had known there seemed like a monstrous perversion of what life should be. There was a dreamlike quality about it and she began to wonder if it actually existed.

"Sorry it had to happen this way," Will said, sitting astride his great stallion. "Nothing I could do about it though. I'm just a messenger boy."

"I understand," Starr replied. David held her hand and she bent to kiss him, then rode away with Will across the pasture among the grazing cattle. She looked back once, and as her eyes met David's she felt her heart lift within her. At that moment she knew that she would always be a part of him, that he always would be with her. And Starr felt the love of God flowing within her like a river of pure light, driving out the darkness where fear and doubt and sorrow dwell—and she remembered, as she would do for the rest of all her life, opening her eyes and seeing Jesus in the face of a child.

✦   ✦   ✦

"Do you know why they're demanding my return?" Starr asked, with a note of concern in her voice. "I'm barely halfway through my research. It doesn't make sense."

They were riding together toward a distant valley with the sun falling toward the purple hills in the west. Their long shadows slipped silently across the contour of the land ahead of them like dark serpents drawing them back to the City.

"They never tell Border Guards the why of anything, little girl," Will answered, moving easily in his saddle with the gait of the horse. "We're little more than slaves to the City Fathers."

Starr was amazed that anyone would speak this way openly. "Aren't you afraid they'll find out how you feel? Those words are tantamount to treason."

"How could they find out?" Will replied, looking all about him at the open countryside. "No one here to tell them."

Starr smiled at him. "I guess you're right," she said.

"Were all of a kind, little girl. Puppets clop-clopping about at the whim of the almighty stringpullers," Will said, throwing his head back and jerking his arms around. "Get people to swallow the big lie, and the stringpullers can control millions."

"You mean that people have to stay inside the Dome to be safe?" Starr asked.

"Exactly. And drugs are the final touch. Make them accessible and no one's got the gumption to stand up for anything," Will said with a growing anger he was trying to control. "Some of us think there are Domes like ours scattered all around the country. Every one with Manuals and Primitives to do the labor."

"Will," Starr asked, still shocked at his outburst, "if you feel this way, why don't you just leave? You do have a certain amount of freedom to come and go."

"You *are* naive, Starr Omega," he said, shaking his head slowly. "A lot of us would like to, but our families are little more than hostages back there. Oh, they treat us well enough—but they make it clear what would happen if someone deserts. They even keep us in our own separate community so we don't infect the general population with what we know about the world outside the Dome."

"It is nice out here, isn't it?" Starr said, trying to steer Will away from the troubling turn their conversation had taken.

His face brightened. "Nice, little girl?" he said, looking about him at the rolling green hills. "Why it's the Garden of Eden."

"Where did you hear about that?" Starr asked, surprised again at Will's words. "Oh, I pick things up here and there," he said, winking at her. "Come on, I'll race you to the creek."

They camped by the creek that night and the sound of it rushing over the stones was the earth whispering to the star-filled heavens. The cry of a whippoorwill calling its mate carried on the evening breeze.

Starr sat with her back against one of the pines in the grove where they had made camp. She thought of what she would face when she returned to the City. All her life she had managed to avoid most of the bureaucratic pitfalls, keeping her career on track. It was the driving force in her life. Now it all seemed unimportant, insignificant, and she desired only to be free of the City and return to the Fields. She thought of Martha Epsilon's wish to go home to her "beautiful green Fields" to die.

Starr looked at Will thoughtfully sipping his coffee while the firelight played on his sunburned face. She had washed their supper dishes and put them away, to his surprise. "My, my," he had remarked. "The city girl's learned something worthwhile."

"Will," Starr began, "why can't I stay out here? Couldn't you tell them you just couldn't find me?"

Will laughed softly, eyes intent on the fire. Then he looked at Starr. "You really have led a sheltered life, little girl."

"Well, why not?" Starr demanded.

Will's face became troubled. "Starr, I saw how things are between you and David. If there's anyone who could keep you safe out here, it's him. Why do you think he didn't try to stop you from going back?"

"Well, you've got that shotgun."

Will laughed again. "David could make me eat this shotgun if he wanted to."

"Why didn't he do something then?"

"Because he didn't want you to die, or any of his family or friends. And that's exactly what would have happened."

Starr looked at Will wide-eyed.

"If you and I aren't back by a specified time, a helicopter gunship will be dispatched from one of the firebases just outside the laser wall and Haven would be nothing but ashes and smoke the next day." Will let his words sink in, then continued. "They did that a lot in the early days of the Fields. Hardly ever happens now. The Primitives meet their grain quotas and the City pretty much leaves them alone."

"No one ever said anything about this, Starr reasoned, "About what could happen to them."

"You grow up 'under the gun;' you don't think about it. You just accept it as a fact of life."

Before she drifted off to sleep Starr saw clearly that her job as a Reliever was as heinous as anything the Border Guards did with their gunships—*but that part of her life was gone forever!* In her dreams, she stood once again with David on the hilltop outside Lazarus' cabin as the moonlight drifted like spun silver over that wild and frightful land, then she smiled in her sleep. In feathered silence, an owl soared above her, its talons bloodied from a night's work.

✦   ✦   ✦

The metal barge shuddered, then jerked forward to the sound of creaking pulleys as it moved out into the River. Starr and Will stood next to their horses and watched the dark water breathe a white vapor into the night air. On the far shore Starr could barely make out the squat figure of Sheila Phi standing in the yellow swatch of light next to the guard station at the ferry landing.

"Welcome home, Omega," Sheila Phi said as Starr led the palomino down the ramp to the bank. "My, don't you look positively radiant after your sojourn among the Primitives?"

"Thank you." Starr said brusquely. "Why was I recalled?"

"All things in due time, Omega," Sheila Phi replied, standing with her legs apart and her arms folded over her ample bosom. "For now, you just come with me."

"What about my horse?"

"Leave him," Sheila Phi said sharply. "You'll have no need of a horse from now on."

As Starr was untying her saddlebags, she noticed Sheila Phi motion quickly with her hand and a Peacemaker seemed to materialize in the darkness near the guard station. He walked over and grabbed the saddlebags before Starr could react. Throwing them over his shoulder, he headed toward a buggy drawn by two black horses.

"Come, come, Omega," Sheila Phi murmured in a husky voice. "We'll have a nice talk on the way back." She took Starr by the arm and led her over to the buggy.

The only sounds were the clopping of the horses' hooves and the creaking of the buggy springs as they rocked through the night toward the distant gleam of the City. Starr was lost in thought when she felt Sheila Phi's hard stubby fingers stroking her shoulders.

"You must be exhausted after your trip, dear," Sheila Phi said, breathing heavily.

Starr tensed at her touch, but remained silent.

"You'll feel much better when you're back in civilization among your own kind."

Sheila Phi's fingers were stroking Starr's neck and when her hand slipped down to unbutton the blouse, Starr shuddered and pulled away with a gasp.

"You dare to reject me, you little trollop!" Sheila Phi snapped, sitting upright in her seat. "I think some time in the Tank might persuade you to be a little more cooperative!"

Oh God! Starr thought. *What have I done now!* She fought back the tears that were welling up inside her.

Sheila Phi took a deep breath and regained her control. "Don't think your reports have escaped our scrutiny, Omega," she said severely. "I felt it my duty to bring it to the attention of the higher authorities."

"I don't know what you mean," Starr said quietly.

"I think you do. Let's just say for now there are indications that you have become—shall we say, particularly enamoured of this spurious philosophy that's rampant among certain groups of the Primitives."

Starr remained silent.

"Christianity, Omega," Sheila Phi blurted. "You are familiar with the term, are you not?"

When Starr failed to respond, Sheila Phi crossed her arms over her chest and they rode in silence.

As they neared the City, Starr saw the Dome shining like a great jewel against the night sky. *"It is beautiful from here,"* she thought. Suddenly, as if someone had spoken them to her, the words seemed to ring out in the night, ". . .whited sepulchres, which indeed appear beautiful outward, but are within full of dead men's bones, and of all uncleanness."

Part Three:

The Flock

Chapter Fifteen

THE WHITE TOWER

The white-suited driver turned the buggy away from the main gate of the City, following a rutted track that ran next to the smooth black base of the Dome. Fifty yards down he stopped before the seemingly blank wall, got out and inserted a thin metal object into a slot. A ten-foot section of the wall slid upward with a slight hum, stopping at a height of eight feet above the hard-packed ground. The buggy creaked from his ponderous weight as the driver climbed back in and drove them into the towering gloom of the Dome.

They traveled along the left perimeter of the Camp where a twelve-foot high sheet metal fence had been constructed to keep the Border Guards alienated from the rest of populace. As they clattered by next to the gleaming fence, a lean man with crew-cut blonde hair, wearing the coarse jacket and heavy boots of the Guards, leaned in a doorway marked Service Entrance. Talking to another guard, he glanced at the buggy with the two women in the back. Starr caught his gun metal eyes with her own and something passed between them that hadn't been there when he put Starr through her training at the Camp.

Although she had lived here all her life, Starr felt like a traveler from another world as they journeyed along this secluded track toward the center of the City. And she sensed something that had been hidden from her before—an almost palpable malevolence that seemed to hover in the dark air. In a few minutes they pulled over next to an open and lighted door set in a dull black tower. Above the door, the single word VERBOTEN gleamed with cryptic intent. The word was used only in direct association with the White Council.

Two Peacemakers stood at attention flanking the sign. In front of them, his bald head shining in the dim light, stood Bernard Alpha. "I see the prodigal has returned. Welcome home, Omega."

Sheila Phi climbed awkwardly down from the buggy, trudging over to Alpha. "Mission accomplished," she beamed.

Alpha held her in the flinty stare of his pale blue eyes. "Excellent Phi. You managed to stay erect in a buggy seat all by yourself for a least an hour. With progress like that you'll be tying your own shoes in no time at all."

Sheila Phi's face reddened as she shifted about uneasily in Bernard Alpha's less than beneign prescence.

Starr gazed at the two of them from the buggy, showing no intention of climbing out. *Things are worse than I thought. I've never known Bernard to act this cruelly before.*

Alpha waved Starr toward him. "You may alight from your carriage, Cinderella. The ball is over."

The three of them entered the vacuum tube, flanked by the Peacemakers. They sat in seats attached to the walls, closed the sliding bars around themselves and zipped upward one hundred feet to the Dome Sled platform. They stepped into the sled itself under another VERBOTEN sign.

Starr leaned slightly out of the window as the Dome Sled rose ponderously on its track following the long, slow curve of the roof. Starlight and the brighter light of the full moon shone through the thick acryllic panels in a muted lustre. The blank walls of the buildings and the narrow canyons between them stretched endlessly below her in angular swatches of shadow and light. There was little movement in these early morning hours. A single carrier, diminished by the height of the Dome to the size of a toy, slid silently along the streets in the vast darkened stillness of the City.

Starr had always had an amiable working relationship with Bernard Alpha and decided to test its waters now. She turned to him quickly. "Where am I being taken?"

Alpha gave her a bleak smile. "To the end of the line."

The White Tower! "Why?" Starr asked, her voice betraying her with its unsteady timbre.

Alpha stared ahead into the murky distance. "You'll find out soon enough."

Shiela Phi remained silent, squirming uneasily in her seat. The two Peacemakers sat like automatons in the rear.

When they reached the final station, Alpha, Phi and Starr disembarked onto the platform. The Peacemakers remained in the sled while it pivoted on its center axis and, with a lurch, began its long descent toward the Rim.

Like most citizens of the City, Starr had never been to the White Tower—nor had she wanted to go. The western station where they stood was one of only four that allowed access, its track extending over to the tower itself—all the other tracks ended from all around the Dome at this circular hub of convergence. Alpha placed his palm on a white circle on the station wall and a narrow door slid open, revealing a tiny four-passenger sled that would carry them over to the tower. "After you, ladies," he said evenly, ushering them into the sled.

As they made the short trip across to the White Tower, Starr looked down more than a quarter of a mile to the walled and gleaming black forecourt that led to its base. Ahead of her two Peacemakers sat in a thick-paneled acryllic guard booth built into the side of the tower. When they were admitted, after the rigid security checks, they walked along a smoothly-polished black corridor to a room somewhere in the interior of the building.

Entering a narrow blinding-white room, Starr noticed a slim man of average height staring at her from a raised, white podium at the far end. His eyes, dark as a ferret's, seemed to soak up the light, and held Starr's with a chilling intensity. As they walked past a gray plastic table with a molded headrest, toward the ferret-eyed man, Alpha motioned for Sheila Phi to remain behind. He then ushered Starr into a slim stainless steel chair directly in front of the podium.

"This is Starr Omega," Alpha said in a level tone.

"You're far more attractive than I was led to believe," Richard Xi said in his precise, clipped speech, glancing at Sheila Phi who shifted nervously about where Alpha had left her. "You look the absolute picture of health. I've never seen anyone other than a Border Guard with a natural tan."

Starr sat erect on the unforgiving steel, trying to avoid contact with Xi's licentious stare. It occurred to her for the first time how pale everyone else was.

"How was your sojourn in the Fields? I understand you made quite an assortment of friends."

Starr cleared her throat nervously. "It was very—enlightening. Vastly different from our society. They have so very few creature comforts."

Xi pressed his hands together in front of his face, rubbing the tips of his joined forefingers back and forth on his pursed lips. "I'd like to hear more about the people—these Primitives."

What's all this leading up to? Why doesn't he just come out and say it? "They lead quiet, simple lives—agrarian mostly, there is some hunting. Everything is centered around the family—the traditional family of OldAge."

Xi gave Starr a bloodless smile. "These—Primitives—what beliefs do they adhere to. They must have some sort of philosophical or religious inclination."

Starr felt a coldness in the pit of her stomach. She knew full well what happened to citizens under the Dome who had even a nodding acquaintance with the precepts of the Christians. "Some do. Mostly antiquated and disorganized."

"I see," Xi mused. "Well, have you gleaned sufficient information from your foray among the Primitives to complete your dissertation?"

"Yes sir. I believe so," Starr murmured, glancing at Sheila Phi over her left shoulder."

Xi smiled again. "You needn't concern yourself with the approval of your *former* academic advisor, Omega. She'll be going on to—other endeavors."

Sheila Phi took two awkward steps toward Xi, her mouth open to speak.

"That's far enough!" Xi barked.

Sheila Phi stopped like she had bumped into an invisible wall. "But, sir! I've—"

"Silence!" Xi said flatly. "You've proven yourself unfit for any furthur academic service—in fact for any service at all, that I can think of." A cold edge came into his voice. "Your last task for the City was to accompany Omega back from the Fields so her recall would look like a routine student-advisor matter to the Border Guards, in case your accusations against her were correct."

Sheila Phi's face appeared as if it would break apart. Her jaw dropped, the skin on her cheeks sagging like melted candle wax as the icy fingers of horror brushed her. "But I've always done as I was told! I informed you of my suspicions!"

Xi fixed his flat dark eyes on her. "Correct! You also, in your inflated egoist manner, told *others.*"

Mystified at the sudden turn of events, Starr revealed it in her expression.

Turning to Starr, Xi explained, "Your stalwart advisor here, took it upon herself to assume some sort of clandestine fact gathering mission regarding your activities in the Fields. She has concluded that, while in residence with a Primitive family, you succumbed to this rather laughable myth of the Crossbearers."

Starr felt coldness in the pit of her stomach spreading outward until she trembled involuntarily.

Sheila Phi, cleared her throat to speak, but was cut off immediately by a sharp glance from Xi.

"Bernard Alpha," Xi continued, "your superior at the Department of Adjustment has assured me that this could not happen— before your trip to the Fields was approved." He stared appraisingly at Starr. "I'm inclined to agree with him."

"Thank you, sir," Alpha offered.

Xi ignored him. "The facts are, however, that the late Sheila Phi has convinced a small, but highly visible group that such is the case—knowing full well that any information regarding dissident factions is handled by the White Council and is, consequently, subject to the strictest rules of confidentiality."

Shiela Phi stared straight ahead, unable to accept what was about to happen to her.

"Therefore," Xi went on, "you must deny any belief in this alledged Messiah by means of a public forum yet to be decided upon. We can't have the general populace thinking that this antiquated philosophy has any merit whatsoever."

Starr sat with her head down, staring at a crescent-shaped scar in the gleaming floor.

"Bernard tells me you would be most eager to return to work, Omega," Xi stated flatly.

Starr looked up into Xi's pallid face. His eyes held an almost saurian appearance.

"We'll begin with a very small task that could reap some very large benefits for you, Omega—a guaranteed Ph.D. in Remedial History to begin with."

Xi nodded toward Bernard Alpha, who led Sheila Phi to the table. She walked with a leaden gait, her eyes glazed with shock, as she lay back onto the hard surface while her arms and legs were fastened with the plastic straps.

Bernard Alpha lay a white box the size of Sheila Phi's clenched fist on the table next to her. "There is only an endless recycling of the soul into body after reincarnated body," he said to her in a tone that lacked all conviction. In his mind he lay under a willow tree on the cool green grass beside the stream, as he left the room.

Xi rose to follow him and, as he passed Starr he stopped, whispering in her ear. "It's a tiny investment for the return you'll receive from it, Omega."

When the door clicked behind Xi, Starr quickly released the straps that bound Shiela Phi to the table. She helped her sit to up, grasping her by the shoulders and shaking her gently. "Sheila—listen to me! They're going to murder both of us!"

Coming out of her dazed condition, Sheila Phi gazed at Starr with a look of panic in her wide eyes. "No—this is impossible! It's not my time—I'm not through with this life yet!"

"Sheila—you must understand! This is your only life—unless you accept Jesus Christ as your Savior." Starr was frantic, but tried to remain outwardly calm. "There is only one God and he gave his Son, Jesus to die for us. His word tells us: 'For God so loved the world, that he gave his only begotten Son, that whosoever believeth in him should not perish, but have everlasting life.' "

As Starr looked into Sheila Phi's eyes, she saw all the grief and suffering and hopelessness that mankind was heir to. She tried desperately to reach into that dark void. Starr took Sheila Phi's face in both her hands. "Sheila—Jesus loves you so much and he understands your fear and your confusion. Just open your heart to him—trust him—call on his name. Jesus! Jesus! Jesus! Remember to call on that name, Sheila. He understands and he loves you so very much."

At that moment, the door swung silently open. Richard Xi, flanked by two Peacemakers, entered the room. Starr turned from Sheila Phi, looking into a face that was outwardly composed, but in those depthless eyes she saw such an intense hatred that she could almost feel it burning her skin.

"A touching scene, Omega—and a costly one for you," Xi declared bluntly.

As Xi flicked a finger at Sheila Phi, one of the Peacemakers lifted her bodily from the table, escorting her from the room. The other Peacemaker took up a position next to the door.

"I'm afraid we've reached an impasse." Xi paced slowly back and forth, his hands clasped behind his back. "You've obviously been enticed by this insidious and demeaning philosophy. This won't do—this won't do at all."

Starr knew what was in store if she didn't denounce her Christian faith publicly. She remembered one woman in particular who had been sent to her from the Pyramid by way of the Intensive Care Unit. (The Healers always tried to restore their patient's health before they sent them to the Relievers.) The woman had told her: "I was nowhere—I was nothing anymore. There was nothing left for me to hold onto. I saw my soul leave my body. It scuttled sideways like a crab out of my breast and down my arm. It brushed my fingertips—I couldn't hold on—and it fell into the blackness."

In her mind, Starr could still see the woman. According to her file, she was twenty-three years old—she looked seventy-three. Her hair was completely white, her skin hung in loose folds on her bones, and she trembled constantly. But her eyes were the worst. Printed indelibly in them were the horrors that filled her shattered mind. Imagine yourself staring through thick glass into the eyes of a man strapped into a chair bolted to the floor of a tiny room— imagine his eyes as the first smothering wave of cyanide hits him.

"I find it incumbent on me to offer you a final reprieve before I turn you over to the Healers, Omega." Xi stopped his pacing and held out his hand toward Starr in supplication.

Starr knew what the words would be before she heard them. They were the same ones she had spoken to Philemon and others in what seemed another life.

Xi stood with his hand outstretched toward Starr. "You need only denounce this insidious philosophy that has seduced you and the City will forgive your rebellion, embrace and nurture you."

Starr could still see the assurance shining in the pale blue eyes of the man called Philemon. *Jesus, keep that same light shining in me—give me that same assurance.*

✦　　　✦　　　✦

In the Rim's Southeast Sector—Unit forty-three, a thin woman with pale blue eyes, in her mid-twenties sat in tube forty-nine watching the steam begin to rise from the spout of a copper kettle that sat on the small one-burner stove. Her straight, blonde hair was tied at the back of her neck with a piece of twine. She wore charcoal gray coveralls and a threadbare blue shawl, faded from countless washings, was draped over her narrow shoulders.

A rumpled little man with keen brown eyes and close-cropped light brown hair sat across from her, leaning back against the steel curve of the tube. His features were sharp and his voice sounded like it belonged to a boy of ten. "I always think of Martha Epsilon when I see you use this kettle, Philea."

"You know what I think of, Lido?" Philea sighed, her voice soft and fragile sounding. "I think of the green Fields she used to talk about all the time. I dream of them at night and I see the tall trees and the streams and white clouds in a high blue sky. And the bright sun, Lido, and the warmth of it. Do you think it really looks like that?"

Lido smiled, his bright eyes twinkling in the perpetual gloom of the Rim. "Today I saw someone who is just back from the Fields. They forced her to return."

"She went there—out beyond the City somewhere?"

"Verily, verily," Lido laughed.

"Who is she?" Lido's smile ended abruptly. "We've got to help her somehow. I don't know what we'll do."

"Don't let your mind wander, Lido," Philea implored, taking his hand. "Who is she?"

Lido's eyes filled with wonder. "Starr Omega."

"This can't be!" Philea was astounded. "Why would she need our help? Why, she's—"

"She's one of us," Lido declared abruptly.

"But—but how do you know this?"

Lido's mind stopped it's wandering. "Because she wouldn't deny Jesus—in spite of what they're going to do to her."

"The Healers?"

Lido nodded.

"Where was she?"

"I saw her in the White Tower."

Philea's eyes grew wide. "How did you reach the White Tower? No one goes there!"

"I go everywhere!" Lido said expansively, spreading his tiny arms. "There's hardly wallspace or crawlspace anywhere I can't go. I go places no one else knows of."

"You're an adventurer, little Lido," Philea smiled. "Most of us just stay to the buildings where we're assigned."

"I can go where Starr Omega is," Lido assured Philea. "I have to help her! She's one of us now."

"She must have heard the Gospel somewhere in the Fields," Philea mused, pouring steaming tea into two blue plastic cups. "I don't think it's gone beyond a few areas of the Fringe here in the City."

"Maybe there's hope for us in the Fields," Lido piped, his eyes shining.

"If we can get to Starr Omega—free her from the White Tower. She could lead us to the Fields." Philea shook her head dejectedly. "No it's impossible!"

"I can do all things through Christ which strengtheneth me." Lido gazed serenely into Philea's eyes, then broke into a smile. "He keeps my mind straight most of the time!"

Philea smiled, her blue eyes filling with confidence. "Thank you for reminding me of that, Lido. It's the only way I could have made it—losing father and Martha on the same day."

Lido sipped his tea thoughtfully. "I'm going to go see Michael Kappa. He'll help me get Starr away from the White Tower. Then we'll have to find a way out of the Dome. He hasn't told me yet, but I think he knows about a secret door."

◆   ◆   ◆

David stood with his arm around Martha, watching Starr ride alongside Will Sigma across the pasture among the grazing cattle. When they dropped out of sight over a rise, he reached in his jacket pocket for the slip of paper Will had handed to him under the table as they ate.

David,

I'm terribly sorry about this. But I must tell you that if I fail to return Starr to the City a gunship will wipe out your entire village. Also the safety of my family is at stake. In these times we do what we have to.

Starr is in terrible danger. She may be taken to the White Tower and forced to deny her faith publicly. If she refuses— they will break her. They break *everyone* sooner or later.

If you come for her—perhaps I should say *when* you come for her—do as follows:

Wait one full day before you leave in case a watcher has been dispatched.

Leave under cover of darkness.

On the third night, I will wait at the barge landing across from the City.

Call my name once from the edge of the light.

Perhaps some day things will be different. Perhaps someday your King will come.

Will—

David handed the note to Martha. She read it quickly, concern growing in her brown eyes for what she knew her son would do. She hugged David quickly, then stepped back, looking up into his dark blue eyes. "I'll start getting some things ready for your journey. You get all the rest you can until tomorrow night."

David smiled at his mother, noticing the shine of her braided hair as she turned, walking quickly to the house. Then he strode toward the big barn located behind the house near a path that led through the woods to the River. He entered through the main door, turning left into the tack room. Opening a heavy wooden cabinet on the wall, he took out several items and placed them on a table under the single window.

Picking up a short crossbow designed for use with one hand, David slipped the crosspiece into it and strung it to make sure it was in working order. Then he dismantled it, put the stock, crosspiece, string and five metal tipped bolts into a leather case, tying it securely. Next he slipped his oaken staff from its case, running his fingertips over the polished wood looking for any sign of a crack. After checking the leather strap, he put it away in its case.

David closed his hand around the bone handle of his knife, its wide blade glinting in the sunlight that streamed through the window. Sitting on a high stool next to the table, he stroked it gently with a whet rock until the blade was sharpened to perfection. Out of the corner of his eye he spotted a cockroach crawling in the shadows along the opposite wall. With a flick of his wrist, the knife flashed across the room, quivering slightly in the heavy pine board as it impaled the insect through the center of its back.

The next evening, having told his sister and brothers farewell inside the house where the family prayed for his safety, David stood with Caleb and Martha next to his horse outside the stables.

The distant cry of a whippoorwill carried to them on a breeze across the evening fields where the last slanting rays of sunlight touched the long grass with an amber gleaming. Cattle were lowing as they headed in for the barns. Smoke drifted upward from the suppertime chimneys of Haven, while mothers gathered their children from play as a hen would gather her brood under her wings.

Caleb threw his son's saddlebags over the horse, tying them securely with the leather straps. "Son, where you're going, you'll face dangers far greater than the wolves of the timberlands or even men like Abbadon. In the City you'll enter into a spiritual warfare much deadlier than the physical one."

David looked gravely into his father's face. "I can already feel it, father. It's like a dark wall is being thrown up in front of me—to keep me away."

"We'll be in constant prayer for you until you return, son," Martha promised.

Smiling at his mother, David leaned over and kissed her on the cheek, embracing her. "Then I'll be under a mantle of light that the darkness can't penetrate."

As the sun dropped behind the shadowed hills in the west, David quickly embraced his father, mounted his horse and rode across the rolling fields. When he reached the top of the first rise he reined in his horse, gazing back toward the only home he had ever known. Martha and Caleb stood together watching him, as he knew they would, until he was out of sight.

The house that his father had built, the other homes and the church with its small white steeple—David drank in the sight of his village, savoring it as a thirsty man would his last drop of water. With a final wave to his mother and father, David turned his horse toward the east where the City, glowing like a smokeless fire in the night, awaited him beyond the River.

Chapter Sixteen

A BRIDGE FROM HELL

Starr could see and hear, but it was not the same.

Somehow she was aware of *two* distinct scenes—both of them clear, even though they were separated. It was not like watching two television screens at the same time. To do that one must shift the vision from one to the other. And when one watched the first set, the mind automatically filtered the signals from the other.

No, she was simultaneously aware of *two* scenes, and each drama came to her with a startling clarity—sharp and defined. *How can I think of two things at the same time—or see two things at once?* The thought arose in her mind, and she remembered a passage from an ancient novel, *Moby Dick,* which marveled over the fact that the sperm whale's eyes do not look straight ahead, but are located on the sides of his head, so that his brain receives two completely different sets of sensations.

One of the scenes was set in a hospital room. There was no mistaking the white-coated men standing beside a bed, nor the patient with tubes running from the nose and other orifices of the body. She could distinctly hear the humming of machines hooked to the still figure by plastic tubes, and she could see the tiny dot that moved across the glowing green monitor, rising to a small mountain peak suddenly, only to drop sharply.

That's a heartbeat Starr knew, though her thoughts were not in words so much as in impressions. *This is an intensive-care ward.* She "looked" around the room, but not as an observer tied to one spot. She was able to see the faces of the two Healers in white coats, and at the same time the man who stood across the bed facing them.

Why—that's Richard Xi! The thought seized her, and then she looked at the pale face of the patient, and realized who it was covered with a white sheet.

That's me, she thought, and the knowledge came not as a terrible shock, but as a confirmation of a truth she had already possessed.

Then one of the Healers, a short, heavy man with a short gray beard said, "We don't fully understand it. As I told you yesterday, she seems to have no serious brain damage—in fact, very little injury."

"Then—why doesn't she wake up?" Xi's voice sounded desperate and his face was gray with strain. "You must have left her on the Blood Siphon too long."

"It's part of the standard procedure for everyone sent to the Healers. It's monitored very carefully."

"Not carefully enough, apparently." Xi paced back and forth next to the bed.

"Well—I wish we could give you a better answer. We've done a great many tests—and to be truthful with you, my colleague and I are just not certain what to do next."

The other Medical, a very tall man with a full head of black hair and dark intense eyes, spoke quickly. "This sort of thing is not altogether unknown. It may be a combination of loss of blood and shock—and she's doing well. I think we ought to do nothing at all for at least twenty-four hours. In my judgment she'll come out of it very soon."

"She must come out of it!" Xi appeared barely able to constrain his rage. "If she dies, we'll have a martyr on our hands. That would only promote the spread of—" Xi caught himself in time. "I have to go before the White Council soon. I need good news to tell them."

Starr longed to return to the Fields—to see David and his family—to see again the rivers and fields and the forests. But there was nothing to be done in the usual way. She knew that, but she didn't know *how* she knew it.

She could see and hear, even smell the antiseptic of the intensive care room—yet she was not there at all.

Where am I then? she wondered. She was mildly surprised that fear was not piercing her—and almost clinically the thought was in her mind *I must be dead.* But even that thought didn't frighten her. To some extent, it was as though she were encased in some invisible bubble, with her senses intact so that she could see and hear—but the sights and sounds from the other world had no power over her emotions. *I ought to be more concerned for that girl on the bed with all the tubes.* That came to her—yet she felt no compulsion to create a pity or compassion for her body that lay so still before her eyes.

That was one world that she was aware of, and it was not exotic or strange, composed as it was of familiar figures and devices.

The other "world" or "scene" was no less ordinary, for it was her own bedroom. But with one difference: she was not looking into the room, as was true of the hospital room, but was actually *inside* the room—but in this vision, she was not looking on, not seeing herself, but was inside her own body.

She was lying on her bed with her eyes closed, and as she lay there the same tinkling music seemed to be in the air, only faintly. The tufts of the chenille bedspread tickled her palms and the calves of her legs. She could smell the faint odor of the cosmetics which she kept on her dressing table.

Even though her eyes were closed, she was aware that someone was in the room with her. As with the other setting (which she was still aware of) she was not alarmed by what would ordinarily have been a frightening situtation; rather she was curious.

But Starr was also seeped in a warm comfort, a state so peaceful that she had no desire to open her eyes for what seemed like a long time. She lay there aware of the room, aware of the girl on the hospital bed—but was reluctant to open her eyes and discover who was in the room with her. *It must be David,* she thought once without being greatly concerned.

Finally a voice came to her, a man's voice, saying, "Starr Omega, open your eyes."

She slowly opened her eyes and saw at once the figure that stood beside her bed. He wore a simple white coat with large pockets and loose-fitting white trousers. It was his eyes and voice that she never forgot—and yet even those two qualities she could not describe to her own satisfaction.

He was rather tall; his face was neither young nor old. Like some orientals, he could have been any age from twenty to fifty—nevertheless, there was such strength in the lean face that age did not seem important. He had very dark eyes that appeared deep as wells, filled with a compassion and wisdom that seemed to overflow as he stood there watching her. He was dark rather than fair; his mouth full and mobile.

Starr sat up in bed, then stood to her feet. "Do I know you?" she asked.

"Not as well as you will later," he said, and his voice was quiet and low. "But I know you, Starr."

She listened, then stared at him. "I'm dead, aren't I?"

"No, no!" he protested at once, and a smile touched his lips as though he entertained an amusing thought. "No great wonder you should think that, I suppose." He studied her carefully, then said, "I've been sent to give you a chance to help, Starr."

"Help? Help who?"

"Yourself, your family, your friends—and many people you've never even met."

She was watching him, and going through her was that feeling that comes when you *know* you've met someone—but have absolutely no idea where or when. "I do know you," she insisted. "We've met before!"

He smiled and laughed audibly. "Well, I suppose that's true— in a way. But for now, it's best that you don't know much about me. Suppose you just call me Goel." A smile touched his lips and he added, "That's an old Hebrew word. It means 'One who stands between me and another.' Are you afraid of me?" he asked suddenly.

"N-no, I don't think so, Goel," Starr said. "But I'm confused. This is my room, isn't it?"

"Yes."

"But—I'm in the White Tower? I've been sent to the Healers by Richard Xi?"

"That's right." He came closer to her and asked, "Starr, do you remember the dreams you've had?"

"Well—I've been having bad ones and good ones."

"I know. I've been coming to you for a while, asking you to go through the mirror."

Suddenly she *was* afraid, for the first time. She cast an agonizing glance at her mirror, then took a step back, anxious to get as far away from the still figure as possible. "No! I won't do it."

He regarded her without moving, but said, "No one is going to force you to do anything, Starr—well, at least *I'm* not." Then he added, "There are others who might try to control you."

"Others?" she cried, and looked around the room. "What others?"

"That's what you will never know—unless you're willing to trust me." He held out one hand suddenly, and compassion was in his voice as he urged, "Starr—you've got to choose! I know others have been trying to control you. But if you'll let me be your guide, I think you'll be able to understand what is going on—not just in your own life, but in the world."

She stared at him, and whispered, "Goel, you want me to go through that mirror, don't you?"

He shrugged and his face was very sober. "Not *that* mirror, Starr." He waved his hand toward the oval mirror beside her bed, adding, "That's just an ordinary mirror, made of wood and glass. If you tried to go through it, you'd probably get some severe cuts— and there's nothing on the other side except the wall!"

She stared at Goel, fear rising in her heart, but the sight of his face and the assurance in his dark eyes caused her to ask, "Then why do I keep dreaming that you want me to go through the mirror?"

"It's just a way of putting it, Starr. Some things can never be put in scientific terms. Love, for example." He studied her and there was something about him once again that looked familiar, though she could not have said how that could be. "You can't say, I love you 354 times 126, can you? Of course not! That's why man has poets, to talk about love in ways that most people can understand. And the world you know, Starr, isn't the world at all—not the real one."

"I don't understand."

"Few people do," he said sadly. "But you know something like it. Because you're here in this room with me—and at the same time you're in the room where your body is, in the hospital. Isn't that so?"

"Y-yes, but that's because I'm—I'm in some sort of a twilight zone!"

"Exactly!" he exclaimed. "A twilight zone is the best way to describe what you're experiencing right now. But most people are aware of only one world. They think little about another world that's just as 'real' as the one they live in."

Starr stared at him, then asked, "But why do I have to go through this—this *mirror?* What *is* it?"

"It's a way that will enable you to see the 'other' world, Starr—that world that only a few poets and a larger number of saints are aware of. A mirror—a *real* mirror—is only a piece of glass with a silver coating on one side. When you look into it, you see a reflection of things. But if all the backing were removed you'd see what was *on the other side of the mirror.*" He nodded and added, "What you are called to do, Starr, is learn to see the world as it is—not just reflections."

"What will happen to me if I do as you say—go through the mirror? Will it hurt me?"

"It might." Goel's face was suddenly stern, and he said evenly, "There are no guarantees, Starr. Those who would do good in this arena must pledge their heads to heaven."

The phrase caught her attention. "Pledge my head to heaven? That means I might *really* die?"

"Will you come with me through the mirror?" he asked, his steady gaze locked on her face. "We never beg, you know, for only volunteers would be any good at this sort of thing."

She wanted to ask who "we" might be, but knew suddenly that he would give her no answers. She understood that somehow the interview was at an end, that either she must go with him through the "mirror"—whatever that was—or go back to the room where her body was in a hospital bed.

She had the feeling that all of her life she had been making her way down a very broad path, in the company of many people, and now she was being asked to step off that comfortable pathway onto a rough, dangerous way that led to an obscure destination. Never had her life seemed so attractive and secure, and she longed to turn her face and flee from the one who stood waiting with longing in his dark eyes.

Though she was not in the body, she felt the weakness that clings to the flesh—the trembling in the knees, the oppressive weight on the chest, the dryness of mouth. She looked into Goel's eyes and pleaded, "If it were only a *physical* danger—it wouldn't be so bad . . . . !"

"No, that's the *least* part of courage," he agreed. "That's because with physical danger, you can only lose your life. But we're talking about something much more valuable than that, Starr. You're risking your soul. I tell you plainly that many who have gone through a 'mirror' such as the one I set before you, have lost everything." Then his voice grew stern, "Choose at once, Starr! There is little time."

She stood poised, ready to flee yet unable to deny the impulse that rose in her. She seemed suddenly to hear her mother's voice saying, "Don't be afraid, Starr! Trust in God!" And she knew, somehow, that wherever her mother was, she was aware of her plight, and was begging her to keep on.

"All right," she said unevenly. "I'm afraid—but if it will help, I'll go with you."

He smiled, and his eyes were filled with a golden joy that shone forth like sunshine. "You will be afraid many times, Starr," he said gently. "But that is not the test. It is not those who have no fear who are able to serve God—but those who go on into the darkness holding their fear in their hands—as you do now." Then he said, "Take my hand, Starr—and I will take you to where you must go."

She took his hand, and it was warm and strong. "Are you real?" she asked curiously, ignoring her fear. "I mean, I suppose you're an angel, aren't you, Goel?"

"Certainly!" he said firmly. "But don't be expecting all angels to look like *me*. We pretty much don't *look* like anything, Starr. We take on whatever form is least likely to startle people." Shaking his head sadly, he added, "But you'll remember in the Bible whenever we appear to one of you of flesh and blood, the first thing we have to say is 'Fear not!' "

"You do look familiar," she insisted.

Then he tightened his grip and said, "We're going through the mirror now—hold my hand. And I'll be holding to you, Starr. Not to your hand, but to the real part of you. Just remember—you've been looking into a flat mirror all your life. All you've ever seen are reflections. Now you're going past that, into the realm where *reality* is present."

And then it happened.

The room faded into a mist and there was a sudden sense of space—immense and vast. Her hand was held tightly, and she knew that it was Goel's way of giving her courage, but she was no less aware of tremendous activity as the last vestiges of her room faded and she found herself in a setting that she could not have imagined.

She was in space, but it was not the cold, empty space reported by science and astronauts. A million glittering points of light greeted her—not icy dots, but all alive with a force that pulsated through the whole cosmos! They were not fixed, she became aware, but were quivering, moving across the sky in a magnificent dance, stately as a minuet, yet joyful as a polka! She had never seen such life; it made what she had seen of earth look dead and dull, and she whispered, "Oh, Goel, how beautiful!"

"Yes, it is. He hath made everything beautiful in its time," Goel said. "You are seeing reality, Starr. All this is the way things *are*—the signature of the Creator who delights in beauty, who makes all things from that galaxy over there trembling like a million diamonds to the segmented earthworm that burrows blindly through the clods of earth. He made them all!"

For what seemed like a long time Starr drank in the myriad burning stars, the moons, the suns and their planets, and knew that no astronomer had ever seen such things—but that she had passed through the mirror that hid the depths of the great creation above the earth.

Then she exclaimed, "What's that?"

"That's your home, Starr," Goel said quietly. "That's earth— the crowning glory of God's creation. It's the one He made for your race—and the one He sent His Son to redeem."

Starr gazed at it, and the beauty of it made her eyes burn with sudden tears. She whispered, "I remember how a man from Old-World named Milton described it."

"One of God's saints, John Milton," Goel said. "What did he say?"

She quoted the lines she had always loved:

> Far off th'Empyreal Heav'n, extended wide
> In circuit, undetermin'd square or round,
> With Opal Tow'rs and Battlements adorn'd
> Of living Sapphire, once his native seat:
> And fast by hanging in a golden Chain
> This pendant world, in bigness as a Star
> Of smallest Magnitude close by the moon.

Goel looked into her eyes and smiled. "It is like that, isn't it—a pendant world hanging in a golden chain?" Then he said gently, "But now I must show you something else. Do you remember in Milton's poem the lines that come just before those you've just quoted?"

"No, I don't remember."

"Come then—and I will show you another reality—the dark side of the mirror."

And they were moving, not in space so much as in another dimension that was not space or time. She became aware again of tremendous activity, everywhere and constantly. All she could say later was that it was like a wind—not a breeze, but a wind that whipped from every direction at the same time. But these were not winds created by the forces of nature, but rather *energies* that crackled with what seemed to be violent electrical charges. Or, she thought, it was like an ocean, where the waves contended with one another, bringing chaos to the sea.

"It's—like a *battle!*" she cried aloud.

"Yes, it is a battle," Goel answered. "A battle that would put Waterloo or Hastings to shame, Starr." Then he seemed to pull her away and they moved to a point where convolutions seemed less— in fact, for the first time, space seemed to be enormous and quiet. She saw again the earth, like a huge pendant, and delighted in the green continents and the dark blue of the seas. Again she said, "It's so beautiful!"

"Yes—but there is a danger, Starr," Goel said quietly. "Not all want it to remain beautiful. There are those who want to use it, to make it a huge ugly dungeon for your people. Look—you see that dark line?"

Starr turned and saw—or seemed to see—a filmy track or line that was attached to the world. It was darker than the blackness of space, standing out against the ebony as an even blacker thread.

And as they moved toward it, the darker it got. And then she saw it more clearly.

"Why, it's some sort of track, isn't it?"

"Something like that. It touches earth, but look where it leads to."

Starr saw that the ribbon of darkness came from space, that it seemed to emanate from some part of space so dark that the rest of the sky was a foil, setting off the utter darkness of that spot.

She looked closer and said, "Something is going from that dark place out there to earth!"

"Yes." Goel answered. "Now, I will quote you a few lines of your poet Milton. In some way that I do not understand, he *saw* this that you see now and wrote about it. You will remember that Satan had escaped from Hell and fought his way through the Abyss until he finally arrived in space. Sin and Death had followed him out of the Pit, and in a few lines Milton described how Satan came to your home. He said:

> . . . Sin and Death amain
> Followed his track, such was the will of Heav'n,
> Pav'd after him a broad and beat'n way
> Over the dark Abyss, whose boiling Gulf
> Tamely endured a Bridge of wonderous length
> From Hell continued reaching the utmost Orb
> Of this frail World—"

"A bridge from Hell!" Starr cried. "I remember that! A bridge that ran right from Hell to earth!"

"Yes," Goel's voice was filled with pain and anger. "And why is it there? The next few lines tell us why for they say that this bridge is the means: '. . . by which the Spirits perverse / With easy intercourse pass to and fro / To tempt or punish mortals, except whom / God and good Angels guard by special grace.' "

"Now you know my task, Starr," Goel said quietly. "I am one who is set to guard you with special grace."

"A guardian angel?" Starr breathed in wonder, staring at him. "I never believed in those."

"But you didn't believe in God—not really." She dropped her head and tears stung her eyes. "Don't cry," he said gently. "You believe now."

"But not everyone has a guardian angel appear to them. It doesn't seem *fair!*"

"All is fair with God," he rebuked her gently. "Shall not the Judge of all the earth do right?"

"Sorry!" she said at once.

"Yes, I know you are—but you see, Starr, not all have the good fortune to see angels—but neither are all called to such a hazardous task as you are."

His words frightened her, and she asked in a small voice, "I'm not very strong, you know. Are you sure there's not some mistake? Maybe it's somebody else."

"We keep very good records," Goel said dryly. "You are the one who has been chosen for this task. Others will have their own calling. Now, let me show you one more thing . . . ."

He waved his hand and she saw that streaks of light were running across the surface of the world. Some of them were mere dots of light; others were much larger. They seemed to come and go constantly, and she asked, "What are those, Goel?"

"It means a battle is going on in that spot. Milton wrote about the war in heaven, Starr, but that war is over. The battleground is not in heaven or in some distant galaxy—but on planet Earth. And the battle is joined. Souls are dying, and the enemy is strong."

Starr studied the globe of her home planet, then asked, "Why are there more flashes of light in some places than in others?"

"Those are areas where the spiritual war is raging most intensely. In those places witchcraft is everywhere. So the Servants of the Lord must be there to protect the people of God."

"All those flashes are angels fighting against demons?"

"No, not all are angels," Goel said, then took her shoulders and looked down into her eyes. "Those flashes of light you see are for the most part believers who have learned how to do battle with the powers and dominions in the service of the Evil One. Come, and I will show you something."

They moved through the reaches of space, and earth seemed to swell and grow. The face of the earth had changed since the days of OldWorld, but Starr had once seen a Classified Document in one of her searches. It showed the world as it now was. They were over the North American continent, and she could see the River cutting its way through the United States. Closer still, and she cried out, "Look! There's where I live, Goel! That's where the City is!"

"Yes. It's your home, Starr—but not all those lights are from the Dome."

She peered closer and the land seemed to rush up, and she saw one area where the flickers of light were clashing with dark splotches. She trembled and whispered, "What is it, Goel?"

"It's the battle that's taking place over you, Starr."

She stared at the flashes, which were like far-off lightning, and whispered, "Why is there fighting over *me?*"

"The enemy knows you have been with us—with the Servants. They know that means you have been chosen to do a work for God. And that is, to the Enemy, a call to battle. The Evil One himself disputed with one of us about the body of Moses. So now there is a mighty gathering of Dark Spirits who are determined that you will *not* return to your body."

"But—what will they do?"

"They will kill you if they can, Starr." The face of the Servant was grim, and he asked, "I will not deceive you. The risk is great—and I cannot help you."

She was stunned by this. Somehow she had assumed that the Servant would make all decisions, and if necessary do all that had to be done. Now she saw that it was not going to be like that—and she cried, "But—why not?"

"I do not know. It is the will of our Lord that the battles must sometimes be fought by human beings." He seemed to meditate on this, was silent for a long time, and they stood there watching the fierce conflict that was taking place beneath. Then he said, "There is a mighty warrior of God down there, Starr. All alone against a phalanx of the Evil One's most powerful spirits."

"Just *one*—against all those!" she whispered. "It seems so hopeless!"

"Do not say that!" he urged. "It is not hopeless. But now—you must decide. Will you be the servant of God, Starr?"

"But, I'm no angel!"

"No, God has many servants—but that is not your problem. The time is this, Starr—will you go back to your home? And will you be a servant of the Lord Jesus—no matter what the cost?"

She was stunned, and could not think. Her mind reeled and she longed to refuse. Yet—something was *pulling* at her—something from that maelstrom of battle far below. And then she realized it was a voice, a familiar voice!

"Come back to us, Starr! Come and serve the Living God!"

"Why—that's the girl I saw in the Rim that day?" she exclaimed. "Is *she* the warrior, Goel?"

"Yes—and a more valiant one the Lord scarcely has in all His host!"

Suddenly Starr felt a surge of hope—and of joy. "Yes! I'll go back, Goel!"

"It may not be possible. The girl is under a terrible strain. If she falters, you will be at the mercy of those vile creatures you saw on the bridge. What will you do then?"

Starr was trembling in every nerve, but the call was strong and clear now—*Starr—you must come back!* She lifted her head, her eyes filled with tears, and she sounded much like her grandmother at that moment.

"Yes! Yes, I'll go back!"

The Servant said with a great victory in his eyes, "To God be the glory!"

They stood there quietly, then she asked, "What will happen now, Goel?"

"You must go back. It will not be easy, but you must trust the girl. She is standing at the bridge where the Evil Ones cross, turning them back. She will not falter."

"And when I get back, will you be there to tell me what to do?"

"Not for a time," he said gently. "It is best that you learn how to be a servant, not from one of the High Ones—but from one of your own nature. We angels know much," he said thoughtfully, "—but none of us are redeemed. That is the *glory* of your race, Starr."

"But I won't know what to do!"

"You will not be left alone. A Teacher will come. He will help you."

"Who is he?"

"That you must find out for yourself," Goel said. And then his voice grew stern, "Be careful, Starr! Many false teachers will surround you. Some will seem so good and wise, but will be wolves in sheep's clothing. Your Teacher will make himself known—but you must choose him."

"But *how?* I don't understand," Starr protested.

"I can give you three signs," Goel said. "Listen carefully and do not forget them. First, he will come by a name you do not know. Second, he—or she, as the case may be—will not be accepted by your family or your friends. And third, he will tell you something about yourself that you do not know—that no one on earth knows."

She moved her lips silently, memorizing them, and asked, "But that's so *vague!* Can't you—"

"It's time for you to go home, Starr," the Servant said firmly. "Are you ready?"

Starr swallowed, then looked down at the dark forms and the flickering sparks of light. Desperately she wanted to go with Goel, to do *anything* but go down and thrust herself into the fierce battle below—but she knew the time had come.

"Yes, I'm ready," she whispered.

His hand closed on hers once more, and he said as she began to rush through space, "Do not fear, my child. You are a Chosen One—and the Lord Himself will be your shield!"

Her ears roared as a wind rose up from earth, swallowing her cries to the Servant who was no longer there, the clasp of his hand gone.

And as she rushed down toward the dark scarred earth below, she heard two voices—one was the girl calling out in pain. The other was a hoarse, formless voice that suddenly tore at her like a physical blow. And then she felt the pain as dark, spectral things ripped at her, and then she cried out to God as the darkness closed in on her.

Chapter Seventeen

WARRIOR

David tethered his horse and waited at the edge of the darkness. He could see the small domes glowing like huge yellow eyes at the tops of the twin black towers, marking the gate through the laser wall. The wind from off the River, just over the next rise, was damp and cool, bringing to him the sound of croaking frogs. He thought of his home with its own River at the foot of the wooded bluff.

"Come quickly into the light," rang out a voice from a speaker somewhere near the entrance. "When this message is complete, you will have ten seconds to pass between the columns. Do not hesitate. You have only this one opportunity." A harsh buzzing sounded the end of the message.

David had expected Will to appear—instead he heard only this metallic sounding voice in the darkness. He glanced at his horse, knowing that once beyond the gate, there was no turning back—there was no recrossing of the laser wall. Sprinting across the field of light, David passed between the black columns and paused at the edge of the darkness on the opposite side of the fence.

"This way!" The voice, coming from the direction of the River, belonged to Will Sigma. David walked through tall grass up a gently sloping hill toward the sound. Halfway up, he saw the silouetted form of a man standing on the summit. "I'm glad you had the good sense to wait that first night, before you started your journey" Will murmured in the freshening breeze. "One of the Special Units was on alert in case anyone followed us. Everything's quiet now."

David bounded easily up the hill. "Is she all right? Where have they taken her?"

Will sat on a crest of rock, motioning for David to sit next to him. "The worst possible place—the place I thought they would—the White Tower!"

"What's that?"

Will explained briefly the structure of the City and what awaited David there. "You'll need some help and there's precious little available under the Dome."

"I've got to get her out of there and across this River," David said gravely, an intense light in his dark blue eyes. "They'll never take us once we make it to the Fields."

Will took a small light from his coat pocket, switched it on and sat it on the rock beside him. Unfolding a sheet of paper, he placed it on the rock next to the light. "This would only be a waste of time for anyone else, but you just may have a chance to pull this off, David. I can get you inside the City—put you in touch with one man you can trust. Now here's what you have to do—"

In a few minutes Will pointed back beyond the gate at the bottom of the hill. "I'll tether your horse and Starr's down in that stand of willows next to the stream tomorrow night and for two nights afterwards. If you haven't made it by then—"

"You have Starr's horse?"

"The Guards keep all the horses." Will switched off the light, slipping it inside his pocket. "No one has ever escaped from the White Tower, David—ever!"

David glanced at Will, then looked down the hill to the lighted barge landing. "I don't go in my own strength, Will, but in the name of the Lord of hosts that delivered Israel."

The long grass on the hillside waved gently in the wind like the surface of the sea. Far beyond the River, the great Dome glowed coldly against the night sky.

There was almost no traffic as David traveled along the dirt track that ran from the City to the River. It had been worn down over the years by boots and horses' hooves until its hard-packed surface was several inches below the ground on both sides. David ran easily along its edge, melting into the underbrush with his gray cloak about him when he heard someone coming. *They've never had to practice stealth,* he thought gratefully.

A quarter of a mile from the City, David climbed to the top of a tall beech tree to get his bearings. The light from the Dome showed him the huge main gate where several Guards, their horses grazing contentedly, slouched around a rough building of weathered lumber. He could barely make out the smaller track skirting to their left. Moving at the edge of the woods, he continued past the small gate where Starr had entered the Dome in the carriage. Two hundred yards further on, after no more than a cursory glance around, he located it.

Brushing back some leaves, David saw the dull metal ring. He lifted on it, the small trap door swinging easily upward. A roughly welded ladder descended into a narrow dark void. With no hesitation, he swung easily into the opening, closing the door over him. The metal rungs of the ladder were cold on his hands as he descended into a darkness that made the night he had just left look like noonday.

✦   ✦   ✦

Lido slid the panel back one inch, peering out over a bale of hay into the gloom of the stables. The horse directly below him, a spirited pinto, smelled him at once and began neighing and shaking his head. After he had quieted, Lido slipped through the panel, closed it behind him and scurried over to the edge of the loft behind several stacked bales of hay. In the back corner of the main stables below him he could see the door to Michael Kappa's small quarters.

Scampering down the ladder from the loft Lido ran across the hay-strewn floor and opened Michael's door. As he stepped into the cramped room he froze in terror. Talking to his friend was a tall man in a gray cape. He had long black hair, dark blue eyes and a look about him that in no way resembled the people that lived under the Dome. It spoke of open spaces and sunshine and rain sweeping across the endless green Fields. Lido felt this, although he didn't understand why as he had never seen any of those things.

"Come in little friend," Michael assured him. "This is David. He's come from the Fields."

Lido looked up into the face of the tall stranger. His elflike appearance and his life in the underground and hidden places of the City were as different from David's as two people could be, but he saw something that transcended all the outward differences between them, something that made him feel he had known David for so long a time that he could trust him. "Have you really come from the Fields? Are there trees and rivers?"

David liked this small, inquisitive intruder and felt immediately the kinship the two of them shared. "Yes there are—and much, much more," he laughed.

"Can I go there with you?"

David sat on one of the two straight-backed metal chairs, resting his elbows on his knees. "I think perhaps you can, my brother. You'd dearly love it out there. But first we have work to do and Michael says you're the man for the job."

Lido looked puzzled. "Job?"

Michael sat down in the other chair. "You can have your usual place." He motioned toward his bunk.

Lido bounced onto the bunk, sitting in the middle of it with his legs crossed.

"David wants you to help him get someone out of the White Tower. Someone they took from the Fields." Michael waited for Lido to bombard him with questions.

"Starr Omega."

"You know her?" David asked, astonished at the response.

"No," Lido answered, bouncing lightly on the bunk. "But I've seen her."

David leaned forward eagerly in his chair. "How did you know it was her?"

"I listened to them."

"You were in the White Tower?" Michael's eyes narrowed in doubt as he stared at the little man who had such a childlike innocence about him. "No one goes there."

"I do."

David gazed intently into Lido's bright eyes. "Will you take me there? Help me get her out?"

"That's why I came here," Lido answered excitedly. "Philea and I were going to get her out ourselves. We needed Michael to help us get out of the City."

"Well then, David makes four of us in on your little caper," Michael mused. "The three of you bring her back here to the Camp and I'll have things ready to get us out of the Dome."

"You're going with us to the Fields?" David was encouraged by the thought of someone like Michael throwing in with them."

Since I became a Christian, it's all I've thought about," Michael smiled. "This is an answer to prayer."

"I'll have to get another boat," Lido piped in. "I just have the one for Philea and me."

David was perplexed. "Boat? Why in the world would you need a boat inside the City?"

✦　　　✦　　　✦

It was like something out of the imagination of a demented mystic, this underground world beneath the City. The deep rumbling drone of the massive generators overlaid everything, making conversation impossible unless you were close to the person you were talking with. The foundations of the buildings looked like giant steel pylons turned upside down, extending from the underside of the buildings themselves. They were attatched to huge metal bases resting on a series of giant springs as protection against earthquakes.

Steam and water pipes of every imaginable size ran vertically, horizontally and diagonally in an incomprehensible maze. The sibilant clouds of escaping steam added counterpoint to the heavy drone of the generators. Shafts of pale yellow light dropped from far above through the grates of the streets, creating the impression of perpetual twilight. Through this spectral world, beneath the stark spires and canyons of the City, flowed a River.

David stood with Lido next to one of the gigantic concrete pillars that supported the City—that provided the stability for all the other networks of systems that sustained it with air and light and warmth. the River flowed before them, warm and languid, and incredibly clear, between the vertical walls of a concrete canyon.

David glanced down at Lido. "Why is the water so clear? There's not even any debris."

"The Rippers." Lido answered as if that should be enough information for anyone.

"The what?"

"The Ripper fish," Lido explained. "They eat anything that gets into the River. I don't think there's anything they don't eat—even if they can't digest it. Nothing seems to hurt them."

David was fascinated. "What do they look like?"

Lido picked up a small chunk of concrete that had broken away from one of the columns. "Watch."

David watched Lido toss the chunk over the concrete bank of the River. As it hit the surface of the water forty feet below, a gray fish, three feet long and shaped like a fleshless barracuda, streaked toward it from a small side channel. Catching the concrete in its mouth, full of razorlike teeth, it chewed and shook its head viciously. Then, like an aquatic shadow, it disappeared back into the dark tributary.

"They keep the River clean," Lido smiled.

"I'll remember that," David remarked, looking up and down the River at the plethora of small channels that either emptied into or flowed away from the main channel.

Lido sat on the concrete bank of the River watching it flow southward away from the center of the City. A hundred yards downstream, the River dropped into a deeper underground channel in the earth, disappearing under the edge of the Dome. The sound of the River's descent into the subterranean darkness was that of a small waterfall.

"When will Philea come?" David asked patiently, learning to adjust his pace to Lido's.

"Perhaps an hour—maybe less. She's been in fasting and prayer for two days. Now she's gone to the Fringe to locate one of the special gowns that the Physic Advisors wear," Lido answered absently. "You can find just about anything in the Fringe if you know where to look."

"I don't understand why she's going with us." David walked over and sat next to Lido, looking down at the river, shivering slightly as he thought of the Ripper.

Lido smiled benevolently at him. "The Physic Advisors are the only ones who can remain in the room at all times with patients under the care of the Healers."

A shadow flickered in David's eyes. "Is it so necessary to have someone with Starr continually?"

Lido answered in a grave tone. "The White Council hates Christians because they fear what they don't understand and because they don't have the absolute control over them that they do the other citizens under the Dome. They think this freedom will undermine their power. That's also why they'll keep Starr alive, as long as they think they can get her to publicly disavow her beliefs."

"Then why do we need someone with her—if they don't plan to kill her?"

Lido stared out across the River at the endless maze of concrete columns, steel pylons, pipes and other structures of abstract and infinite strangeness. His face seemed to change as he spoke. "There is a group in the City that sees Starr as an even greater threat to them than the White Council does."

David stared as Lido's face seemed to become that of an old man. "Who are they?"

"The Coven. And they see the true danger as allowing Starr to remain alive at all—even for a short time. They know her threat to them is not of this world." Lido's face brightened. "That's why we need Philea. She knows how to fight them."

"She must really be something," David declared.

"Oh she is," Lido agreed.

Across the River, in the upper levels of the towering shafts of concrete and steel, a small figure moved catlike across a beam spanning an open space. He hooked a belt around one of the supports and slid down it to a platform where he began some sort of repair work, using tools from a bag attached to his waist.

"Who's that?" David asked, fascinated by the agility of the small workman.

Lido glanced upward. "Oh, he's just one of the Shadowmen. They keep things in working order down here."

"They come all the way down here every day?"

"No." Lido watched the man as he made his repairs. "They live down here."

David looked about him at the absolute lifelessness of the surroundings. "Here—all the time?"

Lido smiled benignly at David. "It's better than the Rim. At least down here no one bothers them."

"From what I've seen of the City, they must be under the scrutiny of someone."

"Oh, they were once—a long, long time ago. Then, over the years, their overseers came down less and less until they more or less forgot about them." Lido waved to the little man on his high, precarious perch. He put his tools away and waved back. "The Shadowmen found out if they kept things running well, no one bothered them. I doubt there's anyone left who's even responsible to check on them anymore—and that's the way they like it."

"It must be a lonely life," David murmured, watching the repairman scramble back up the support.

"Oh no!" Lido answered quickly. "They have their families with them."

Shaking his head gently, David stared at the Shadowman as he disappeared into the murky recesses of the City's substructure. "The resilience of the human spirit never ceases to fascinate and amaze me, Lido."

"They're just doing what it takes to survive like the rest of us," Lido remarked staring back into the River. "And they're very good at it. I think they have access to every building in the City from down here. That's how they get their food and anything else they need. They take just enough to survive so no one will come looking for them."

"Did they show you how to get into the White Tower?" David asked abruptly.

Lido smiled, nodding his head. "And a lot of other places too. It's fun to go with them sometime."

Looking about him at this forbidding and complex world with its own River and aerial pathways, David said, "I guess it's an interesting life down here—and a safe one."

"Maybe not for much longer." Lido remarked cryptically.

"What do you mean?"

"Christians trying to get away from the Peacemakers are coming down here—more and more of them. I believe they'll soon find out about this place."

"What makes you think that?" David asked, turning his attention to Lido.

"The things I've heard in my journeys under the City—especially in the White Tower and the Department of Adjustment." Lido frowned. "It's going to be very bad."

David heard the swish of soft shoes on concrete and turned to face her—and his spirits fell! Thin and pale and fair-haired, she was more girl than woman, having a fragile look about her as though she should be protected behind glass. She wore a diaphanous gown sprinkled with gold that gave her an ethereal air. Incongrously, she carried a heavy canvas bag over her shoulder. In her free hand, she held a small blue cloth bag with a drawstring.

Seeing her in the stark and murky environs beneath the City, David felt she was a vision rather than a person, expecting her to disappear any second.

"I'm glad to meet you, David. My name is Philea."

With the first soft sound of her voice, the vision became flesh and blood.

"How—how do you know me?"

"I could never mistake you for anyone who lives in the City—and neither will anyone else." Philea handed him the canvas bag. "That's why I brought you a present."

As David took the bag, he gazed steadfastly into Philea's light blue eyes and began to sense that there was far more to her than her appearance suggested.

"It's perfect!" Lido exclaimed with sudden insight, before David had opened the bag.

"How do you know?" Philea smiled.

Lido shrugged knowingly. "There's only one way David could go undetected in the City."

David pulled a shiny helmet and the white uniform of a Peacemaker from the bag. "You expect me to wear this?"

"I think you'll cut a dashing figure in it," Lido teased, trying on the helmet.

David laughed at the sight of the little man in the huge white helmet with its black visor. "Maybe so, but I think I'll wait until we get to the White Tower to put it on."

"We'd better be going," Philea urged. "It's a long trip and we have very little time to spare."

The three of them made a strange amalgam: David, wearing his buckskin shirt and boots with his weapons slung on his back; Lido, tiny and agile in his gray coveralls; and Philea, in her shining gown; climbed down the steel ladder to the small ledge at the edge of the River. Tied to a pipe that ran along the concrete wall forming the River bank, were two canoes made of a black plastic material. They were eight feet long and narrow, having no seats in them.

David looked at the unsteady craft, glancing about for a sign of the Rippers. "Are you sure they're safe?"

"No," Lido muttered, a wry smile on his young-old face. "But they're all we've got."

David dropped the canvas bag into the front of the lead craft, climbing carefully into it. He positioned himself on his knees and took up a small gray paddle made of the same plastic material as the boat. Lido and Philea boarded the other craft with Lido in the rear handling the paddle. With the soft swishing of the hulls against the water, they began their journey through the perpetual gloom of this surrealistic world beneath the City.

Paddling with a smooth, steady stroke, David noticed a movement in the cellophane-clear water beneath him. Three Rippers had appeared almost magically several feet below the surface—one just in front of his boat and two others flanking it closely on either side. They were all six feet long or more and their bony frames shimmered in the dim light as though they were made of metal—the yellow eyes gleaming with a patient and malevolent light.

◆　　　◆　　　◆

"You assured me that Starr Omega could be trusted implicitly, Bernard." Richard Xi sat behind his white desk in his formally cold office in the White Tower. "It seems your assurances are worth little more than Shiela Phi's vow of silence."

Bernard Alpha always preferred offensive tactics rather than defensive. "I merely provided you with irrefutable facts regarding Omega's performance, Richard. I admit to championing her cause, however, I had no authority to sanction it. That, my old friend, required your approval."

Richard Xi's eyes, dark as a ferret's, fastened on Bernard Alpha. "I believe we've reached an impasse, Bernard."

"It would seem so," Alpha replied.

"It's also appallingly obvious that we both have a vested interest in the psychic remediation of Starr Omega," Xi continued. "The White Council frowns on anyone even remotely connected to a conversion such as Omega's."

Alpha clasped his hands together, resting his chin between the knuckles of his forefingers. "I've given this a lot of thought. I don't plan to be sacrificed on the altar of Omega's insanity. The Healers are bungling this with remarkable ineptness—even for them. With their reliance on the Siphon and the Pyramid of Darkness, Omega's imminent death is virtually certain."

"You have an alternate plan?"

"That depends on the information you give me. I've heard only rumors so far."

Xi leaned back in his chair, his close-cropped white hair glinting in the harsh light. "What have you heard? Maybe I can assuage the anxiety that rumors usually spawn."

Alpha smiled knowingly. "Well, rumor has it that there's to be a purging, or maybe we should call it by a more accurate name, an inquisition of the Crossbearers. My sources tell me this is to be under the direct control of the White Council."

"We prefer to call them Disciples of Treason, the name used when the first outbreak of this blight occurred. The Action of Enlightenment is to begin in the not too distant future."

"Action of Enlightenment—I like the sound of it," Alpha grinned sardonically.

"Now that you're *enlightened* as to the current and rather precarious status of the Disciples of Treason, what are your ideas for dispensing with the bothersome Ms. Omega?"

Alpha propped his elbows on Xi's desk, but jerked back in the face of his menacing glare. "What I propose is to let the Coven have their unholy way with her. They have absolutely no tolerance for Christians. And, since there's to be this Action of Enlightenment, the need to have her publicly recant her beliefs would seem to pale in significance. Even I know members of the Coven have infiltrated the power structure, at least as far as the Healers."

"Perhaps you're right," Xi mused, studying Alpha intently. "Of course we couldn't overtly endorse such an action. That would be tantamount to barbarism."

"Of course," Alpha smiled coldly. He sensed then a sudden, almost audible thud, like a door closing forever in his heart. The gleam in his pale eyes became incredibly like that of the Rippers, moving silently in the shadowy depths a thousand feet below him.

Chapter Eighteen

THE COVEN

Her body tingled from the salt water bath, and she was shaken by an inner agitation as she joined the others who were assembled around a nine-foot circle of rope. The only light came from two tall candles which rested on a crudely constructed altar—and she was glad that the room contained no bright lights, for despite her boldness, it had been harder to remove her clothes and join the twelve other naked worshippers than she had imagined.

By the flickering candlelight, she could see that the others were paying little heed to her—except for Natas Molech. The darkness behind the eye slits of the iron mask seemed to come alive as he looked directly at her—and she had to exert every ounce of will she possessed to hold his gaze. His breath was a cold vapor through the mouthpiece as he then nodded to a middle-aged woman standing to his right. She at once turned and went to a low table where a very large silver cup rested, picked it up and took it to Molech. He lifted it high with both hands, and raised his voice in a high-pitched incantation in which the others joined from time to time, then raised the cup to the slit in the mask and poured the liquid in. He passed the cup to the young man on his right, who drank eagerly before passing it on, and one by one, all thirteen of the members of the coven shared in the cup.

When the newest member lifted the cup and took a swallow, she knew exactly what it was—a highly potent psychedelic drug. She knew this because she herself had smuggled it out of the dispensary of the ward where she was the Head Nurse. Molech had told her that he preferred belladonna or a brew made from the amanita mushroom. "But the mushroom brew takes time—and we have a crisis that will not wait," he had said.

After the potion had been swallowed by all thirteen members, there was a reading from The Book of the Shadows by a tall elderly man—that she recognized instantly as the executive assistant to a member of the White Council. By the time he was finished, the drug had taken hold, and as the ritual progressed she could not be sure if things were actually happening—or if they were creations of her brain inspired by the drug.

She swayed back and forth noting the items that rested on the altar with the silver chalice—a hazelwood wand and a small caldron. A brass censer of burning incense, a five-pointed metal star engraved with signs, a bowl of salt, a black-handled sword (which she knew was called "athame") and a length of cord that symbolized the spirit that unites all the elements.

Molech called on a young woman to come forward, and as she stood in the center of the circle, he gave her a ceremonial scourging, after which he allowed an opportunity for anyone to share a personal request with the rest of the group. Several spoke their requests, including an overweight matron of forty who pronounced a curse on her Loving Friend and seemed to take great pleasure as the rest of the members chanted a vigorous and optimistic anticipation of the result.

Molech said in his shattering voice, "For our newest member, I must explain that the requests we speak result in a combined thought wave, and this we call 'The Cone Of Power.' It is a neutral force which can be directed only by a head witch or warlock, and *can be a healing process—but can also be directed against a person or group of people." His voice fell to a low pitch, almost a guttural snarl and his features twisted into a mask of hate, as he added, "Tonight we are come together to do battle against a threat to our Master!"*

A low murmur ran around the circle, and the eyes of those in the circle seemed to glitter in the candlelight, the newest recruit noticed. She felt very important, suddenly, her spirit seeming to swell within her, and she could not tell if it were the result of the drug—or the fact that Molech had fixed his penetrating eyes on her expectantly.

Then he said, "We have been given the means to crush this new danger—and the instrument will be our newest member." His eyes glittered, and he said, "Orion—we will have the sacrifice!" The tall man whirled and left the circle. He was back in an instant with a struggling young goat held firmly in his hands. He placed it on a rough table that one of the others had produced, and Molech was there, a gleaming knife attached to his stump of a hand. He began to chant and the others offered a refrain from time to time. Then he suddenly reached out and slit the throat of the struggling animal.

Though she was a nurse and innured to the sight of blood, the sudden gush of crimson brought a quick revulsion to her throat. But the others all released a cry of victory, and then Molech was standing before her, his hand reeking with the hot blood. He suddenly reached out and she felt the leathery stump on her face. It seemed to burn her flesh—and she was filled with an emotion she had never known—a mixture of sensuous joy, a sense of infallible power, and the raking of raw terror across her nerves. She would have fallen, but two of the members caught her, held her fast, and she heard Molech say:

"You are the instrument of His Majesty's wrath! Go to the girl. She is being kept alive only by the persistence of one woman— who cannot last much longer. She hasn't slept or eaten in almost three days! Your assignment—bring back to me a lock of the girl's hair and some fingernail clippings. And be quick! We must destroy this girl—for we know that she has been chosen to be used by the Enemy. Even my Masters do not know exactly how—but we are commanded to destroy her at once. Now—go!" Then he added in a voice that was hard as steel and colder than anything she had ever heard: "If you falter—you will find out that our Masters can be cruel to those who fail—or even draw back!"

She stumbled from the room, washed the blood from her face, dressed and managed to get to the carrier. Her hands were trembling so violently it took several tries before she could open the door, and when the carrier began humming along the track, she wondered if she could even remain erect. Rolling down the window, she took in huge gulps of air, and finally the terror subsided. As she sped through the City, she planned in her mind exactly what she must do when she was in the same room with Starr Omega, and her lips were curved by an exulted smile as she thought, "It will be easy. Who would suspect the Head Nurse of belonging to the Coven?"

"Really, Philea—you *must* go home and get some rest!"

Philea raised her head slowly, looked at the tall form of the Healer who stood beside the nurse. Philea knew how she must look, for she had seen her reflection in the bathroom mirror an hour earlier when she had bathed her face with cold water. Face pale as paper, eyes ringed with red from weeping and from fatigue, mouth pale and drawn tightly together, great dark blotches under her eyes which seemed to have withdrawn into the cavities, giving her a skull-like appearance.

Every nerve in her body cried out for rest, for she had not closed her eyes in sleep since she had come to stand guard over Starr. Her limbs, she knew, were so weak that she didn't dare try to stand up and face the three who had come to persuade her to go home. Instead, she took a tighter grip on the blue bag in her hands, and spoke in a voice that was firm as stone—though raspy with fatigue.

"I will stay until Starr comes back."

The Healer shifted uncomfortably at the words, for they didn't seem *right* somehow. *Until Starr wakes up* would have been more correct. He caught a warning shake of the head from the other Healer, who stepped forward and put his carefully manicured hand on Philea's frail shoulder, saying in a soothing voice, "Now, Philea, we don't want to have you here as a patient, do we now? We don't have enough good Psychic Advisors as it is. Go home for some rest. Starr will receive the best of care—you know that, don't you?"

Philea did not move, but something about her face caused the Healer to remove his hand from her shoulder very quickly—as if it were a dangerous location. A light flickered in her dark blue eyes, and she said, "The best of care for her body, yes. But there are other dangers."

The tall Healer shook his head, then bit his full lower lip. "There are fine Spiritual Healers on call, Philea. As soon as Starr wakes up, we'll see that they are available."

"No." Philea gave that monosyllabic answer, then forced herself to say, "Thank you for coming by."

"Certainly!" The Healer had lost some of his smooth assurance. His smile was forced and he was thinking *I'd like to take this crazy woman and wring her neck!* But he merely shrugged, saying, "Call me if you need me—anytime."

The two Healers left the room, and Philea sat down beside Starr. Her lips were dry and she was obviously at the end of her rope emotionally. "I'll wait until God does something," she murmured quietly.

Until God does something—but was God *going* to do anything?

The thought fell into her mind, lay there like a stone—a tiny lump of doubt—like yeast in a loaf. And the longer she sat there struggling, the larger it seemed to grow.

Then the voices began.

Thoughts, really, but they came to her almost audibly. She knew it was the humming of the air conditioner, but the steady sound was overlaid with thoughts:

Maybe it's not God's will to bring her back. Maybe He's done this out of His sovereign will.

You're tired. You're not able to think or pray properly. Go home and get some rest—then you'll feel much better. You'll be able to pray better.

"No!" She forced her gritty lids open, opened the blue bag and tried to read the worn pages it contained—but her eyes were burning. She stared at Starr's face, and a bitterness rose in her, and anger boiled within:

It's not fair, God! I can't do it alone—why don't You send someone to help?—If she dies, it won't be my fault—You're asking too much!

If it had been a physical battle, that would have been easier—for although the pain of a fleshly wound could be fierce, it was as nothing compared to the warfare that had racked her spirit for so many hours. Her spirit seemed to be isolated in a cold, alien place, and all around were fierce, cruel beings that ripped and tore at her without ceasing. She thought of Prometheus chained to a rock and the vultures that came each day and tore at his liver, and she thought of the lone trapper lost in the woods surrounded by a pack of green-eyed slavering wolves, keeping them at bay by a single torch, knowing that if he dropped that small firebrand for one moment, the pack would be at his throat instantly.

She had fought this battle before, long ago in the Rim, but her father had been beside her. The two of them had stood against witchcraft and the black magic of the covens that had taken root even there—but now she alone kept one small flickering flame of faith held high. She alone knew of the darksome creatures, the powers and dominions that strained to move into Starr ripping her soul with their fell powers. As Moses' arms had grown weary held high to God, her spirit and her faith were dragged down as the long hours and days plodded by,—and there was no Aaron or Hur to hold *her* hands high!

She struggled against the anger and bitterness, but it swept over her like a current, choking her attempts to pray. She had the sensation that she was being sucked down into a dark, resistless maelstrom, being drawn into a world of terror and fear. She uttered a small cry, and rose to her feet, tottered over to take the limp hand of Starr, and through parched lips quoted the ancient words: "Have mercy upon me, O Lord; for I am weak; My soul is also sore vexed; but thou, O Lord, how long?"

She fell across Starr's still form, like Elijah of old, and for a long time lay there sobbing and calling on God.

Finally she rose, wiped her eyes, then made her way to the bathroom taking the pitcher of ice from the table. Closing the door out of habit, she took a clean cloth and began bathing her face with cold water, then made an ice pack and held it over her burning eyes. She never was able to remember how long she stood there, but she did remember hearing the door close. The nurses and aides came in from time to time, and she thought nothing of it—but usually whoever came said a word to Starr, knowing that she could not hear, but out of habit.

But there was a silence in the room, and suddenly Philea dropped the ice pack and stood bolt upright—for the presence of something evil came to her, icy and deadly!

She whirled, threw open the door and saw instantly the head nurse bending over the still form of Starr, holding a pair of gleaming scissors in her hand, poised to snip a lock of Starr's long hair! The nurse had always been cheerful, her round face honest and sincere.

But it was not the same, Philea saw instantly, for the simple face and honest eyes were transformed by something inside the woman that narrowed her eyes to slits and turned her lips into a snarl. At once Philea felt the same presence of evil power that she had felt years ago when she and her father had faced a painted witch doctor—for the eyes of the nurse had the same diabolical light that had burned in the eyes of the black magician.

"Leave this room!" Philea said instantly.

But the woman snarled in a voice not at all like her usual tone, "Get out while you can, old woman!" She dropped the lock of hair and reversed the scissors, holding the gleaming instrument like a dagger, and took a step toward Philea. "I'll kill you!"

Philea stood straight, looking into the woman's frenzied eyes, knowing that she stood on the brink of death—but there was no fear in her. She lifted her voice and cried out, "In the name of Jesus Christ of Nazareth, I rebuke you!"

The nurse faltered and the hand holding the scissors dropped slightly—but she shook her head and hissed, "You cannot stop us! Don't stand between me and what I've come for!"

Philea began to speak, and it was with a voice of authority, "In the name of Jesus Christ, I command you, evil spirit, begone! You have no power, Satan! The Lord Jesus Christ overcame you at the cross!" Then as the woman in front of her began to writhe and twist, her eyes burning, Philea cried out, "The blood of Jesus! The blood of Jesus Christ of Nazareth!"

The nurse dropped the scissors, covered her ears with her hands, and then ran out of the room making incomprehensible moans. The door slammed behind her, and suddenly Philea felt that every drop of strength had been drained from her. Her legs began to tremble and she staggered forward, falling on her knees beside Starr's bed. Her head swam, and she clutched at the sheets, fighting the weakness, knowing that she must not fall to the floor!

She felt herself slipping in a warm comfortable darkness, and cried out, "Lord, God! Strengthen me!"

And then—she felt a hand on hers!

A thrill raced along her nerves, for she thought for one panic-stricken instant that the demonic nurse had returned! But then she heard a thin, reedy voice:

"Mother! Mother!—where are you?"

She pulled herself to her feet, and saw that Starr had found her hand and was clinging to it. "I'm with you, Starr!" she cried out. "I'm right here!"

The translucent eyelids of the girl on the bed fluttered, then opened wide, and Philea saw the panic in the girl's eyes. "Who are you?" she cried out, and Philea threw her arms around the girl, saying, "My name is Philea. I'm a friend. It's all right, Starr! It's all right! We've won! The victory is the Lord's on this day!"

She felt the girl's body move, and when she leaned back, she saw that tears were running down Starr's cheeks—but they were tears of joy! The eyes were clear, completely free from fear, and Starr whispered, "Philea—you brought me back! They were all trying to drag me down, but I saw this little light and I heard your voice—so I struggled to get to it." She looked at Philea with wonder in her eyes and said proudly, "You held them back! They were all horrible and black, coming across the bridge to drag me back with them—but you stood there and they couldn't get me—because of the light you held!"

Philea didn't understand the allusion to a bridge—but she knew that the girl had been saved, and she held her tight, rocking her back and forth, making a comforting noise. Finally Starr drew back and her eyes were huge as she said, "We won, didn't we, Philea?"

Philea nodded slowly. The glory of victory was in her pale blue eyes, but she said, "Yes—we won, Starr. but this was only one battle. The war will be long, and the enemy is strong. He will come again, and he is legion." But there was victory in every line of her face as she whispered, "But God is going to do a mighty work, Starr. He is going to raise up an army! It will be like no army you ever saw—and the world will laugh at it. But if we will be faithful to Jesus, we will see His banners flying in glorious triumph over this city!"

"An army, Philea?"

"Yes, Starr—and you are called to be a part of it!

Chapter Nineteen

THE PROPHET

"Hurry, hurry! This way!" Lido waved frantically to David and Philea from the opposite end of the long corridor, glaring brightly under the florescent lights. He still felt uneasy at the sight of David in the uniform of a Peacemaker—although he had had twenty four hours to get used to it.

David carried Starr, still dressed in her white hospital gown, in his arms as she clung to his neck, only half-conscious, her face almost the same color as the gown. Philea held to his right arm, dragging along behind him, weakened from three sleepless days and nights of fasting and prayer.

"Down here, in the Closed Ward! Show some life you lumbering idiots—they're escaping!" Bernard Alpha turned the corner just in time to see the four of them disappear into the storage room.

Lido led the way to the furthest corner of the cluttered room, piled high with boxes and crates of medical supplies and machinery. Throwing aside a large white box, he bent down and slid open a panel at the bottom of the wall. Philea went through first, turning to help Starr as David lowered her from his arms.

The door burst open with a sudden light—the huge man in the white uniform pointing a shotgun into the room. He spotted David bent over in the far corner and raised the weapon to his shoulder. Lido scrambled to the top of a crate, a rubber tipped hammer with a shiny steel handle raised in his hand. He flung it at the Peace-maker with all his might, striking the hand that held the stock of the shotgun.

BOOM! BOOM! BOOM! The shotgun blasts shattered the quiet of the ward, but the hammer had deflected the barrel just enough, the heavy pellets striking four feet to David's right, ripping out sections of the wall. While the man reloaded, David threw off his helmet, reaching inside the opening where he had left his weapons. He strung the small crossbow, inserting a bolt as he spun to face his attacker. In one smooth motion, he swung the bow around, leveling it at his assailant as he squeezed the trigger.

The tall man had David in his sights when the iron-tipped bolt struck the front of his helmet, burying itself up to the feathers. A stream of blood gushed forth beneath the dark visor of the helmet just before he crumpled to the floor. Four other Peacemakers rushed over the fallen man as David followed Lido through the small opening, closing the panel behind him.

The darkness of the subterranean world beneath the City, sliced with pale striated light from above, enveloped the four fugitives like a damp, heavy blanket. Lido led them along a shelf of rough concrete that formed part of the foundation of the White Tower. David carried Starr with Philea bringing up the rear.

"Can they get to us down here before we make it back to the boats?" David breathed easily.

As if in answer to his question, a heavy door swung open fifty feet in front of them, the uniforms of the two Peacemakers shining in the glare of the florescent light as they stepped onto the concrete walkway at the base of the door. David saw with great relief that they both carried long slim swords rather than shotguns.

Easing Starr down beside Philea, David handed Lido the crossbow and bolts. The two men in white, their heavy muscles bulging under the shiny uniforms, advanced carefully toward David, swords held in front of them.

David glanced at the long iron staircase that descended from the concrete ledge at the base of the door, down into the twilight world where their boats awaited them. Twenty feet away now, the giants in white prepared to make their move. David unslung the oak staff from his back, balancing it easily in both hands.

Turning his head toward Lido, David whispered quickly, "When I finish here, take the girls down to the River. There may be more coming—I'll follow soon."

The first man had barely begun the thrust that would have plunged his blade through David's chest, when the oak staff whipped under his outstretched sword arm, shattering his right knee. Sudden pain paralyzed his whole body as the leg caved in, sending him tumbling down the steep concrete embankment that fell away from the ledge. His scream of agony rose up from the darkness far below.

With a roundhouse motion, the other man swung his sword at David's head, just missing as the blade clanged against the wall of the White Tower. At the same moment he heard the ringing of steel against concrete, his breath left him in a whooshing outrush as the butt of the staff struck his solar plexus. He doubled forward, his sword lost and sliding down the embankment.

Laying the side of his staff under the man's left shoulder, David flicked him after the clattering sword. "Down the stairs," David barked to Lido. "I'll meet you at the boats."

With Lido on one side and Philea on the other, they half-carried Starr down the long, steep staircase toward the River.

"Don't be long," Lido called back over his shoulder. "The Tower's full of those big bullies."

Stripping off the white uniform, David watched the three of them descend into the murky depths below the City. Through the open spaces between the concrete pillars and steel beams, he could see the wide clear channel of the River, thrown into shadow by the high banks, as it ran straight as an arrow shot toward the south, disappearing into the purple distance.

Hearing a noise behind him, David whirled to face another giant of a man rushing through the door. He lowered the barrel of the shotgun as soon as he spotted David, but coming out of the glaring light it took a fraction of a second too long. Before he could squeeze off a shot, David sliced the weapon from his hands with the staff, sending it rattling off into the darkness.

The man bellowed in pain as the polished oak cracked against the knuckles of his left hand. In a blind rage, he got his huge hands around David's neck, squeezing with a strength born of desperation and a hatred of anyone who dared defy his masters.

David felt himself slipping quickly into a smothering blackness under the viselike grip of the grunting giant. Holding to his attacker's arms for balance, he stomped the heel of his right foot down on the man's left instep, crushing it with a sound like a limb snapping underwater. Releasing David, the man screamed in pain as he fell to his knees. David slammed his right fist into the man's temple. He rolled over on his side, lying perfectly still.

Hearing the muted thunder of dozens of footsteps rushing down the hallway toward the open door, David looked quickly about him. Taking his staff from the ledge where it had fallen, he put his shoulder to the door and closed it, wedging his staff between the heavy metal door and the corner post of the railing. A tremendous pounding came against the door with the sound of shouting as the pursuers tried to break it down. With a brief look back to make sure the staff was secure, David bounded down the stairs, taking them three at a time.

"You go ahead, Philea. I'll try to help Starr across after you." Lido stood on the east side of the River, easing Starr into a sitting position on a pipe that paralleled its bank.

"You'll never make it alone," Philea insisted, breathing heavily after their long descent.

Lido glanced at the eight-inch wide I-beam that spanned the hundred-foot width of the River. "We'll make it," he muttered with feigned confidence.

Philea reluctantly stepped out onto the cold surface of the beam. Almost immediately, a half dozen Rippers appeared in the River, as if by magic, along the route she would take over the water.

How do they know? How do they always know when someone is over the water? Lido stared with a mounting dread at the spiny, gray shadows, circling ominously beneath the surface, their eyes reflecting the dim light like cold fires.

Looking down and taking a deep breath, Philea began the walk across. Slowly and carefully, her arms outstretched for balance, she gained the opposite bank.

Lido struggled to get Starr to a standing position.

"You next!" David leaped down the last of the stairs, sprinting across the open space to the River bank. "Go ahead—don't stand there! I'll bring Starr."

"Thank God, you're all right!" Lido declared excitedly. "Are they coming?"

"They're coming," David shot back, glancing over his shoulder. "It's just a matter of how long we have."

Lido scurried across the beam in a flash, running over to Philea to help her down the ladder to the boats.

Lifting Starr like a child in his arms, David crossed the narrow bridge and climbed easily down the ladder, where Philea and Lido were already in their boat. David lay Starr gently in the small bow of the boat, climbing in carefully and paddling strongly out into the current ahead of his companions. Below the fragile crafts, the Rippers glided like the antithesis of guardian angels.

David kept to the middle of the River so they would be as far as possible from a threat on either bank. Moving with the current, they passed swiftly under lofty girders and beams and past the huge concrete pillars. The anemic light from the high vaulted ceiling glinted like slivers of ice in the depths of the River and off the armour plated backs of the Rippers.

Glancing ahead and upward David noticed movement in the shadowy heights. A small man, bald and wearing a light brown tunic, stepped out onto a girder a hundred feet above the River. David recognized him as one of the men who had visited Starr in the Closed Ward. Almost instantly, a Peacemaker appeared next to him, handing him a shotgun. The small man took the gun, jacked a shell into the chamber, and aimed it directly at Starr's prone form. David leaned forward, gripping the gunwales for balance as he shielded Starr's body with his own. He felt fire in his left shoulder as two of the pellets ripped through the fleshy part at the edge of his ribcage. The hollow roar of the gun reverberated through the high framework like a distant cannon.

Bernard Alpha had miscalculated the distance, but seeing that his victims were helpless, he pumped a fresh round into the chamber and took deliberate aim. He heard a soft thunk—his right thigh exploded with a scalding pain as the bolt from the crossbow buried itself into the soft flesh. Alpha's leg collapsed under him. Losing his balance, he clutched at the dark air around him. With a piercing wail of despair, he plummeted toward the River. The last thing he saw before he plunged beneath the surface, were the gleaming yellow eyes of the Rippers.

David glanced back at Lido, who lowered the crossbow and inserted another bolt. In front of David where Bernard Alpha had hit, the water appeared to be boiling, changing color quickly from a deep pinkish tint to bright red.

The Peacemaker, seeing Lido reload the crossbow, stepped behind a wide steel brace, bringing his shotgun to bear on the tiny man in the second boat. As he tightened his finger on the trigger a small shadowy figure swung from a rope tied to a support high above him, slamming his feet into the big man's back. The shotgun thundered as the man, arms and legs flailing, pitched forward down to the surface of the River. Again the clear water became a boiling, crimson cauldron.

The Shadowman, still holding his rope, stood where the Peacemaker had been; a bright smile on his dark face. When Lido waved his thanks, the man tipped his greasy cap, disappearing like a vapor back into the dim recesses of his home under the City.

✦　　　✦　　　✦

"They'll blanket the City with searchers. We've got to get out now." Michael Kappa paced back and forth in his cramped quarters, a restless light in his eyes.

Starr sat next to David on Michael's bunk. Her pale, almost ghostly face reflected the horror of the past few days. A streak of pure white ran through her thick auburn hair from her left temple along the side of her head to her shoulder. She smiled up at David, grateful that his wound, now cleaned and bandaged, had not been serious. Leaning back against his chest, she allowed herself the luxury of relying on his strength rather than her own.

David put his arm around Starr, feeling her fragile softness against him. "Starr's in no condition to travel—neither are you for that matter, Philea, but Michael's right. We've got to get across the River and through that laser gate before they block off everything."

Lido and Philea walked over next to the others from their temporary seclusion in the corner. Philea placed her hand on Lido's shoulder, a soft light in her eyes. "We've decided to stay."

Michael spun toward them. "Why—that's insane. They'll hunt you down like animals."

Lido returned Michael's look with a newly found confidence. "We're going underground—to live with the Shadowmen and the other Christians who've had to escape there."

Michael opened his mouth to respond, but was waved gently to silence by Philea.

Sitting next to Starr, Philea smiled at each of her four companions. "The dark night of the soul is come upon us all, my friends. It will begin here in the City, but I can see now that it will also extend to the Fields and wherever else Christians may be."

"We can escape them in the Fields, Philea!" David offered fervently. "It's the one place where they're at a disadvantage—even with all their weapons. They're soft from all the easy living and having no one in the City stand up to them. The Border Guards are our only real threat and from what Michael tells me, a lot of them won't try very hard to hunt us down."

Philea gazed intently into David's eyes. "They would be at a disadvantage, David—if they played by the same rules you do—but they don't. They'll try to destroy you by hurting the weakest and least suspecting of your people. They'll come against you with no sense of honor."

"Do you really think you'll be safe down there under the City?" David asked gravely.

"Lido does," Philea smiled. "Anyway, we must stay. Our people will need us more than ever now. Not just in ways to help them escape the inquisition—but most of all with prayer. It's the most powerful weapon we have—the only way we'll be victorious."

As Philea spoke, a sudden, chilling picture filled Starr's mind. She saw herself walking down the corridor between the high stacked cylinders of the Rim toward Martha Epsilon's home in number seventy-three. A pale woman in her mid twenties sat above her at the edge of cylinder number forty-nine. She had blonde hair tied at the back with a piece of twine and her light blue eyes were fixed on a picture she held in both hands.

Starr felt soft hands on her head and, glancing upward, saw that Philea was praying for her—for God to give his angels charge over her to protect her in all her ways. She lay hands on each of the other three in turn, praying for God's grace and protection over all of them. When she had finished, she sat down next to Starr, as if the last of her strength had been exhausted.

Taking Philea's hand, Starr felt hot tears flow down her cheeks as the horror of what she had done rushed in upon her. The three men left the room to make final preparations for the trip as if bidden to do so by someone unseen.

Overwhelmed now by grief, Starr was sobbing, her body shaking as she gasped for breath.

Philea put her arm around Starr's shoulder, letting her cry herself empty. "It's all right, my child," she murmured, her voice no more than a whisper in the still room. "It's all right now."

Although they were the same age, Starr felt that Philea was somehow much older than her although she had the face of a child. "But, Philea, you don't know what I've done."

Philea touched Starr's cheek with her hand, turning her face toward her.

Starr looked into Philea's blue eyes and saw a love and an understanding that were beyond her comprehension. "Philea!" she whispered, turning away. "I murdered your father the same day I—went to Martha Epsilon's. Oh, please forgive me—forgive me!"

Philea took Starr's hand again. "I already have my child—that same day."

Starr gazed at Philea, her eyes wide in disbelief. "You—you already knew what I had done! And you risked your life in the White Tower to save me!"

"I was only able to forgive you by the grace and love of Jesus Christ, Starr," Philea said in a steady voice. "I had to fight the battle in His strength that day, for I knew the bitterness would destroy me if I didn't. By His mercy, it's all gone."

Starr put her arms around Philea, and as they embraced she felt like warm oil was flowing through her, cleansing and healing all the old wounds and hurts.

Sitting back, Starr looked again into Philea's eyes. "I—I haven't told David what I've done—what I was. I just couldn't do it."

"The right time will come," Philea assured her. "God has forgiven you and David will too."

Lido slipped quietly into the room. "They're ready."

Starr looked down at the little man with the big bright eyes. "Thank you so much for what you've done. I do so wish you were going with us." She bent down and kissed him on the cheek.

"I want to see the Fields very much," Lido murmured, smiling up at Philea. "But we've got work to do here. Maybe we can both come to all of you later."

"Oh, I hope so," Starr said, turning to Philea. "I'll pray for both of you every day."

"And I you—and for all of those in the Fields," Philea replied as they embraced. She stepped back, holding Starr's hands and gazing intently into her eyes. "God will send a special annointing upon you Starr Omega. He has chosen you among all His other children for a particular work. Go now in His grace."

Starr squeezed Philea's hands gently, feeling the tears come to her eyes as she turned and left the room. As she hurried toward David who waited at the foot of the ladder, it occurred to her that perhaps it was not by accident that this healing and cleansing of her spirit had happened in a stable.

As they crossed the small river that bordered his home—further north where it joined the much larger one, David saw the huge column of smoke. Rising against the hard blue sky it became an ominous harbinger of the wolf-lean years ahead, bringing to mind with a chilling finality Philea's words spoken in the stable, "They'll come against you with no sense of honor."

David rode ahead along the path through the trees next to the bluff that looked down on the River—Starr followed on her Palomino with Michael acting as rear guard. As they came to the vegetable gardens, David saw the first of the bodies. Women and children had been hacked to pieces, thrown carelessly among the carefully tended rows like so much garbage.

On the opposite side of the path from the gardens, the livestock had been slaughtered and lay scattered among vast pools of blood. Smoke eddyed from the burned pens, wafting upward as the breeze off the River caught it.

The three travelers looked straight ahead as they continued down the path toward Haven, dreading what they would find there. The heavy drone of hundreds of blue-bottle flies overlay the grisly scene like some ghastly soundtrack.

"There's where the gunships landed," Michael remarked, struggling to keep his voice steady.

Starr looked at the open field where the long grass had been flattened by the helicopters. She saw David staring at something beyond the field next to the pond. His face paled suddenly, as he kicked his horse into motion, racing through the tall grass at breakneck speed. She and Michael followed at a gallop, knowing that speed no longer mattered in this holocaust called Haven.

When Starr climbed down off her horse, David sat on the hard-packed ground under the ancient sweet gum tree, cradling in his arms the body of his butchered mother. Timmy's small lifeless form lay next to him, where David had placed Timmy's head on his knee as though he were asleep.

Together they walked up the slope toward the charred remains of the house, David carrying his mother and Starr carrying the child. Michael followed, leading the horses. He was glad to no longer be a servant of beasts calling themselves human—those who could committ such atrocities, even if it meant death at their hands.

Near the house, under a huge oak blackened by the fires, Obadiah sat next to the body of David's father. His face and chest had been ruined by shotgun blasts.

Obadiah looked up at the three travelers, recoginzing two of them. His face was slack, the eyes glazed by grief and shock. "Your daddy fought as hard as he could to protect his family, David," he muttered, pointing to the bloody sythe still clutched in Caleb's work-hardened hands. "But I reckon he didn't stand much of a chance."

David lay his mother's body next to his father's. Starr lay Timmy between them.

As David took Obadiah's hand, helping him to his feet, he looked about the village where several men, just back from their time in the fields, were wandering aimlessly amid the smoldering ruins. "Come on old friend," David said softly. "We've got work to do."

◆　　　◆　　　◆

Late that night, their grisly work completed, the survivors sat around a fire under the tall pines on the bluff that overlooked the River. The flames crackled with a friendly warmth, the night wind sighing high in the crowns of the trees. Beyond the edge of the firelight mounds of fresh earth stretched in orderly rows.

"Light of the World!" Obadiah spoke softly, but with an unmistakable authority. He rose to his feet, this small black man wearing a rough homespun cloak. His face seemed transformed, shining with a strength eternal and immutable.

Starr moved closer to David, holding to his arm as Obadiah spoke. The others lifted their faces in rapt attention at the compelling sound of his voice.

"I have a word from the Lord," Obadiah continued. "We are the Light of the World and that Blessed Light must not be darkened by thoughts of revenge against those who have slain our loved ones. 'Recompense to no man evil for evil. Dearly beloved, avenge not yourselves, but rather give place unto wrath: for it is written, Vengence is mine; I will repay, saith the Lord.' "

Obadiah paced around the fire. Looking into the upturned faces, "Jesus said that we would be hated by all men for his sake. Some of us will be betrayed by those closest to us: parents, brethren, friends—and some of us will be put to death. There will be great earthquakes and famines and pestilences—fearful sights and great signs from heaven—signs in the sun and in the moon and in the stars."

A smile of great joy came to Obadiah's shining face. " 'And when these things begin to come to pass, then lift up your heads; for your redemption draweth nigh.' Our redemption is very near my dear brethern and my sister. Jesus is coming soon. Some of us will be witnesses for him here in the Fields—others will journey to the City where you may be called upon to preach the Gospel to those who would murder you."

"Brethern, let us love one another. Let us rejoice in the grace and mercy of Almighty God. Paul said that he had suffered the loss of all things that he might know Jesus—'and the power of his resurrection, and the fellowship of his sufferings . . . For I reckon that the sufferings of this present time are not worthy to be compared with the glory which shall be revealed in us.' "

Obadiah lifted his arms toward the great black dome of heaven sparkling with thousands of stars and the shining planets. "Father, into your hands we commend our lives—our hearts—our spirits. Jesus prayed for us not to be taken out of the world, but that You would keep us from the evil. We trust in this prayer and in your eternal love for us which is in your son, Jesus."

With a smile that would not allow fear in its presence, Obadiah turned again to the remnant gathered around the fire. "I leave you now with the words of Jesus, 'Fear not, little flock; for it is your father's good pleasure to give you the kingdom.' "

Sitting down at the foot of a pine, Obadiah, a small black man in rough clothes, insignificant and of no value in the eyes of the world, lay back and closed his eyes.

As the little group settled down for the night, Starr lay next to David on a bed of fragrant pine needles, her hand securely clasped in his. She thought of the great and terrible things that were to come, but strangely, there was no fear in her heart—there was only peace and joy and a deep longing to see the face of Jesus.

She imagined Jesus in the hills of Galilee with his rough band of followers, gathered around a fire such as this. She could almost see him standing before them—could almost hear his voice as she drifted off to sleep.

Fear not, little flock.

Books by Starburst Publishers

(Partial listing—full list available on request)

Beyond The River   —Gilbert Morris & Bobby Funderburk

Book 1 in The Far Fields series is a a futuristic novel that carries the New Age and "politically correct" doctrines of America to their logical and alarming conclusions. In the mode of *Brave New World* and *1984,* **Beyond The River** presents a world where government has replaced the family and morality has become an unknown concept.

(trade paper) ISBN 0914984519   **$8.95**

A Candle In Darkness   —June Livesay

An exciting and romantic novel set in the mountains of Ecuador. The first in a series, based on fact, the story begins on market day in a small Indian village in Ecuador. Rolando, the eldest son of an alcoholic landowner and bedridden mother, is overprotective of his little sister Elena, who eventually runs away with her lover Carlos, a boy from "the other side of the tracks." Dragged home by her brother, Elena again runs away with Carlos only to find short-lived happiness—for lurking in the shadows of their life together is the kidnapping of their firstborn child, emotional breakdown, and death. Depression and alcoholism eventually drive Rolando to consider suicide. While on his way to commit the act he encounters a friend who offers him hope and help which leads him on the road toward happiness.

(trade paper) ISBN 0914984225   **$8.95**

The Quest For Truth   —Ken Johnson

A book designed to lead the reader to a realization that there is no solution to the world's problems, nor is there purpose to life, apart from Jesus Christ. It is the story of a young man on a symbolic journey in search of happiness and the meaning of life. Eidell, a student of an unnamed university, accidently receives an invitation to a festival to be held a long journey from his home. He decides to attend, thinking that at the festival he will find the meaning of life. On the way to the festival Eidell meets a variety of individuals, some unsavory, who delay his journey and bring about his near destruction. Each one tries, in one way or another, to influence him to accept their own philosophy of life. Finally, Eidell is broken to the point where he is willing to give up his notions of how things are supposed to be and accept the right way—God's way. It is as this epic journey unfolds that the reader realizes the setting is after the rapture of the Church, during the great tribulation.

(trade paper) ISBN 0914984217   **$7.95**

Books by Starburst Publishers—cont'd.

The Beast Of The East
—Alvin M. Shifflett

Asks the questions: Has the Church become involved in a "late date" comfort mode—expecting to be "raptured" before the Scuds fall? Should we prepare for a long and arduous Desert Storm to Armageddon battle? Are we ignoring John 16:33, *In this world you will have trouble?* (NIV)

(trade paper) ISBN 0914984411 **$6.95**

Except For A Staff
—Randy R., Spencer

The ancient *staff* was not merely an implement used by shepherds but also was employed by rulers, teachers, travelers, the physically impaired, and warriors. In each instance, closer examination reveals that the specific use of the common *staff,* or rod, was intended by God to be a foreshadowing of the power of the Holy Spirit. Numerous accounts in scripture reveal this beautiful typology of the Spirit's ever-present ministry and manifests His truer character. **Except For A Staff** parallels the various functions of the Old Testament shepherd's staff with the Holy Spirit and sheds new light on the role of the Holy Spirit in the life of the Christian.

(trade paper) ISBN 0914984349 **$7.95**

A Woman's Guide To Spiritual Power
—Nancy L. Dorner

Subtitled: *Through Scriptural Prayer.* Do your prayers seem to go "against a brick wall?" Does God sometimes seem far away or non-existent? If your answer is "Yes," *You* are not alone. Prayer must be the cornerstone of your relationship to God. "This book is a powerful tool for anyone who is serious about prayer and discipleship."—Florence Littauer

(trade paper) ISBN 0914984470 **$9.95**

TemperaMysticism—Exploding the Temperament Theory
—Shirley Ann Miller

Some Christians have found the Temperament Theory (Sanguine, Choleric, Phlegmatic, and Melancholy) to be extremely fascinating, if not addicting. The mysterious and intriguing sense of "self-discovery" has undoubtedly contributed to the overall excitement generated because of this "new" personality system. **TemperaMysticism** answers the questions: (1) Where did the Temperaments and the Enneagram originate? (2) What is the truth about the Sanguine, Choleric, Phlegmatic, and Melancholy personality theory? (3) Are the temperament teachings of some Christian leaders introducing New Age philosophies into the Church? **TemperaMysticism** (authored by a former astrologer) is an indepth investigation of the Temperament theory and other personality typologies.)

(trade paper) ISBN 0914984306 **$8.95**

Purrables
—Alma Barkman

Subtitled: *Words of Wisdom From the Life of a Cat*. This book was derived from the antics of the family cat, Sir Purrcival van Mouser. The author has taken anecdotal material used in a weekly humor column and combined it with Scriptural truths from the book of *Proverbs*. **Purrables** is an inspirational self-help book, with a very unique slant. Sir Purrcival van Mouser draws the reader into consideration of spiritual truths as they apply to everyday living. The humorous behavior of the cat is used to draw a parallel with our own experience or attitude, and the application is summarized by an appropriate proverb. **Purrables** especially appeals to anyone who loves a cat and would therefore enjoy reading truth from a different *purr*spective.

(trade paper) ISBN 0914984535 **$6.95**

Man And Wife For Life
—Joseph Kanzlemar

A penetrating and often humorous look into real life situations of married people. Helps the reader get a new understanding of the problems and relationships within marriage.

(trade paper) ISBN 0914984233 **$7.95**

Like A Bulging Wall
—Robert Borrud

Will you survive the 1990's economic crash? This book shows how debt, greed, and covetousness, along with a lifestyle beyond our means, has brought about an explosive situation in this country. Gives "call" from God to prepare for judgement in America. Also lists TOP-RATED U.S. BANKS and SAVINGS & LOANS.

(trade paper) ISBN 0914984284 **$8.95**

Purchasing Information

Listed books are available from your favorite Bookstore, either from current stock or special order. To assist bookstore in locating your selection be sure to give title, author, and ISBN #. If unable to purchase from the bookstore you may order direct from STARBURST PUBLISHERS. When ordering enclose full payment plus $2.50* for shipping and handling ($3.00* if Canada or Overseas). Payment in US Funds only. Please allow two to three weeks minimum (longer overseas) for delivery. Make checks payable to and mail to STARBURST PUBLISHERS, P.O. Box 4123, LANCASTER, PA 17604. **Prices subject to change without notice**. Catalog available upon request.

*We reserve the right to ship your order the least expensive way. If you desire first class (domestic) or air shipment (overseas) please enclose shipping funds as follows: First Class within the USA enclose $4.00, Airmail Canada enclose $5.00, and Overseas enclose 30% (minimum $5.00) of total order. All remittance must be in US Funds.